PRAISE FOR E.A. AYMAR

When She Left

"*When She Left* keeps you guessing with breakneck pacing and unexpected twists, but what truly stands out are the characters: quirky and flawed but endearing as hell. But be warned: in an E.A. Aymar novel, no character is safe. Ever."

—Alma Katsu, award-winning author of *The Hunger* and *Red Widow*

"E.A. Aymar is an exceptional talent. You'll be riveted by his uniquely realized characters, immersed in his high-intensity plot, and blown away by the poetry in his voice. At once a harrowing story of power, escape, and raw courage and a heartbreaking tale of family, love, and necessity, *When She Left* reveals the soul-crushing desperation of facing mortal danger while attempting to undo the past. Superb, thought provoking, and propulsive and, in the end, touchingly redemptive."

—Hank Phillippi Ryan, *USA Today* bestselling author of *The House Guest*

"E.A. Aymar steps on the gas within the very first pages of *When She Left* and doesn't let up throughout this wild ride of a thriller. Relentlessly paced, with characters that are complicated and feel real enough to talk to, this book will keep you up well into the night as it speeds and twists toward its surprising conclusion. Read it!"

—Alison Gaylin, Edgar Award–winning author

"What a churning cauldron of intrigue and human complication. Love, loathing, and lies abound. A real page-turner. Aymar bats a thousand with *When She Left*! This one will stick with you."

—Tracy Clark, author of the Cass Raines and Detective Harriet Foster series and winner of the 2020 and 2022 Sue Grafton Memorial Award

"An action-packed story with well-drawn characters that will make you laugh, gasp, and keep turning the pages."

—Cate Holahan, *USA Today* bestselling author of *The Darkness of Others*

"*When She Left* is perfect for fans of Elmore Leonard. It's darkly funny and packed full of richly drawn characters and gasp-out-loud twists, and the writing is gorgeous. Get your copy now."

—Jess Lourey, Edgar-nominated author of *The Taken Ones*

"Cliff-hangers and plot twists abound in this intriguing page-turner. From a nail-biter of an opening scene, E.A. Aymar deftly propels the unconventional cast along an adrenaline-jolting narrative to a gratifying finale. This is crime fiction at its finest, a seamless fusion of character study with mystery/thriller. Don't miss it!"

—Wendy Corsi Staub, *New York Times* bestselling author of *Windfall*

"Aymar is at the top of his game in this bold, high-stakes thriller where no character is safe. It's excellently written, thought provoking, intense, and gripping, with enough shocking twists and turns to keep you fully immersed until its stunning end. Don't miss this one!"

—Lisa Regan, *USA Today* bestselling author

No Home for Killers

"This is a bold, relentless, breathtaking thriller from start to finish. E.A. Aymar writes about complex, damaged characters with incredible grace, anchoring the heart of this book in family conflict and trauma. Taut and twisty, with intense pacing and perfect plotting, *No Home for Killers* is a remarkable read. I absolutely loved it."

—Hilary Davidson, bestselling author of *Her Last Breath*

"Tough, haunting, full of surprises and vivid characters, *No Home for Killers* is hard boiled and thoughtful, riven with pain and spiked with humor, and never less than a pedal-to-the-floor thriller. A gripping read."

—Meg Gardiner, Edgar Award–winning author of the Unsub series

"I had so much fun reading *No Home for Killers*. It's an action-packed thriller filled with characters you root for and bad guys you love seeing go down. I couldn't stop turning the pages. One of the best books I've read this year!"

—Matthew Farrell, bestselling author of *We Have Your Daughter*

"E.A. Aymar's *No Home for Killers* is a breathtakingly paced thriller, a character-driven journey of rage and justice that will leave you pondering the subtleties between good and evil and right and wrong. Violent yet sensitive, Aymar's command of the noir thriller is on full display here, in what is absolutely his best book yet."

—Jennifer Hillier, *USA Today* bestselling author of *Things We Do in the Dark* and *Little Secrets*

"Aymar skillfully blurs the line between justice and vengeance in a gripping tale of crime and its consequences. His masterfully drawn characters are at times both relatable and brutal as the tension builds through each shocking turn until the final twist that will haunt you long after the book is closed."

—Isabella Maldonado, *Wall Street Journal* bestselling author of *The Cipher*

"This book is a delight from start to finish—by turns funny, poignant, and action packed. Twists and turns to keep us guessing the whole way. E.A. Aymar is a master storyteller, delivering fascinating characters in a realistic setting. Make a home on your shelves for this one!"

—Eliza Nellums, author of *The Bone Cay* and *All That's Bright and Gone*

WHEN SHE LEFT

OTHER BOOKS BY E.A. AYMAR

No Home for Killers

The Unrepentant

They're Gone (written as E.A. Barres)

WHEN SHE LEFT

A THRILLER

E. A. AYMAR

This is a work of fiction. Names, characters, organizations, places, events, and incidents are either products of the author's imagination or are used fictitiously. Otherwise, any resemblance to actual persons, living or dead, is purely coincidental.

Published by Thomas & Mercer, Seattle

www.apub.com

Amazon, the Amazon logo, and Thomas & Mercer are trademarks of Amazon.com, Inc., or its affiliates.

ISBN-13: 9781662504532 (paperback)
ISBN-13: 9781662504549 (digital)

Cover design by Faceout Studio, Amanda Hudson
Cover image: © Dusica Paripovic / ArcAngel; © Grant Faint / Getty; © The Good Brigade / Getty

Printed in the United States of America

To John William Hart
What a gift you were.

Part One

And it came to pass, when they had brought them forth abroad, that he said, Escape for thy life; look not behind thee, neither stay thou in all the plain; escape to the mountain, lest thou be consumed.

Genesis 19:17

Chapter One
Melissa

Melissa Cruz realized she was trapped the moment those two men sauntered into the twenty-four-hour diner.

"They found us," she whispered to Jake Smith. Hope had finally begun to seem like a possibility, and now it was over, the abrupt ending of an interrupted prayer.

Her fists tightened helplessly in her lap. Breath was hard to come by.

Jake sat across from her, his back to the door, oblivious. He didn't look up from his camera as he spoke. "Who what?"

Melissa brought her hand to her forehead to hide her face, hoped the movement wasn't obvious. "The people hunting us," she said, low and intense. It was difficult for her to say the whole sentence, fear nearly turning it into a question. *Hunting us?*

Jake swung around.

"Jake!" Melissa whispered desperately.

He ignored her, kept looking at the two men who had entered the diner. Stared as they sat at a booth near the door.

"Turn around!"

Melissa's high hiss broke through, and Jake turned. The bruises coloring the left side of his face, a faded map, were already less apparent than they had been yesterday. But Melissa still noticed them.

And, despite her fear, they still caused her heart to ache—love and guilt wrestling inside her like a pair of angels tumbling to earth.

"That's not them," Jake announced.

Melissa wanted to believe him, wanted to let that wave of relief wash over her. "How do you know?"

He shrugged, unconcerned. "They don't seem the type. Polos, slacks. One of them has a lanyard. Probably here for some kind of convention. Came to get food after a party."

Men always had this sense of certainty, of working in absolutes, the world defined by their perspective. *Nothing's wrong. We're fine. I thought so.* Sometimes Melissa found this confidence comforting, even if she knew it was misplaced.

She peered again at the two men. "Or they're trying not to look suspicious."

Jake grinned, that easy smile that always softened everything inside her. "Honestly, if the Winterses made custom polos to find us at midnight in some random diner, then they deserve to catch us."

He lifted his camera and snapped a pair of pictures of the half-eaten food on their table, the soft apple pie and finished dinner and empty coffee cup in front of him, the cooling bowl of tomato soup and nibbled grilled cheese sandwich in front of her.

He reached across the table with his free hand.

"No one's after us," Jake insisted.

Her hand was cold in his. Melissa had accidentally left her jacket in the car, and the diner wasn't warm. She could feel the chill coming in from outside, from the thin glass window alongside their booth. "No one just leaves them. Especially the way we did."

Melissa had heard stories about men and women who'd tried to leave the Winters crime family, how they'd been caught. The parts of them that had been found.

"And you need to be more careful," Melissa went on. She disliked the bossiness in her voice but couldn't help it. "You can't just stare at someone when I tell you they might be watching us."

"I do that?"

"You just did!"

"Must be a guy thing," Jake mused.

"I think it's a *you* thing."

Jake looked like he was going to say something else but caught himself. He returned to his pie.

Melissa watched him, her mind split with worry about their current situation and self-exasperation at how brusque she was being with him.

"The Winterses have every cop in the area looking into them," Jake said, between bites. "The last thing anyone in that family can do is follow us. It was the perfect time to leave."

"There's never a perfect time to run off with another man."

Jake nibbled from the piece of pie and abruptly pushed the bowl next to a plate of chicken-fried steak he'd turned into crumbs. "That's a really good point," he admitted.

Chris Winters was going to find them, and Melissa knew, intimately, the impact of her ex-boyfriend's anger. She could almost feel it—a rope binding her to him; the two of them forever connected.

"Do you regret it?" he asked.

"I don't," she said honestly. "I just wish I wasn't so scared."

Talking with Jake helped. Reminded Melissa why she was running off with him.

"And I don't feel comfortable in public," she continued. "I feel like I should be looking everywhere, and my shoulders are tight, and I keep having to pee. Although maybe that's all the water—"

"No one at some diner at midnight is going to remember us," Jake interrupted. "All they'll be able to say is we were some random white guy and a hot Spanish chick."

"Panamanian," Melissa corrected him.

"See?" That easy grin. "I'm saying!"

And again, Melissa remembered how that grin used to relax her, its offhand assurance.

It didn't work now.

When she'd imagined running off with Jake, love had been their North Star, rightfully guiding every decision, their devoted accomplice. And she still did love Jake. Melissa looked at him, and it was like sunrise in her chest, but she hadn't realized how much her fear would weigh.

Melissa wondered where the waitress was. She hadn't seen her since their food was brought out.

The only customers were her and Jake, a middle-aged couple in the back, and the two men quietly talking in the booth near the entrance. And it was likely to stay that way. This remote diner, somewhere outside Frederick, Maryland, didn't seem like it would draw a crowd, much less on a cold late-December night. That was why she and Jake had picked it, the first time they'd left his old Honda Accord and the safety of its enclosure, the opportunity to speed away from danger.

"Those men in the front," Melissa said slowly, thinking as she was speaking, "with the lanyards. No one helped them."

"What do you mean?"

"They just walked in and sat down. And they haven't ordered anything. They haven't even looked for the waitress."

Jake was back to examining his camera. "People do that."

"No one comes to a diner at midnight just to sit and talk without ordering anything. No one . . ."

A door opened with a sudden whisk, like a ghost was gliding by. The waitress emerged from the kitchen, headed over to the two men in front.

Melissa let out a shaky breath. "Maybe I do need to chill."

"Maybe." Jake snapped another quick picture of her, frowned at the display on his digital camera.

Melissa had grown used to the constant presence of his camera. *Just don't pay attention to it,* Jake had told her when they'd first met, and that seemed impossible at first—impossible to ignore the way he needed everything documented and memorialized, and then intensely scrutinized. Often reshot. Jake's hopeless annoyance when he didn't get the exact picture he wanted, his contagious cheerfulness when he did.

"You really think we're going to be okay?" Melissa couldn't help the skepticism in her voice.

"It's not like we stole money from them or anything," he offered. "And Chris took his anger out on me already." Jake touched his cheek, his fingers grazing the bruises.

"I know." Her voice small and childlike, far younger than her twenty-three years.

Melissa had seen violence before, horrible images that tugged at her like lecherous hands. She carried them with her, memories like a small frantic germ, determined to infect. But she felt dizzy when she thought about Chris's fists slamming into Jake's cheek, that weird, happy light that almost seemed to illuminate Chris's face as he knelt over Jake's body. The anguish—and the anger—she'd felt for Jake. She remembered the wine bottle in her hand. The thick glass as she stood behind Chris and raised it high.

"Melissa?"

She was bombarded by memories, unbalanced between two different worlds, not fully present in either. Vertigo climbed her body like hungry spiders. "I'll be back."

Melissa slid out of the booth and headed to the restroom. Pushed open the door for the women's room, made her way to the sink. She pressed her palms down on the cold counter, closed her eyes, and breathed slowly, deeply, the kind of hypnotic breathing the counselor she'd once briefly seen had recommended.

Deep from the diaphragm. Hold it for five seconds.

Exhale slowly, like a quiet stream in a wooded area. Imagine sunlight through shadows.

Three slow breaths.

Melissa opened her eyes, walked into one of the stalls, covered the seat with toilet paper, slid her pants and underwear to her knees. Unhappily leaned forward, elbows pressed into her thighs.

She pulled her phone out of her purse and checked her messages. She'd texted her friend Carla Acosta hours ago, asking if she'd heard anything from Chris or the Winterses, and Carla kept telling her no:

Ellos tienen otras cosas preocupado.

But Melissa didn't buy that Chris or the Winterses would be focused on anything else.

She thought about contacting Carla again but decided against it, knew it couldn't calm her fear and uncertainty.

Or that other thing, the tiny feeling darting inside her like a pesky gnat.

Guilt.

Melissa felt sorry for Chris, despite how viciously he'd hurt Jake. A four-year relationship was a lot to leave, even if that last year had been spent arguing, so often on opposite sides that a breakup seemed inevitable.

At least, it had to her.

She'd been able to hide her guilt from herself, smother it in justification and Xanax. Those mornings when she'd leave Jake's apartment, the summer sun emerging hotly, like snarling honesty forcing her to confront what she'd done with Jake the night before: that was when

Melissa had told herself that she was going to end it soon. That this wasn't the kind of thing she'd ever do when she was eventually married.

Of course, she'd suspected Chris of doing the same, even if she had no proof. But the idea of blaming Chris made her feel better.

All the justifications, desperate to appease herself, those hot mornings after sweltering evenings.

Now there was no hiding who she was or what she had done.

Melissa flushed, left the stall. She glanced at herself in the bathroom mirror as she soaped her hands. Pulled a wrinkled brown paper towel from a dispenser, dried off, dropped it on top of an overflowing wastebasket. The paper fell to the floor and Melissa grimaced, delicately picked it up by an edge, set it back on the trash pile.

She stepped out of the restroom, and her breath vanished as quickly as a hook yanking a small fish from the water.

A stranger was sitting across from Jake, in the same spot where she had been, a large paunchy man with a ruddy complexion and curly brown hair. The stranger smiled and waved to Melissa, ushered her over. Jake's camera was in the stranger's other hand, tiny in his palm, a toy.

Jake's back was to her, his head bowed like a child being punished.

She thought about her gun, sitting in the glove compartment of their car outside.

"Your boyfriend kept trying to take my picture," the stranger told Melissa as she walked over, fear slowing her steps. "I had to take his camera away."

Jake looked miserable.

"Sit down." The stranger patted the seat next to him.

Melissa glanced around the diner, hoped someone was paying attention, that she could catch another person's eye. No one noticed her.

"Sit," the stranger said again.

Melissa did, felt his large body next to her.

"Chris wanted more than a note," the man told her.

And with those words, everything Melissa feared came true.

There had been a hope she hadn't fully realized, a chance this man wasn't connected to them, just someone upset that Jake had photographed him as he had walked into the diner. That happened, Jake had told her. Often.

This wasn't that. The stranger knew Chris Winters.

"How'd you find us?" Melissa asked.

He ignored her question. "The good news is Chris wants you alive." The stranger inclined his head toward Jake. "Doesn't much care what happens to your boyfriend. But I'll let you finish your dinner first. The pie looks delicious."

Melissa stared sadly at the pie, retracing every step she and Jake had taken, every mistake they'd made. Using his car. Not running farther away. Charging credit cards at gas stations. His insistence that they stop at this diner.

Leaving the gun outside.

Too many mistakes.

"Can I have my camera?" Jake asked.

The stranger turned it over in his hands. "I'll bury you with it," he said. "Good enough?"

The door to the kitchen swung open, and the waitress approached their table. A jolt of hope went through Melissa.

"Get you anything?"

"Darling," the stranger said, and Melissa noticed the waitress's back stiffen, her face tighten. "Your pie looks delicious. I bet I could eat it all night."

The waitress glanced at Melissa.

Melissa wanted to communicate everything she could in her eyes, her fear and desperation, the secret empathy between women. *This man isn't with us. Please help.* But the waitress just looked annoyed.

"So you want the pie then?" she asked. Her tone was impatient but practiced. She'd dealt with men like this before.

"I said I *could* eat your pie," the stranger replied. "But not tonight. We'll just take the check."

"Fine." The waitress left, and Melissa's hope left with her.

The stranger turned back toward her with a smile.

But his smile abruptly changed as he looked down, saw what Melissa had snatched off the table and pressed against his leg.

"Well," he said. "Look at you."

Jake half rose to peer at the steak knife Melissa was holding against the stranger's thigh.

"You really think you're going to stab me?"

"I can't go back," Melissa said.

The stranger rubbed his bristly chin.

"The knife will hurt," he admitted. "But not enough to stop me from pulling my gun. You two won't make it out of here. And, in the end, Chris won't care."

The table fell silent.

The stranger stared at Melissa, his eyes clocks winding down.

"We can give you money." Melissa didn't know if this was true. She couldn't keep her thoughts clear enough to recall how much money she had, what remained in her purse. She and Jake had run off and taken nothing.

"There's no money that can save me," the stranger said, "if Chris learns I let you go."

"But we can give you—"

"No." Those twin clocks ticking. "You two jumped off a cliff. There's nothing to grab on the way down."

Melissa couldn't maintain the stranger's gaze, couldn't keep staring into his utter confidence. Jake hadn't moved since she'd grabbed the knife. Melissa looked at the kitchen door, hoped the waitress would reappear. The door stayed closed.

Maybe, she hoped, the waitress had somehow understood their situation. Sensed the fear emanating from Melissa, decided to tell someone. Called the cops. Of course, the Winterses had the cops, but at least it would give them time to—

"Time's up," the stranger said.

"Melissa," Jake told her, strained. "Give him your money."

"You tune out just now?" the stranger asked. "I don't want your—"

"Give him your money," Jake repeated, "and get out of here."

"What?" Melissa asked.

"Leave without me," Jake said. "He can take me, but you go."

"Sorry?" the stranger asked.

"You get me," Jake told him. "And she gets a chance. That's what we're buying."

"I'm not leaving you here," Melissa said resolutely.

Their gazes wrestled across the table.

"You don't have a choice," the stranger said. "And—"

He didn't get to finish speaking. Without any of them realizing it, the waitress was back. Standing next to them. Looking wide eyed at the steak knife Melissa was pressing into the stranger's leg.

"What are you doing?" the waitress asked.

Photography is all about the moment, Jake had once told Melissa. *You have to know the right one to capture.*

And Melissa chose that moment to shove the knife into the stranger's thigh.

He swore in surprise and bent over while the waitress screamed.

The middle-aged couple in the back rose, a shriek from the wife.

The two men in the front turned, their eyes and mouths dark, wide circles.

Melissa heard her own screams as she rose and saw the stranger's gun in one hand, his other grasping the handle of the knife in his thigh. Blood spread over his jeans like evening shadow. He lurched out of the booth and grabbed the waitress for balance. She jerked away, and he dropped his gun. Grabbed the knife handle and fell to the floor.

Hands on Melissa's arm, pulling her. Jake telling her something lost in the commotion.

Melissa felt light headed and unsteady. But she couldn't stop looking back as Jake tugged her, the waitress stumbling to her feet, the older man standing like a shield in front of his wife, the two lanyard-wearing men in front still staring.

The stranger on the ground, trying to wrench the knife free.

Jake let go of her hand halfway to the door. He hurried back to the booth, stepping around the stranger as the wounded man frantically searched for his gun.

Jake grabbed the camera.

Then he and Melissa ran to the door, the waitress behind them. The first shot exploded like a giant angrily slamming its hands together.

Melissa turned and saw the waitress fall.

Jake pulled her to the door. Melissa looked down. The waitress's face was a stark white as she tried to crawl.

Another shot, and the diner's front window cracked.

One of the men who had been in the front booth lunged forward, his lanyard swinging. He reached the door at the same time as Jake and Melissa, but the doorway was too tight for all three of them. At the gun's third shot, that man's hands slipped from the door handle. He fell heavily to the ground, his left hand waving as if desperately calling for attention, his right hand clutching the bullet wound in his neck. On his knees, he crawled back to the safety of the table.

The diner door swung open and Melissa ran out, felt the cold rush of December, heard the heavy silence of night. Jake spent too long at her car door but finally forced it open. The cloth seats, the dust-stained console, the interior light a halo. Jake's door slammed closed and the old silver Honda Accord jerked backward.

The parking lot receded somewhere behind them.

After a few minutes the car slid to a stop on a hill, off the road. Jake's hands stayed tight on the wheel. He was breathing loudly, in spurts.

"Jake?"

Moments later, Melissa sat alone.

She watched Jake's silhouette in the dark, a tall figure with a camera just outside the light from the car, snapping endless pictures of the carnage in the diner below, like an artist standing on the edge of the earth and painting a picture of hell. Melissa closed her eyes, desperately wanting to run, even as Jake made this moment last forever.

Chapter Two
Lucky

"You know he drank!" Sheila Banks exclaimed to whomever she was talking with on the phone. She was sitting on the living room couch, an outdated floral-print sofa the homeowner had refused to place in storage for the open house.

Lucky Wilson gazed at Sheila from the kitchen, his hands absent-mindedly spreading his *Lucky Wilson: An Agent You Can Trust!* business cards in a fan on the linoleum counter, stacking them like a blackjack dealer, fanning them out again in a practiced wave.

"I heard it was a lot!" Sheila shrieked.

To Lucky, her voice felt like a drunk bear stumbling inside his skull.

The first time Lucky had murdered someone—well, someone he hadn't been paid to kill—was when he had just started working for the Winterses. This had been a car accident late at night on an empty road, a minor fender bender, and the man driving was belligerent, yelling a stream of expletives so colorful that Lucky was impressed. But the man hadn't stopped there. He'd engaged Lucky physically, and Lucky had ended his life with a single gunshot.

The other unpaid killing happened nearly a decade later. A new teacher at his daughter's day care had been fired after it was discovered he was inappropriately touching the children. A week after he had been fired, Lucky had gone to his house past midnight, slipped inside wearing a ski mask and gloves.

Only two occasions.

So far.

Sheila's irritating manner was driving him to a third, and Lucky's dejected state of mind didn't help. In addition to everything else in his life that troubled him, Lucky hated holding open houses. He especially despised neighbors strolling through only to judge and gossip. He'd known Sheila was going to be trouble, could tell by the way she'd hurried over to introduce herself as one of the heads of the homeowners' association.

"I'll make sure you get the right buyers," she'd promised and winked.

He fanned his cards again and stared at Sheila through the kitchen pass. Her phone was tucked between her shoulder and ear. A long brown coat wrapped tightly around her, even though Lucky had kept the house invitingly warm, almost as if she wore it to shield herself from the unflattering surroundings.

Sheila glanced up and met his eyes. Surprise or concern crossed her face. Lucky wasn't sure which.

He picked up a bottle of water from the counter, twisted off the top. Sipped and stared.

Sheila looked away. He heard her clear her throat and continue. "I'm sorry?"

Lucky turned and gazed at the dismal kitchen. White paneling needing a coat of paint, sluggish yellowed appliances, loose knobs too worn for a screwdriver to tighten. The houses in this Falls Church neighborhood of northern Virginia had been built in the 1940s but, given their proximity to DC, still sold near or over a million when renovated. But this owner, a widower in his eighties who had reluctantly settled into an assisted-living center, had no interest in spending a dime on updates. Lucky would be fortunate to get 90 percent of its worth.

Sometimes, of course, there was a surprise. Full ask or higher on a property that didn't warrant it, the new owners harried because of the competitive DC-region housing market. Properties sold in almost complete states of disrepair. Imaginative buyers seeing promise in a shining rebuild.

Lucky imagined the excitement of a young couple in a house they'd just bought, and tears welled in his eyes.

He forced himself to focus on the job, and not his marriage.

"I don't know who would buy it!" Sheila exclaimed into her phone, and, with that, Lucky walked to the knife rack and pulled out a long chef's knife.

"He's in the kitchen!" Sheila shrieked.

Lucky hadn't even heard the front door open. He slid the knife back into the rack. Wiped his wet eyes on his sleeve and left the kitchen for the living room.

A couple waited in the entrance, watching Sheila as she beamed at them from the couch, like rabbits warily regarding a leering wolf. Lucky sized them up. White, late twenties or early thirties, wearing Sunday church clothes, the man clean shaven, the woman in heels.

The man, still slim before the softening effects of middle age, wore a dark-blue suit with tan leather shoes and a matching belt.

She was pretty with a thin, sharp face and looked around the house with quick birdlike intensity. A dark-blue ankle-length dress. The princess-cut diamond on her wedding ring glinted.

Yuppies, Lucky figured, who rented in DC or Arlington and were looking for a bigger home to fill with family.

Young and married and happy.

Lucky hoped he'd be able to speak past the lump in his throat. He used to be so much better at compartmentalizing.

"Is the open house still going on?" the man asked.

Sheila watched them appreciatively from the couch. Lucky figured this couple fit the bill for her, especially after a Black family had come by a half hour earlier, and Sheila's face had held nothing but distress. Lucky had cheerfully imagined slapping her with a hammer.

"It is," he answered. "Come on back to the kitchen and sign in. My name's Lucky."

"Lucky?" the woman asked.

Sheila barked out a laugh.

"My father was a gambler," Lucky explained. He'd done this his entire life. "He said that having a son was like—"

"And I'm Sheila Banks." Sheila rose from the couch. "President of the homeowners' association. Do you mind if I join the tour? This is such a lovely neighborhood."

"Well . . . ," Lucky began.

"Only three houses in the neighborhood share this model," Sheila said, and the couple followed her into the kitchen. "And this is such a great community for families like yours."

Lucky's hands tightened into fists.

There was no way to get rid of Sheila Banks. If he asked her to leave, then he risked offending her and losing any shot of selling homes in this affluent community. He'd heard stories of that happening to other agents.

So he and Sheila guided the couple up the carpeted stairs to the second floor, Lucky hoping they didn't notice the loose railing.

"Watch out for the loose railing!" Sheila told them.

They stopped in the primary bedroom, a bare narrow room that Lucky knew could be salvaged with a nice clean coat of paint.

"The bedrooms are a little small—" Lucky began.

"And in *desperate* need of new paint," Sheila added.

"But smaller bedrooms were the style at the time this house was built," Lucky continued. "Now, you knock out the second bedroom, expand this room, connect it to the bathroom at the end of the hall? That gives you a sizable primary bedroom with an enclosed bath and—"

"But they'd lose a bedroom," Sheila interrupted.

"Right, but they'd still have two, and if they convert the basement—"

"I'm sorry, but that doesn't seem like a good idea." Sheila smiled at the couple. "I can't imagine losing a bedroom is going to help resale. Can you?"

"It gives the house a more modern look." Lucky's voice was strained. "And you have to consider—"

The phone in his left pocket buzzed.

Lucky always carried two phones. The phone in his right pocket was for family and real estate. It was the phone where Lucky kept photos of his wife and daughter and a bulging library of real estate and puzzle apps.

Lucky loved puzzles.

The phone in his left pocket had nothing on it. It was a generic phone that had been given to him by the Winterses last night, buried in a plastic bag next to a certain tree in the woods behind his house.

He stopped talking, pulled out the new phone, stared at the screen.

"You take that," Sheila told him. "I'll continue the tour."

He gazed at the message for another minute, then slipped the phone back into his pocket.

The young couple and Sheila were heading back to the stairs. "The basement," Lucky said as he hurried behind them, "is right through the kitchen. In the door next to the pantry. Now, it's not finished, and there was a possum, well, more like a community of possums, but—"

In his rush, Lucky's foot slipped on the stairs. He caught himself before he fell, but nearly yanked the old banister from the wall.

"I think we've seen enough," the husband said. He and his wife glanced at each other.

Lucky knew that glance well.

"Are you sure?" he asked. He could tell the sale was lost, but, after fifteen years in real estate, pushing back was habit. "The basement isn't finished but—"

"We're sure," the husband confirmed.

"I'm sorry it didn't work out," Sheila told them.

Asking Sheila to leave would be a poor choice, Lucky decided. Better to lock the front door, choke the life out of her with his bare hands, hide her body in the basement. Come back in the night and drive her corpse away. Toss Sheila Banks in the bottom of a new home site being built down the street and bury her deep. He smiled at the fantasy.

Lucky placed his hands in his pockets, felt a reminding vibration from the phone in his left pocket. The phone from the Winterses.

> My husband and I are moving to DC from California in a couple of months and are heading up soon to look at houses. Are you available for showings? Can we talk later?

"Hopefully we'll have better luck next weekend!" Sheila called.

He heard the front door open and close.

Lucky kept staring at the message.

How about tonight? he wrote back.

The response came right away.

> Midnight.

Sounds good, he replied.

Another quick response.

> This could be a life-changing sale for you.

◆ ◆ ◆

"I'm sorry," Renee said sympathetically, after Lucky finished telling his wife about the open house. She was sitting on their kitchen counter, legs crossed, a glass of wine in hand. "Sounds like a waste of a day."

Lucky examined the plate he'd pulled from the dishwasher, searching for water spots, avoiding looking his wife in the face. "I did almost kill the president of the HOA. That would have made me feel better."

Renee took a sip. "Sometimes you have to do something just for yourself, you know?"

"But I do have interest on the place in Sterling. Meeting with a family and their agent next week."

"The rambler?"

Renee had a terrific memory for details. Lucky's memory, as he strolled further into middle age, was dulling. He'd even started carrying a little notebook filled with scribbled details about showings . . . details he now needed glasses to decipher.

"That's the one." He put away the plate, pulled out a coffee mug. "How about you? Ready for tomorrow?"

Renee was an assistant headmaster at Eastwise, a private elementary school in Annandale. One of the school's largest funders was touring soon, and the staff had spent the weekend prepping for his visit.

"We found *so many* vape pens. But on the bright side, now a bunch of us know how to vape. I felt so cool. Also, your special package arrived today."

He nodded.

"You okay? You look so angry."

Lucky kept staring into the clean mug. "Just thinking about work."

He'd discovered Renee's affair by accident, a startling revelation weeks ago via their maps app one morning as Lucky was trying to find directions to a new client's home. The address in the app's archives surprised him, given that he was the only one who used it—their seventeen-year-old daughter Marybeth had just earned her license, and they rarely allowed her to drive, and Renee generally only went to work and back. As he researched the address, wondering if it was one he'd forgotten to clear, he discovered who it belonged to.

William McKenna. A teacher at Renee's school. Lucky knew him from occasional dinner parties at their house. White and blond with reddish cheeks and a heavyset bearing, on the edge of being overweight. He'd seemed inconsequential, the kind of man met and promptly forgotten.

Lucky had also noted the date that the address had been accessed. A Tuesday. A day that, supposedly, Renee was at work.

Lucky had asked her about him later that night—"How's that William McKenna doing?"—and she'd replied with a vague, "I don't really talk to him."

But Renee had paused before she answered, and Lucky had interrogated too many people to miss those kinds of signs.

"We need to talk about your daughter," Renee said now, gently swirling the remaining wine in her glass.

"Our daughter."

"Not for this, I'm too annoyed. She's been lying to us, even more than usual. She didn't go to the movies the last two weekends. Instead she went to parties at some friend's place in Herndon. Who do we even know in Herndon?"

"No one." Lucky closed the upper cabinet, which was filled with mugs from Marybeth and Renee with sayings like "Best Farter Ever" and "#1 Dad at Going #2."

"How'd you find out about the party?" Lucky asked.

"Snoop-E." Snoop-E was an app Renee and Lucky used to track their daughter's social media and email. "I don't know what's happening at these parties, but if she isn't telling us about them . . ."

She set her empty glass down, let the sentence hang, the silence explaining itself.

A bottle of wine on Sunday nights had become a tradition for Renee, dating back to when Marybeth had entered her preteen years. Lucky rarely drank, especially compared to how much his parents had.

"I'll talk with Marybeth," he offered.

"Tonight?" Renee asked.

"We can't have her sneaking out and going to parties."

Renee reached for the bottle. "Now that's just good parenting."

Lucky left her in the kitchen. He wondered if someone watching their conversation would have noticed the tension, how Renee drank alone. How he hadn't once looked at her face.

Or if it just would have seemed like the familiar trappings of a twenty-year marriage.

Lucky didn't know what a happy marriage was supposed to look like. His own parents had stayed married until cancer had come for both of them when Lucky was in his early twenties and stationed overseas. He didn't remember any instances of either of them straying, even significant fights . . . at least, not when they were drinking. And in his memories, they were always drinking.

Lucky headed upstairs, knocked on Marybeth's door, waited for a "Yeah?" before walking in.

"Hey," Marybeth said, without looking up from her phone.

It was odd to Lucky how much Marybeth resembled Renee, as if their family had relatively unimaginative genes. Marybeth had her mother's angular cheekbones and wide eyes, like long brushstrokes had been used for their faces, and her mother's dark hair. But where both Lucky and Renee were no longer trim, Marybeth had an easy thinness. Even now, she casually sat in a yoga pose, one he recognized as the lotus position from the virtual classes Renee and Marybeth did together, each of her heels propped up on the opposite knee as she sat cross-legged.

She glanced up. "What's wrong?"

"Wrong?"

"You look so sad right now. Didn't Mom tell you your special package came?"

Lucky closed her door behind himself. "Just looking at you sitting like that hurts."

His daughter grinned, and he settled in the chair opposite her bed. In addition to her mother's looks, Marybeth also had her approach to tidiness. Clothes were in piles throughout the room. Renee was the same way, and it had taken a while for Lucky to realize that there was a method to her disorganization, and every pile had some relevance: a pile of clothes she'd bought that needed to be returned, another for outfits still tagged that she wanted to try on and hadn't yet, a heap of older jeans and shirts that were eventually going to be donated.

And, in addition to the piles of clothes, school papers and folders and books and various beauty products Lucky didn't understand were all over the dresser, desk, and floor, and the walls were covered with posters of musicians: Billie Eilish, the Weeknd, Atmosphere, Markus Peña, Lizzo, BTOB, all performing, their expressions strained. Being in Marybeth's room always made Lucky feel like someone was shouting at him.

"So what's up, Dad?"

"Tell me about the parties."

"Parties?" Marybeth tried to keep her voice composed, but he noticed she'd stopped scrolling.

"The parties you went to the last two weekends. Instead of the movies."

Marybeth set her phone down, glared at her father accusingly. "Were you looking at my accounts again?"

"Yes."

"You had no right—"

"The parties."

She relented.

"I didn't want to tell you because older guys were there."

"How old?"

"Like . . . college?"

"College?" Lucky couldn't hide his incredulity. "You're still in high school!"

"I'm a *senior*." As if he was unaware. "And, I promise, I didn't know they'd be there the first time."

"And the second?"

"Yeah, I knew then." A small smile, despite herself. Something Marybeth was keeping secret.

She liked one of these older boys.

Lucky wondered if Renee had similar moments, times when she was lost in thoughts about William. Found herself smiling.

"You can't go to parties with college boys," he said.

"I know," Marybeth replied, her eyes earnest. "I'm sorry."

Far too easy.

"And no more phone tonight." He held out his hand.

Marybeth was going to protest, but she looked at him and something in her face changed.

Lucky generally kept his patience, his tone even. Renee was the one who raised her voice.

But he was the one Marybeth feared.

Lucky wasn't sure why.

Lucky heard Renee head upstairs to bed, but he didn't follow her. Instead he sat on the leather recliner next to the couch in their living room, the lights off and the room dark.

And he felt tears.

Tears at the thought of Renee with someone else.

Tears at how easily Marybeth had lied to him.

Lucky reached for the controller on the end table. He turned on the lights of the Christmas tree and it blinked to life, green and red lights illuminating the ornaments, a mix of glass and wood and plastic, children pulling sleds, smiling *Peanuts* characters wearing stocking caps or holding wrapped gifts, silver-and-red balls, fake tan gingerbread families, Disney figurines Marybeth had treasured when she was a little girl.

Another button turned on the lights of the garland over the fireplace mantel, fake plastic holly and berries and soft white lights, wise men accompanied by camels and sheep as they voyaged from one end of the mantel, a barn in the center lit from inside, a small window showing Mary and Joseph kneeling over a bundle of straw.

And, of course, the Christmas Village, spread out on the living room table and fireplace hearth. But Lucky couldn't think about that now.

He sat in the chair stiffly, trying to corral the emotions tormenting his chest, the thoughts polluting his mind.

He couldn't be in his house anymore.

And that was a terrible thing to realize.

Lucky turned off the lights and rose. Headed through the dark living room and dining room, completely unable to see, but with the comfort of someone who has lived in the same home for years.

Or someone used to walking through the dark.

He opened the patio door and headed outside, rubbing his arms in the brisk cold. The exterior office hadn't been entirely necessary, but Renee had been helping out her school by teaching classes virtually during the pandemic, and she'd said the separate, quiet space helped.

For some reason that sentiment had made Lucky feel terribly lonely.

The quarantine at the start of the pandemic had been a shocking adjustment for their family, as it had for everyone else. Renee's and Marybeth's schools abruptly moving to online education. Lucky's showings placed on hold, and homeowners, worried about the uncertain future, deciding not to sell. Groceries delivered, along with everything else. Their home suddenly also a business office and classroom and rec center. Renee and Marybeth had been distraught, but the dramatic lifestyle change had affected Lucky differently. Despite the news reports of crowded hospitals and rising death tolls, Lucky had found a warmth in seeing his wife and daughter more than he ever had, a joy during newfound game and movie nights, enchantment when observing his wife and daughter at their respective schools. They'd complained that they needed more room, and, over that first summer when a return to in-person schooling was still improbable, he'd had the backyard office built for Renee.

Lucky loved the square one-room building. It had been designed to look like a miniature version of their house: a small sloped roof, faux white bricks, even a tiny dormer.

He unlocked the door to the backyard office—now his, since the concept of remote learning for children had long ago passed—and walked in. The office was nondescript in the way Lucky preferred: nothing but a rug and a desk and a chair. He pulled out his second phone, sat and waited, idly spinning back and forth.

It would be a few hours before the Winterses called, but Lucky didn't mind. He felt calmer now, removed from the house and his family, his adulterous wife and deceptive daughter.

Lucky needed something else, even an assignment from the Winterses, anything that offered reprieve from pain.

This could be a life-changing sale for you, they had written.

Lucky wasn't sure why he believed them, but he did. And in his agitated state, any path toward peace, even a bloody path, held promise.

CHAPTER THREE

RUBY

Once upon a time, the Winterses ruled the triangle of DC, Maryland, and Virginia.

Their operation was, like the most callous criminal enterprises, ostensibly legal, a business powered by ruthless capitalism and tireless expansion, gods in American religion, profits fervently praised, tactics hotly defended from criticism. The Winters Holdings Inc. was a proud commercial real estate development firm familiar throughout DC, the name plastered on new construction where old buildings had once stood: "Coming Soon: A Winters Property."

The Winters Holdings Inc. focused on DC but stretched into Maryland and Virginia, visiting neighborhoods decimated by poverty, their logo of a flying angel the promise of a soul being saved, a sinner guilty of the offense of financial duress now forgiven. Gentrification tied to the enticement of a Black-free block, the photos of new gyms and grocery stores and condominiums on their advertisements showing cheery white families. High-end retailers and cherished businesses that famously overcharged rumored to eventually take up residence. No one discussed what would happen to the current occupants of these neighborhoods; the politicians and police were paid, the media enamored, the plight of the current homeowners silenced.

And their plans quietly worked even when, ostensibly, they failed: buildings in the midst of neighborhoods eroded by poverty and routinely ignored, the construction endless or stopped, structures barricaded by chain-link fences and graffiti-strewn wooden panels. These properties were intended to be forgotten, a tax write-off waiting on a never-to-come future buyer or economic revitalization—for all purposes, abandoned.

Inside these buildings, if you chose to look, you would find things you didn't want to know about. Women, barely dressed and shivering. Cases of pistols and rifles and ammunition. The Winterses had an empire, yellow bricks laid throughout the DC region, led by one man who, for years, had no public presence other than a Wikipedia page with the following information:

> Victor Winters is the owner and founder of Winters Holdings Inc., a commercial real estate development company based in Washington, DC.[1]

It wasn't until Victor's assassination, along with his associate and girlfriend Isabel Pike, that anyone asked questions. Victor Winters was wealthy, and Isabel was beautiful, and they had been murdered, and so the media and public were helplessly intrigued. And when ties were found to illegal activity, to human trafficking and gun smuggling, it was like a crackling fuse reaching a red bundle of dynamite.

There were some arrests: a Black city politician who was already notoriously corrupt; a group of women at a high-end massage parlor, their male customers unidentified and freed; the owner of a local professional sports team tied to sex trafficking, although that story ultimately faded from attention. Victor Winters, who had switched from a shadowy figure to a revered criminal, like Al Capone or John Gotti, was dead, and without a living person to attack or blame, the media and public's concerns waned.

The signs for Winters Holdings Inc. stopped appearing throughout the city. The existing signs were taken down.

But the buildings remained. And the work inside them continued.

◆ ◆ ◆

Ruby Smith was, in many ways, the voice of the Winterses.

For all the romanticization of the anonymity and danger of the dark web, the Winterses preferred the old days of hiding in plain sight, like the signs on their buildings, a taunting "Here I am." And they chose a simple process to communicate with Ruby.

On Sundays Ruby would walk three blocks from her house in Winchester, Virginia, to a nearby church, where she would pray. Sometimes, during prayer, she would be so overcome by anguish that she would weep.

On the way back home, she would stop at a liquor store, eyes downcast. The liquor store was closed on Sundays, but the back door was always open for her. She would slip inside, and a man called Joe would give her money and a cell phone and a message. Joe would repeat the message three times.

The first time Ruby comprehended what Joe was saying.

The second time she absorbed it.

The third time she remembered it.

As often happened with colleagues over the years, regardless of circumstance, Ruby and Joe developed a cordial relationship. Sometimes it took her more than three tries to remember the message, and they laughed at this. Sometimes Joe told her about the long drive from wherever he lived to the liquor store in Winchester, playful exasperation at having to come this far.

And then, after Victor Winters was assassinated, Joe told her about the organization.

He told her about the death of Victor Winters, the rumors that it had come at the hands of a rival gang, a specialized police unit, a government agency, a masked vigilante. He told her about the uncertainty among the soldiers, the problems of a vacated leadership, the fears of raids or federal investigation now that they were no longer concealed, the errors that had begun to occur. Four naked girls stumbling outside a warehouse, blinking in afternoon sunlight as passersby took photos. A shoot-out with a gang that left two civilians dead. The unshipped crates of weapons, the recipients worried about receiving anything related to the Winterses.

It was a mess, Joe confided, and it lasted months. He still visited Ruby weekly, even without a message or money, just to keep her apprised. She enjoyed these visits, the way he turned to her for his unburdening.

Aside from the Lord and Joe, Ruby didn't have anyone else. She devoutly but quietly went to church once a week, maintained a cordial relationship with the lawyers at the small bankruptcy firm where she worked as an office manager. Her nights were spent eating on a TV tray and watching old game shows: *Jeopardy!* from when Alex Trebek was alive, *Who Wants to Be a Millionaire?*, school quiz shows with uncomfortably dressed students nervously offering answers.

And then she would prepare the codes for the messages the Winterses had given her.

It was a lonely life, Ruby realized, but a fulfilled one.

One Sunday she went to the liquor store and Joe wasn't there.

"Joe's not coming back," the man waiting for her said.

"What happened to him?"

The man shook his head. He was older and tall and thin and wore yellow-tinted glasses. Black curly hair contrasted with pale skin. An open brown leather jacket over a dark shirt and dark pants.

Ruby didn't know why he looked familiar to her.

Then he told her his name.

"You look different than your brother," Ruby said.

"You met Victor?" Frank Winters asked.

"Once."

"If Victor had lost two hundred pounds and not gone bald, he'd have looked like me."

"So you're running things now?" Ruby asked.

He nodded.

"Is Joe dead?"

"No one knows what happened to Joe," he replied. "But you're one of the last people who saw him. Anything seem different to you last Sunday?"

Ruby thought back to the prior weekend. Joe telling her the usual. The anxiety he'd confessed to months ago, after Victor's assassination, had been replaced by frustration. Soldiers grumbling about unclear directives. Money slowing.

Ruby thought it best not to reveal any of that.

"Not really."

He stared at her from behind those yellow glasses. Ruby almost felt his gaze prodding her mind, searching for answers. Eventually he sniffed, pulled his nose, shrugged.

He gave her a phone and money, enough money to make up for the weeks when she hadn't been paid, even more than that.

And he gave her a message to share. Frank only said it once, but Ruby remembered it.

"Make the calls tonight," he said. "This is urgent."

◆ ◆ ◆

"Is this Lucky Wilson?" she asked hours later, her voice unrecognizable to anyone who had ever spoken to her, high pitched and young.

Lucky's guarded tone: "Yes."

Ruby remembered a show she'd seen on television years ago, a *60 Minutes* special about a young popular minister who spoke in tongues. The reporter's skepticism did nothing to deter her fascination with the program or the video of the minister preaching to the congregation. He paused suddenly, his eyes wide and worried, and took uncertain steps, then collapsed as the crowd stood. And then the minister rose, voice and face strained as the camera closed in on him, words emerging that had an ancient sense to them, as if this was a language he had once known but forgotten. It reminded Ruby of the incomprehensibility of modern paintings and poetry she'd come across in a high school class, hidden messages on the verge of being deciphered.

And so, when she spoke on the phone on behalf of the Winterses, Ruby was always reminded of that young minister, compelled to speak words he couldn't comprehend, delivering an untranslatable message that, nonetheless, was understood. Ruby closed her eyes, and an identity filled her, a young woman she didn't know but welcomed and gave her body to, as if her body was a vessel for a wandering ghost.

"Hi, Lucky! I'm Marie Cross. Thanks for talking to me so late! My husband couldn't make the call." She laughed, excited and chatty, a contrast to her normal speaking voice. "So you just get me."

"That's not a problem." Ruby heard faint pencil marks on the other end. She imagined him scribbling notes as she dropped certain clues: *Marie Cross, so late*, and *husband couldn't make call.*

"What can I help you and your husband with?"

"Well," Ruby went on, "we're moving to DC because of my husband's job. And I was looking at listings in the *Post* on Saturday and saw some nice areas in Frederick. Do you work in that area?"

Scribbles.

Husband's job.

Saturday Post.

Frederick.

Work in the area.

"Yes, I'm licensed in both Virginia and Maryland."

"Oh, good! We're looking for a single-family home, just one bedroom. We don't need two."

One bedroom.

Don't need two.

"Are you looking for something new or used?"

"We prefer new. I mean, we always hear that if you buy an old home, then you're just buying someone else's problems. But we're just starting out, so we don't have a ton of money. We're open to a condo." She offered another laugh. "I mean, we don't mind having neighbors. As long as they're not playing loud music or anything. We like it quiet."

New.

Condo.

Quiet.

"The other thing is, we're only going to be in DC for a little bit. Seven days."

"What's your budget?"

"We want to stay between three to four? That's for a one-bedroom. Maybe up to five for a two-bedroom, but it'd have to be in really good condition."

7 days.

3 to 4 for 1.

4 to 5 for 2.

She paused.

"Can you help us?"

"Let me do some research," Lucky said, "but I think so. I'll text you."

"That's great! It was nice talking with you!"

She hung up.

Ruby thought back to the conversation, tried to remember if she'd missed anything.

Saturday Post

Frederick

It had been an article in the *Washington Post* on Saturday, an incident at the Heartbreak Diner in Frederick, Maryland. Two people murdered in a shooting, two others who escaped. The story hadn't identified the names of the two who had fled, just that they were young, but it had identified the man they'd stabbed, who had accidentally killed two people in his attempt to stop them: Bruce Parks, a clumsy soldier for the Winterses.

Marie Cross: A stand-in name for someone with the initials M. C.

Ruby had never called out for a job that required multiple contractors before—that's what she'd meant when she said *condo*. And that spoke to the urgency, and to the new management. So much about this job was unusual.

Seven days to complete the work.

The money was good. Between thirty to forty thousand for M. C., forty to fifty for both her and her partner.

Can you help us?

Just then, her phone buzzed with Lucky's reply.

I can help.

Ruby felt the power of a spirit well within her as she prepared to share the message with another killer.

Chapter Four

Jake

Jake drove most of the night, he and Melissa without conversation, just the nearly silent sounds of her crying. Once he pulled over and took a picture of her as she sat curved in the passenger seat, arms wrapped around her head, knees to her chin, a highway light revealing how her fingers clutched her own hair. And then Jake kept driving, deeper into Maryland, away from the cities and down dark highways and toward the Eastern Shore.

He couldn't stop thinking about how Melissa had pushed the knife into that stranger's pants and the way it suddenly glided into his thigh, could swear he'd heard the scratchy sound of blade scraping bone. The man's face when he and Jake looked at each other, his surprised expression just before the pain.

The man with the lanyard crawling away from the door, blood running down his body like a broken fountain.

Tears threatened. Nausea tugged.

Jake drove.

They reached the Bay Bridge and climbed its high unsettling arc. Jake was compelled to take a picture, not of the bridge but of Melissa's worried reaction. Jake was mesmerized by her expressions; he'd never met someone whose emotions so naturally played onto her face or body, like a silent actor from a black-and-white world.

But Melissa stayed huddled away from him.

"Once I went skydiving," Jake said, "and the instructor strapped me to him, and I asked, right before we jumped, why he got into training people. You know, parachuting with a student? He said he did it to face his biggest fear. Dying alone."

She didn't laugh.

"Okay, I've never been skydiving." He glanced over the side of the narrow, high bridge.

"Hopefully this won't be my first time."

They cleared the bridge, and Jake pulled to a stop a mile away and took pictures of the road behind them, trying to capture how the dark resembled a giant snake swallowing the world.

Finally he saw a sign. An old wooden billboard, lit from underneath by two spotlights, offering a location in a town called Wharfside and an idea. He stopped and photographed the billboard, the aged brown boards like a religious promise to pilgrims.

Jake followed the sign's direction down a side road, drove until he saw the warehouse for Best Boats Storage, nothing else around but the occasional faint lights of houses in the distance. Jake parked in the warehouse's empty lot.

The front door was locked and chained shut. He took a picture of it, the chains impenetrable vines. Walked around the back of the building and saw that the warehouse was surrounded by trees, branches bare in the winter, limbs of frozen giants.

No sign of an alarm on the window.

Worth a shot. Jake removed his shirt, wrapped it around his fist.

It took two punches to break through the window; the glass shattered and fell to the floor below. He peered into the dark warehouse, listened intently, legs and arms tense, ready to run in case an alarm cried.

No sound but water lapping nearby, somewhere unseen through trees.

A gasp of breeze.

Jake flashed back to the diner, the way the waitress had suddenly stopped crawling. The gurgling sound she'd made.

He shook the glass out of his shirt before putting it back on. Cleared out the broken shards from the windowsill. Climbed into the building.

The warehouse was a place for boat owners to store their ships in winter, so they didn't have to leave them in driveways or docks, the building a giant indoor parking lot under a metal arched ceiling with rows of lights hanging from the rafters. Many of the smaller boats were covered by fitted tarps, packed so closely together that Jake had to squeeze sideways between them. It was a mismatched fleet, everything from Jet Skis to tiny motorboats to a row of small yachts lining the back. It was the yachts that interested Jake the most. He walked over to them, ran his hands over their smooth sides. Looked up high to their decks.

Melissa was standing outside the broken window when he returned.

"I think we're home."

Melissa looked away.

"And, if we get hurt," Jake added, "now we can go to the dock."

Nothing.

"Get it? Dock, like doctor?"

Still nothing. Jake aimed his camera at her, his left eye wide so his lashes didn't crowd the viewfinder. He took a picture of Melissa looking away.

◆ ◆ ◆

The next afternoon Jake sat on the edge of a pier and photographed the Chesapeake, sunlight shining on the water like diamonds bouncing on the surface. He reached into the paper bag next to him, pulled out a white powdered doughnut, bit into it. Breathed in cool air as gulls above called and swooped and soared.

There wasn't much to the fishing town of Wharfside. A small community, quiet and closed during the winter. He'd found a convenience store near the town's edge, the kind of store for people driving past and fast. The kind of place where it wasn't likely a person would be remembered.

Jake had heard about towns like this, places where Marylanders with money would visit over the summer to sail. Off-season, now in December, it was shut down, little more than one small street of businesses, most of the stores dark with signs announcing a spring reopening. The nearest houses were isolated from each other, buried within the woods.

He took another bite from his doughnut and pulled out his phone. Shifted so Melissa's gun, stuffed in the pocket of his hoodie, stopped poking him in the stomach.

There was something Jake wanted to do, and he wasn't sure if it was a bad idea or not. He thought about it, tapping his phone against his chin.

"Call Eric," he told his phone.

There was no way, Jake reasoned as the line buzzed, that the Winterses had somehow tapped his phone.

Probably not.

"Jake?" Eric Liu, his best friend, asked. "You all right? Is Melissa okay? Why are you calling me? That's such a bad idea."

Jake swallowed, wiped powder from his lips with the back of his hand. "The Winterses don't know who I am, so there's no way they know my phone number."

"You sure?"

"Definitely." Jake hoped he believed himself. "We're hiding in a town called Wharfside, in a warehouse for boat storage, after almost getting killed in a diner. And Melissa's not talking to me. Things are really good."

Jake told his friend about the diner, the stranger, the dead people. Eric listened quietly. Jake imagined the tension in his friend's face, the grimace that seemed to appear whenever Jake talked about Melissa. Wished he could take a picture of it.

He and Eric had known each other since they were children, their moms in the same business, the boys brought together by circumstance and need. Often staying together in their disheveled apartment building in a distressed area of Alexandria, Virginia, when their mothers went to work.

Jake tended to wander, his life like a winding path through thick tangled woods, but Eric held firm. Eric was that one calm kid in class reading a textbook while a hurricane of students gleefully screeched around him. Jake was close friends with him until Eric's mother died and he was suddenly whisked away to live with his family down south. But Eric had returned a few years ago, and he and Jake had easily fallen back into friendship.

For so long, Jake had been immersed in photography. Learning the mechanics of cameras, the whimsical nature of light, seeing a photograph the way others heard a song. But Eric's return—a surprise meeting at a grocery store when Eric walked up behind Jake, touched his elbow, said that he swore he knew him—had given Jake something he hadn't realized he missed. Friendship. Eric taught him how to love someone else; without Eric's example, Jake didn't think he'd ever have had the courage to let in Melissa.

"Can't you two do anything quietly?" Eric asked once Jake finished his story. "You're leaving a trail."

"Quiet's what I want," Jake replied. "What Melissa and me both want."

"Two women came by my place," Eric said. "Twins. They asked me where you were."

"Cops?"

"No. I think they were with the Winterses."

"They came to your place?"

"Yeah."

"What'd you tell them?" Jake asked.

"The truth. That I had no idea where you and Melissa are." Eric paused. "But you have to listen to me. If you want to save Melissa and yourself, you need to go farther away."

"Do you remember their names?" Jake could feel panic rising.

"They didn't give them. And it didn't seem like I could ask. But just be careful. Something about them seemed . . . off."

Their conversation ended.

Jake no longer had the same confidence he'd had moments ago, before he'd called Eric, or when he'd assured his friend that this call was safe.

Men and women were hunting him and Melissa and nothing was safe.

Jake was scared, the type of fear he'd felt when he was four or five, and Eric and his mother weren't around, and Jake's mom would leave him in their apartment at night, Jake curled on the couch under a blanket with the television on because he was too scared to sleep alone in his room. This was that kind of fear, when Jake had to watch TV and lose himself as deeply as he could in the shows, ignore the shadowy apartment around him, the noises from the hall outside.

He wanted to call his friend again, confess his fear, find sanctuary in honesty. Shake away the sense of failure creeping behind him, something that had always lurked in the shadows of Jake's life, the flip side of artistic ambition.

Jake suddenly realized how tightly he was holding his camera, as if trying to bend it into some other shape.

He relaxed his grip. The Lumix DC-FZ80 was a sturdy little digital camera, but Jake didn't want to risk warping the frame. It was the only camera he'd been able to grab when he and Melissa had fled. The man he'd bought the camera from had told Jake the lens was powerful enough to show the craters on the moon, and he'd been astonished to discover that this was true. Jake wished he'd thought to bring a tripod or other flashes, but he imagined this camera would be enough for however long he and Melissa needed.

He felt a little better thinking about that, the idea that a future for them existed.

◆ ◆ ◆

Melissa was slouched in a folding chair on the deck of a yacht, wearing a big floppy hat and sunglasses when Jake returned.

"You doing okay?" he asked.

"No." She gazed at him evenly. "A cop came by."

"What?"

Melissa nodded. "A rent-a-cop. I saw him looking through that window you busted. Shining a flashlight through."

Jake felt overwhelmed. "Did he see you?"

"Yeah, he came in, and we talked about sailing."

"What?"

Melissa lifted the brim of her floppy hat, looked at him from behind the sunglasses. Her earlier numbness seemed to have dissipated. "No," she said patiently. "He didn't come in, and we didn't talk, and he didn't see me. But he's probably coming back. Or someone will to check out the window. And they'll search the boats."

"Dammit."

"That's what I said." Melissa paused for a moment. "But it's weird. I was happy when he was here. Like . . . I hoped he'd arrest us."

"Why?"

"We killed those people at the diner."

"We didn't kill them."

"They'd be alive if we hadn't been there."

Jake didn't know how to respond. "Where'd you get the glasses and hat?"

"A closet down below."

"You going to keep them?"

"They're cute." As if that answered his question.

Jake waited a moment before he spoke again, worried about how Melissa would react to what he was going to tell her.

"I called Eric."

Melissa yanked off the sunglasses. "What?!"

"I'm sorry," Jake said sincerely. "It was a mistake. I didn't think about it. I'm sorry."

"Jesus, Jake."

"I know, I just wanted to talk with him. To make sure he was okay."

Melissa still looked upset but didn't press her irritation. Jake loved her for that, the way she always seemed to understand his impulses and inhibitions, even now. "What did he say?"

"He told me the Winterses asked him about us," Jake replied, "but Eric didn't say anything. I'm hoping they give up."

"Chris won't be happy until we're both dead," Melissa said simply.

Jake didn't know how to respond.

Again, failure whispered.

"I moved my car." Jake hoped this would offer some reassurance. "Parked it off the side of some dirt road. But we can't risk driving anywhere, and we can't take a train or plane with everyone looking for us. I figure we stay here tonight and find someplace new tomorrow."

"I guess we should." Melissa pulled off the hat, examined how it was woven. "Had you ever seen someone die before?"

Melissa's question was a shovel plunged into his ribs. She kept talking before he could reply.

"I didn't know it would be like that, with that much blood. It was like blood was being pulled out of their bodies."

Jake didn't respond.

"I wish I hadn't seen them. I don't ever want to see your pictures."

Jake nodded. He couldn't look at them either.

"It feels like we're corrupt," Melissa said. "Too dirty to ever be clean."

"I'm sorry," he told her quietly. "I'm sorry I got you into this. That I brought you to that diner . . ."

"I shouldn't have let you stop."

Jake walked to the other side of the deck and looked over the railing at the swarm of dry boats.

"Should we go back?" he asked. "Try the cops?"

"We have to run. That's the only way we'll be safe."

Jake turned toward Melissa, but he didn't look at her.

"Do you want to run without me?" he asked.

"No. Do you?"

"It'd feel like drowning," he told her. "And when I feel like I'm going to drown, I just want to hold you."

"So you'd pull me down with you?"

"Well, yeah, but . . . romantically."

Jake explored the warehouse. A dozen skylights were spread throughout the ceiling, the late-year sunshine straining through dirty glass. A locked door led to an office from which, Jake assumed, the large bay doors could be opened. He went through the other boats, hunting for food, drinks, clothes, anything they could use. All he found were cases of water, some scuba diving gear he figured they could pawn, heavy boating equipment he didn't understand.

Jake walked back to their boat, a case of water balanced on his shoulder.

"Hello?"

A man's voice.

Jake stayed statue still, trying to control his breathing, listening hard.

He set the case down.

"Hello?" That voice again. Older and quaking. Scared. "Anyone here?"

A grunt. A crunch of glass.

Someone had climbed in through that broken window.

Jake touched the gun that was still awkwardly stuffed in his hoodie's pouch.

Footsteps approached, unsure and slow.

Jake pulled the gun free, held it unnaturally in his hand. He'd only fired a gun once before, when he was in his early teens and a friend had taken him into some swamp in Alexandria, and they'd found a deer's dead body and filled it with bullets, the animal's long black eyes staring until, finally, Jake was too shaken to shoot anymore.

"Jake?"

Melissa's voice from inside the boat, probably still in the bedroom, wondering where he had gone.

That man's footsteps again. Quicker now. Coming toward them. Following Melissa's voice.

"Where'd you go?" Melissa called out.

Jake slipped behind the yacht. He walked around it, the bow that nearly touched the warehouse's back wall. Hurried past the long side with "The Constellation" painted on it in red and blue.

Jake circled the boat until he saw an elderly man, a security guard in tan pants and a red polo, staring up the ladder. No gun or weapon on him. Nothing but a flashlight in his hand. His back turned.

Oblivious that Jake was walking toward him.

"Um, hi," Jake said.

The guard's shoulders hunched like an arrow had suddenly dug between them. He yelped and turned, still in a flinch.

His frightened gaze didn't leave Jake's gun.

"Who are . . ." The guard's voice faded, and he tried again. "Who are . . ."

"Turn around," Jake told him. He heard the quaver in his own voice. "Please."

"Don't," the guard whispered. "You don't have to."

Jake pushed the other man's chest with his free hand, the shove harder than he'd expected. The old man stumbled, caught himself before he fell. Jake almost reached out to steady him.

"Jake?"

He and the guard both looked up. They saw Melissa on the deck, staring down.

"Help me," the guard said to her. "Please."

"What do we do?" Jake asked her.

"He's seen us," Melissa said. "He'll tell them about us."

Her voice broke as she spoke, the same sudden anguish on her face as when she'd stabbed that man at the diner.

Jake's hand trembled as his fingertip touched the trigger.

Chapter Five
Lucky

Lucky peered through binoculars as dawn broke over the Heartbreak Diner. The parking lot was empty, signs on the window announced that the diner was temporarily closed. Lucky wondered if the closure would be permanent. When he was a kid, a murder at a business meant that the business could never continue.

But times changed.

He locked his car and walked across the parking lot. It would have been easy enough to sneak inside, but there was no need to draw attention to himself. Lucky often found that a direct approach was best in most situations. And if he was stopped and asked, he could produce the business card that identified him as a licensed private investigator from the sixty-hour course he'd completed years ago. Not that he had any interest in working as an investigator, but it did help when accessing crime scenes.

To know what cops were looking for.

He'd left his house at 4:00 a.m. for the drive, a time of day that—ideally—ensured no one else would be here. Renee thought he was scouting properties somewhere outside northern Virginia, and she'd sleepily murmured a goodbye after he kissed her on the forehead. She was used to his early mornings and late nights.

Lucky thought about that forehead kiss as he drove here. It had been habit, reflex conditioned over years.

So much of his marriage consisted of an intimacy that had become casual. Quick kisses. Monthly lovemaking. Even his appearance was intentionally unmemorable—light-brown hair always parted to the right, forever cleanly shaven, no tattoos or other markings. He was seemingly designed to be forgotten.

Should life have been less casual?

Had that been his mistake?

Lucky forced himself not to think about that, tried the door to the diner. Locked. He glanced around, pulled out his lockpick, slipped on a pair of thin gloves. Fortunately, the lock looked new—like people, old locks often aged into stubbornness. He used a tension wrench and pick, popped the tumbler like a held breath suddenly exhaled.

At this point in Lucky's life, picking a lock was as easy as using a key.

He opened the door, stepped inside. Switched on the lights.

Lucky walked up the small aisle between the counter and booths. Of course, the bodies and blood and markings from the investigation were gone, but Lucky wouldn't feel satisfied until he saw the crime scene with his own eyes. He went from one end of the diner to the other, peering under each booth, looking up at the ceiling. Pushed open the door leading to the kitchen, walked around the smudged steel ovens and refrigerators, the crumb-filled counters that had yet to be cleaned. The seating area of the diner seemed undisturbed. The kitchen, in contrast, looked like someone had rushed out.

Curious, Lucky thought, that the waitress had tried to leave through the restaurant and not the back door.

But panicked people rarely made the best decisions; Lucky had witnessed many of these mistakes. Victims running out the wrong door, pulling open an empty drawer when they went for a gun, hiding halfway under their bed, hopelessly praying with their eyes shut as he approached.

He found nothing but stains in the microwave, a cold tinfoil-covered pan of something unidentifiable in one of the ovens, Saran-wrapped bowls in the fridge.

A beep from the phone in his right pocket.

Lucky pulled it out, opened the WatchFull app, and his screen filled with an image of the front of William McKenna's house.

The lump in his throat throbbed.

Lucky had gone to William's neighborhood weeks earlier, parked a few streets away from his house and loped through the woods. Climbed a tree across from William's home and attached a lipstick-size camera to a high branch.

The same technique he used when tracking someone he was going to kill.

Lucky stared into his phone as the front door opened and William walked to his car, the way he did every morning at this exact time. Wearing a dark-blue business suit, leather satchel slung over his shoulder. William opened the door to his silver BMW, the house and car relics from William's divorce years ago from a wealthy woman, and tossed the satchel inside. Lucky had learned long ago that people, often unconsciously, followed the same pattern every single day. And William's pattern was to leave at approximately six fifteen in the morning for Eastwise Private School.

Lucky kept staring down into his phone as he stepped back into the dining area.

"Freeze!"

He stopped as if cold water had suddenly splashed his face.

For a crazy, confused moment, he wondered if William McKenna was here.

"Don't say *freeze*." Lucky realized there were two men in the dining room, both focused on him.

"Hey, Lucky."

It took a moment, Lucky still coming down from surprise, his mind adjusting like he'd walked from a dark room into light.

"Chris Winters?" Lucky asked.

Victor Winters had been a glowering mountain of a man, a giant force of nature. His nephew was markedly different. Shorter and slim, hair that nearly covered his eyes, arrogance in his expression.

And a shiny white bandage on top of his head.

The only similarity, Lucky noticed, between Victor and Chris was a sense of lurking danger. Like wading into ocean waters that turn darker and colder the farther you swim.

"This is Marley," Chris said, indicating his associate, a squarish muscular man with a cold gaze. Marley just stared at Lucky and pushed open the long black jacket he wore. Lucky saw a pair of pistols with silver grips holstered on his waist.

"How'd you know I was here?" Lucky asked.

"There's a reason we give you a phone."

Marley walked past Lucky, stood directly behind him, and Lucky fought the urge to turn.

"You're an early riser, Lucky," Chris said. "I hate that. But Marley here told me what my uncle used to tell him: successful men don't wait for the world to start; successful men start the world."

"Good advice," Lucky said, still bothered by Marley standing behind him, those twin silver pistols. His shoulder blades tightened.

"So this job," Chris went on. "Things changed. You got an order to bring the girl in alive, right?"

"Yeah."

"Dig two graves."

A touch of eagerness in Chris's voice at that. Lucky could tell he'd wanted to say that line.

"What changed?" Lucky asked.

Instead of answering, Chris walked over to a booth. Looked like he wanted to sit but thought better of it.

Marley stayed behind Lucky.

"You worked freelance for my uncle for years, right?" Chris said. "But you never wanted more than that? Never wanted to get . . . an employee badge?"

"No."

Chris seemed to be waiting for Lucky to say more.

Lucky stayed quiet. He never told cops or crooks more than they needed to know.

"Everything fell apart after my uncle was killed," Chris said, and Lucky saw a moment of vulnerability in the younger man, that arrogance turned indecisive, a young lion with a limp. "We're still putting everything back together."

Lucky had heard stories about Victor Winters's death, the dark rumors of his murder coming at the hands of a rival crime organization, a mysterious vigilante, a secret law enforcement unit that went beyond the books, a group of trafficked women who had finally fought back.

Or a member of his family.

People always whispered around the dead.

"And now my other uncle is out here, from Vegas," Chris said. "You met Frank yet? Slim guy? Wears yellow glasses like he's from the seventies?"

Lucky shook his head. He heard Marley breathing behind him, imagined he could feel the other man's breath on his neck.

"He's out here because after Victor died, no one knew what to do. We lost people. Lost money."

Lucky's phone shivered, but he didn't dare move and risk surprising Marley.

Chris was still talking. Lucky tried to listen, despite his utter certainty that his phone was alerting him to movement at William's house.

Maybe William had returned home with Renee, his morning plans changed because of Lucky's early departure, the two of them hurriedly seizing a quick opportunity for sex.

For love.

"Too much has happened," Chris was saying. "Our men dying, some just disappearing. Suppliers worried they aren't going to get paid. Territory being lost. It's time I took over, brought the Winterses back to the place where my uncle had us."

Another notification from his phone. Lucky imagined the screen showing Renee's car parked, the driver's side door hanging open in her rush, one of her shoes kicked off and left on the porch, the shape of her leg as William lifted her skirt, the two of them embracing in his open front door.

"And Chris Winters can't do that if everyone knows he got cucked and knocked out."

That distracted Lucky. "Wait," he said, confused. "I thought you're Chris Winters?"

"I am." Chris looked just as confused.

"The third person thing threw me off."

"I told you, boss," Marley said to Chris, still behind Lucky. "It's weird when you do that."

"My uncle did it!"

Nobody would have dared correct him, Lucky thought.

"Anyway," Chris went on. "We don't need some outsider from Vegas taking over, even if he is family. Chris . . . I need our soldiers to know who's in charge. So I need to make an example out of Melissa."

Lucky noticed the burn in Chris's eyes as he spoke, the flush in his cheeks, the tremble as he said her name. Hate from scorned love.

Lucky didn't care about Chris's youth. He'd accepted that, as he aged, the people he worked for would be younger. But in that moment, Chris was suddenly a kid, impulsive and rash, a look on his face similar to his daughter's when Lucky confronted her about the parties.

"Her name's Melissa?" Lucky asked.

"Melissa Cruz," Chris said, that venom still there. "She ran off with some photographer. Brained me on the way out the door." Chris touched the edge of the white bandage on his head. "We're here to give you photos, information, anything else you need. No one escapes Winter."

A moment of silence.

"Is that a new motto?" Lucky asked. "There's a slogan now?"

"Do you like it?" Chris asked.

"Well . . . I mean . . ."

"It's not great," Marley offered. "I told you that, boss. It sounds like *Game of Thrones* or something."

"Honestly, I'm not in love with it," Lucky added.

Chris's expression darkened. "No one escapes Winter, or Winters, whatever," he said, his voice firm. "And killing Melissa is our priority."

"Got it."

But Lucky knew this effort was misguided. If Chris was worried his men were having doubts, taking revenge on his ex-girlfriend wasn't going to reassure them.

Lucky remembered a homeowner last year who, rather than update his primary bathroom, had opted to spend money on landscaping. Lucky had attempted to convince him that the yard—which admittedly needed work—wasn't going to deter buyers, especially once they got inside the house. But this homeowner, an advertising executive, had insisted, and the house had finally sold, but for less than Lucky knew it was worth.

Sometimes, when success is small, it's a sign of larger failure.

"I got the message that I'm not working alone," Lucky said. "How many others are on this job?"

"The Rusu twins. You. Your boy Seth."

Your boy Seth.

Lucky tried to keep his expression impassive.

"Why so many?" Lucky asked. "Any one of us could find them."

"And now maybe you'll find them faster."

Lucky didn't like that answer. More people in the field meant more chances for mistakes, loud clumsy incidents like the one at this diner. Victor Winters would have done things differently.

"I thought the twins were out of the area," Lucky said. He knew of the Rusu twins, Bianca and Adriana. Pretty and blonde and from some eastern European country. Came to the states posing as sex-trafficked teens, but they were secretly working with the trafficker to keep the other women in line. Once that trafficker was killed the twins went on their own, and eventually ended up with the Winterses.

"The twins go where the work is," Chris told him. His sense of malice, a bullying sort of mischief, was back. "Speaking of that, you going to call Seth, work with him on this?"

"No."

"He said the same thing about you."

Lucky didn't reply.

"I want to give you something, Lucky."

It sounded like a threat. Lucky's poker face was starting to ache.

"What's that?"

"A promise," Chris said. "You do this job, you take out these two, and you can leave."

"What?"

Chris smiled. "I know why you're working for us. I know what happened with the army. Why my uncle wouldn't let you stop."

"You do?"

"You want to live your life with your family," Chris said. "Retire from this and just sell houses, right?"

Lucky's heart hammered, but not with fear. Something else, excitement, as if he was digging and his shovel had just uncovered the edge of a treasure chest.

"That's right."

Lucky hadn't realized, until that moment, how much he wanted what Chris was offering. He'd worked with the Winterses for so long that being free from them was a forgotten hope.

And then, suddenly, Lucky felt the wind knocked out of him.

Was this how Renee felt about their marriage?

"My uncle threatened people to get what he wanted," Chris was saying. "It all came through fear. And that worked for him. I'm different. Chris doesn't want to threaten you. He wants to give you what you want. If you do this for me, then . . ."

Chris stopped talking, squinted into Lucky's face.

"What is that?" Something like horror in the young man's voice.

At Chris's tone Marley stepped around Lucky, looked him in the eyes.

"You're crying!" Marley exclaimed.

Lucky wiped the tears from his cheeks. "I'm sorry."

Chris and Marley seemed dumbfounded. They exchanged uneasy glances.

"You're crying," Marley said again, as if this was something contagious.

"It's just . . ." Something inside Lucky had been turning over, deep in his gut, and now it rose. An earthquake rattling his emotions. "I'm so sorry."

"This is . . . weird," Chris said.

A terrible clenching pain seized him and Lucky bent over, wheezed.

"Are you going to hurl?" Marley asked. He and Chris took a quick step back.

"It's my wife." Lucky couldn't stop himself. This was something, a distant part of him realized, that he needed, the rare kind of calm that only comes through confession. It seemed the only way to quell the panic scrambling inside him.

"She's sleeping with someone else. I just found out."

Lucky was crying too hard to see either Chris or Marley clearly, gasps shuddering through his body.

"When you said I'd be free to go to my family," Lucky told them between hard breaths, "well, I just don't know if my family will still be there."

Lucky's face was on the floor, the cold linoleum like balm. He stretched out and flattened his body.

This wasn't the first time anxiety and grief had overwhelmed Lucky. Three days ago, while shaving in the morning, alone in the house, Lucky had burst into tears. Only for a few minutes, but those tears were uncontrollable. So were his sobs, deep, body-wrenching sobs.

He didn't know why Renee's transgression stayed in his thoughts, tugging like an untrained dog on a leash. But he couldn't stop imagining how often she must think about William, their secret texts and whispered phone calls, the irresistible attraction when they saw each other at work.

Lucky had never felt that type of excitement before.

But he could imagine it in Renee.

"Hey." A foot nudged his shoulder. "Bro?"

Lucky rose to his knees, shuffled toward Chris and the napkin he was offering.

"I'm so sorry," Lucky said. He noisily blew his nose. "I don't, I don't know what's happening to me."

"I think you're having a panic attack," Marley said.

"Yeah." Lucky nodded, shakily rose to his feet. "Would one of you do me a favor? Would one of you hold me? Or maybe both of you?"

Marley and Chris glanced at each other. "I think it'd be weird if I did it," Chris said. "Since I'm in charge."

"Boss," Marley replied, "it's not like we have HR or something."

"Then you hold him!"

"Please?" Lucky asked weakly. His knees felt like they might give out.

"Here," Marley said, and he hurried to the door, brought over an empty coatrack. "Try this."

Lucky wrapped his arms around the rack, his tears wetting the wood. "This is better. Thank you."

And, truthfully, there was something strangely comforting about the wooden rack. Lucky had never been particularly given to emotions, but he'd often had longings he was able to ignore. One was the sense, when he embraced Renee or Marybeth, that he didn't want to let go. The emotion in the embrace was like a blanket to him, and when they pulled away, the blanket was tugged off. And Lucky was left cold and alone.

But the coatrack didn't pull away, and it didn't judge him or make him feel needy. There was a resoluteness to the wood that Lucky recognized, and he held on to it the same way a child might clutch a doll, as if this was one of the only things they could fully trust.

"Hey, Lucky," Chris said, and Lucky realized he'd momentarily forgotten about the other men.

He stepped away, wiped his eyes.

"We'll find someone else for this job, okay?" Chris told him. "You've been good for us, but you're . . . cracked? You need to take care of yourself."

"No." Lucky shook his head. "I can do it. I'm fine. I promise."

"You were, like, blubbering," Chris said. "And really having a moment with that coatrack."

"That made me so uncomfortable," Marley added.

"I'm okay." Lucky's voice was ragged. "Don't take this chance away from me, Chris. Please. I want to do this. I need to do this."

"Christ, okay," Chris said. "Just don't . . . don't ever do that in front of me again. I feel gross. Marley, give him the information and let's go."

"Yeah, okay," Marley said. "Jake Smith and Melissa Cruz. I got their pictures here."

He pulled out his phone and scrolled through it.

And at that moment Lucky was grateful that his face was a blurred mask of tears, that Chris and Marley were too uncomfortable to look directly at him. Otherwise they would have seen his surprise.

Jake Smith.

Lucky knew exactly who Jake was.

Chapter Six

Melissa

"Did you tie those right?" Melissa asked.

Jake looked up at her from where he was kneeling behind the elderly security guard. "I have no idea."

"Trust me." The guard grimaced. "It's tight."

She and Jake had decided to bring the old man on board the yacht and to the empty second bedroom. They weren't sure what to do with him, but, if there was one thing they'd found when exploring other boats, it was rope. Corded, braids, thick and thin strands, fishing wires. And ropes perfect for tying someone up.

They'd tried to tie the guard to a folding plastic chair, using a framed guide for fishing knots helpfully hanging on the wall . . . and couldn't figure out any of the knots.

So instead Jake and Melissa had used endless amounts of rope and dozens of small shoelace knots throughout. Small rabbit ears drooped up and down the guard's arms and legs.

Melissa wasn't confident in their work.

"I'm going to keep searching the warehouse," Jake said. He handed Melissa the gun. "I'll see if there's something else here we can use."

Melissa sat on the floor of the small room after Jake left, her back against the wall.

Helplessness was spreading through her, the same feeling as when she'd learned the depth and violence of Chris's crimes.

When she'd realized she needed to leave him.

Or when she'd pushed the knife into that man's leg at the diner.

It was a trapped feeling, the urgency to make a choice. And, no matter which choice she made, the consequences would alter her life in ways she couldn't predict.

The only certainty was, regardless of her choice, things would get worse.

"My name's Harold," the guard told her. "Harold Thompson."

Melissa didn't respond. After a few moments of silence, Harold stared despondently into his lap.

Melissa felt sorry for him. She thought he was a cute old man, short with a little belly touching his thighs, disappointed eyes behind thick, square glasses. White hair combed into a faded crew cut.

"I'm sorry that we had to tie you up," she told him.

"You could let me go."

Hope touched Harold's voice. Melissa was sad to take it away. "We can't do that. But I promise you, we're not criminals. We don't want to hurt you."

"You broke in here, stole supplies, kidnapped me, and you're holding me at gunpoint. But you're not criminals?"

And he doesn't even know about the diner.

Grief fluttered like a wounded bird.

Melissa abruptly stood. Crossed her arms tight over her chest, started pacing.

"Hey," Harold's voice was soft. "You can just let me go. I won't tell anyone you two are here."

Melissa didn't look at him, kept pacing, thinking. "We can't let you go. Not until Jake and I know what we're doing next."

"His name's Jake?"

That was probably a mistake, but she was too stressed to care.

"What's your name?" Harold asked.

"Melissa."

"Jake and Melissa," he said slowly.

And where was Jake? Melissa wished he would return. Not that Jake would be better in this situation but at least she'd be out of this room. Maybe she could take a walk while Jake stayed with Harold. Get food. Look for help. Think clearly about what they could do next.

"You ever shot a gun?" Harold asked.

"My ex took me shooting." Melissa knew she shouldn't share more, knew this information would potentially come back to haunt her, but she didn't care. Like Jake's desperate, ill-advised outreach to Eric, she needed to talk.

"You don't seem like you want to hold it," Harold said.

Melissa stopped pacing, glanced at the gun in her hand.

"I can help you," he went on. "All you have to do is let me go. I'll be out of here, and you'll never hear from me again. You and Jake can stay as long as you need. I won't tell anyone."

"Why would you help us?" Melissa asked.

"Because I don't want trouble."

"Aren't you a security guard? Isn't stopping trouble your job?"

"Yeah, well, Wharfside isn't exactly Gotham."

She couldn't help a small smile at that.

"Please, Melissa. My granddaughter—"

The door to the room flew open and Jake returned, his camera bumping his chest. The smile on his face, its simple joy, was at odds with the urgent conversation Melissa and Harold were having, like a sudden sunny day in the middle of a rainy week.

"Check this out!" Jake beamed. He lifted his arm to reveal rolls of duct tape circling his elbow to his hand. "You think this will work better?"

His enthusiasm slipped when he saw Melissa's face. "What's wrong?"
She'd seen duct tape used to bind someone before.

◆ ◆ ◆

Melissa walked along the water's edge, following the path Jake had told her about.

They'd strapped Harold to the chair, his hands and feet securely bound by duct tape.

The same way she'd seen Chris do it.

Melissa tried to push that memory away, but doing so was impossible. Almost as if Chris himself was walking beside her.

She'd met him five years earlier, during her last year of high school in Silver Spring, Maryland. Chris was a year older, a high school dropout who would hang out with friends at the school's parking lot during lunch, guys gathered around his brown pickup truck like neighbors congregating on a porch. He saw her walking by and left his laughing friends behind to talk to her.

"Hey!"

"Hi."

Despite the admiring way the other boys had swarmed around him and his cocky stride toward her, Melissa realized that he didn't know what to say next.

"I'm Melissa," she said.

"Oh." Speaking quietly, shyly. Soft eyes gazing out from under long brown hair, thin face, reddish haze of faded acne on his cheeks. Knife-sharp lips. "I'm Chris."

She liked his uncertainty and nervousness, especially because he was older, the clear leader of those boys watching from his truck.

But her girlfriends didn't trust him, and her mother didn't either. Melissa's mother was overly protective of her only daughter. She'd been in America over twenty years, moving from Panama for marriage with a soldier that quickly ended in divorce, left to raise Melissa alone. The two women were never close, and Melissa's teenage years were full of fights, almost always because of Melissa's mediocre grades. Her mother tried to encourage her through shouts, threats, punishments, abuse. None of it worked. Melissa stumbled through high school, and shortly after graduation, her mother had to return to Panama to take care of her own mother. She entrusted Melissa into the care of a good friend who gave her a place to live while Melissa attended Baltimore County Community College.

By that time Melissa and Chris had been together almost a year and he was comfortable around her. But her worried mother saw his nonchalance as arrogance.

"You're beautiful, but you're not smart," her mother told her. "He'll take advantage of that."

Those words and their wariness took a toll, a concern that slowly crept in and became Melissa's own. She worked at the college bookstore in between classes or hung out with girlfriends, and it didn't help that her friends often wondered aloud why she and Chris rarely saw each other, what could possibly keep him so busy.

But Melissa knew the reason.

He was with his family, and he'd told her about his family. About the Winterses and who they were and what they had done. The constant arrests of their associates, the whispers about his uncle Victor, their wealth and the rumors of how it had been gained. He would never join them, Chris promised her, but he had to spend time with them.

And she understood the power of family, even one you distance yourself from. Family pulls you like water circling a drain.

Four years ago Chris told Melissa that, even though the used car dealership where he had taken a job was a front for his family's business, none of their work was anything he was involved with. He was excited about the job, his first real one, and she was excited for him. He showed her his first paycheck and they marveled over it together, thousands more than she earned at the bookstore. She had no idea car mechanics made that much.

And no idea they actually didn't.

Three years ago, Chris admitted his growing involvement with the Winterses to her but promised it was on such a small scale that anything he was caught doing would result in nothing more than a slap on the wrist. And so the threat of danger was there, but distant. Like walking down a dark alley you're certain is empty.

There was a thrill to that.

And Melissa could see the thrill in him. Chris confessed all this during dinner when they were celebrating her graduation from BCCC. The celebratory feeling of the dinner had already been dimmed by the email she'd received earlier that day, informing her that her only attempt at a scholarship at Towson University, one of the few universities to which she'd applied and the only one that had admitted her, had failed. She couldn't afford a loan and, despite his insistence, didn't feel comfortable borrowing from Chris. But she didn't let that disappointment, or the worry she detected in Chris's eyes after he'd told her more about the Winterses, ruin their dinner.

Two years ago Chris had promised that the house he bought—an actual house just outside Baltimore with a yard and fence and basement and walk-in closets—had been paid for with money from his new role as assistant manager at the dealership and not from his family. Melissa had growing doubts about Chris's work and the secrets he kept, but she moved in with him anyway. Her mother had died months earlier, while crossing the street in hectic Panama City, looking to her left, not seeing the city bus barreling toward her from the right. Melissa went to Panama for the funeral, a fast weekend when Panama's thunderous hot rains soaked everything. Her aunts had stared at her balefully, strained politeness and pointed side comments Melissa did her best to ignore. Her cousins were more cordial. Melissa's mother had often complained about them, telling Melissa what her sisters said about their children's work ethic and laziness. Maybe it was true. Or maybe, in Panama, parents distorted love and worry, turned them into a sharp-edged relationship with their children, one defined by the most dramatic elements of each emotion.

The loss of her mother amplified something else for Melissa—her distance from Panama. Her mother had been her only significant connection to the country, and now that she was gone, that connection seemed tenuous, bordering on artificial. Even her grasp of Spanish was failing. Melissa and her mother usually spoke in English, given her mother's hope for fluency. And so over the years, without practice, Melissa's Spanish had dulled. That first day in Panama was devoted to fierce concentration, deciphering the words of her weepy grandmother, red-eyed aunts, hushed cousins. Some of the language returned by the end of her trip, but Melissa knew that wouldn't last.

She had a couple of close Latina girlfriends, but like her, there was an embarrassed loss of identity, Spanish only spoken when they wanted to convey something secretive—and, more often than not, they didn't use the right words. By almost all measures, Melissa and her friends had been raised in what approximated to a clichéd view of typical Americana. English-language television. Books that she enjoyed but that were written by and about people who looked nothing like her. Even famous people who weren't white—newscasters, celebrities, politicians—often spoke in a way that had a universality to it, lacked distinction.

That distance from Panama had only furthered when she dated Chris. Most of her friends had mentioned an uneasiness they felt toward him, or, if they kept quiet, she noticed their tight reactions whenever she talked about him. But Melissa knew Chris better than they did, saw the conflict inside him to be good despite the evils of his family. He needed her; she was the anchor to what was honest in his life. But her relationship to him still separated her from those friends, until only

Carla remained, a quiet Mexican-born girl Melissa only spoke with sporadically.

And so when Melissa returned to Maryland and Chris, it was as if she was leaving what remained of Panama within her behind. And he was waiting for her, in the ways she needed, attentive and concerned that she was going to collapse.

And she did collapse but only once. After that she didn't cry again. Instead, another revelation surprised her, that of trying to adjust to a life without her mother's reprimands. Her schooling, her work, her relationship . . . all of Melissa's life was now purely, solely, her own.

Almost.

Chris was increasingly caught up in his family's business, and that business distanced him from her, weighed on her. She sensed the danger increasing.

Months passed, and Melissa wasn't working anymore; instead, she lived off the money Chris gave her every month, and she spent her days watching television and exercising and talking with the girlfriends and wives of Chris's friends, who also didn't work. They relaxed her, these new friends, other women also tangentially involved with the Winterses. These women who offered the comfort of surviving, models of how to adjust to their men.

Because it was then that the killers came.

They were quiet, serious men with harsh scars and broken fingers and haunted eyes. Men who smelled of death. Men who looked at Melissa in ways that went beyond want, to someplace darker. These men frightened her, especially when she started to sense their presence in Chris. The shyness she'd first loved in him was long gone. Now he was withdrawn and curt and often angry.

Sometimes Melissa was scared he would hurt her.

"I'd never hurt you. Or anyone," Chris insisted when she questioned him one night, a rare moment of communion between them.

But a week later Melissa's worry got the best of her. She awoke in bed, alone, even though Chris was home. She left the bedroom, saw a light in the kitchen. Walked downstairs, holding the banister to make sure she didn't make any noise. Unsure why she was being secretive, but some instinct telling her it was necessary.

Chris was sitting at the kitchen table, his back to her, headphones over his ears. Hunched forward and staring into his laptop.

Melissa saw part of the video he was watching. She quickly walked away.

She couldn't go back to sleep, terrified of what she had seen, frightened of what her life had become. She lived with a sense of foreboding, a constant premonitory feeling shadowing her, the light of the world obscured. The work Chris did was kept secret from her, and she was too scared to ask questions, worried about his answers. Almost hoping that, if she did ever ask, he'd lie.

But there was another feeling in her—doom approaching, footsteps in the dark. The insistent voice from her dead mother, cruelly chastising Melissa for her mistakes, coldly assuring her that she had chosen poorly. And, rather than rebel as she had always done, Melissa had a realization.

This wasn't her mother's voice or advice. This was her own.

And with that, Melissa decided to act. She woke hours later, wondering if she'd even gone to sleep, unsure what was a dream. She headed downstairs, walked through the quiet house. Chris was out, she assumed, but his laptop was still on the kitchen table. She opened it, logged in with his password—he'd written it down, carelessly left it on his nightstand a year ago, and never changed it—and found the video he'd been watching.

The video opened to a room of a man duct-taped to a chair, the camera apparently stationed in front of him. It took Melissa a moment to realize the room was in their basement, an unfurnished side room for storage that they didn't use.

In the video Chris approached him.

Melissa couldn't stop herself from watching Chris's practiced ease, his ruthless persistence as he used a razor to dig out screams from the man in the chair. Until that tortured man's head finally fell forward.

She switched off the laptop.

Her throat felt like it had been chewed.

Melissa was too scared to confront Chris about what she had seen and too frightened to run. Their once-heated love, already distant, now disappeared, like phone calls that came further and further apart.

And then Jake showed up in her life, a burning light indicating some safe shore. A place Melissa realized she'd never been.

When Jake asked her to run off with him, she took his hand.

And now she was here, hiding with him in an Eastern Shore town, desperately running from the world.

Melissa pulled out the burner phone she'd bought, used an app she'd discovered to read the texts on her other phone, the one she'd left behind so Chris couldn't track her. It had been a lot to leave her phone: thousands of photos and videos she sometimes scrolled through, retail and social media apps with saved passwords she no longer remembered, contact information from people she may never have the chance to speak with again. A lost life.

The texting app was her only link, and it showed a text from Carla checking in, not worried yet, just wondering where she was. The message read as dutiful, as if she wanted to inquire but didn't want to be drawn in further. Or maybe that's how Melissa imagined it.

Texts from clothing and makeup stores offering sales, reaching out to Melissa as if her life had continued uninterrupted. She savored these texts, the way they brought normalcy.

Texts from her other set of girlfriends, the ones involved with Chris's friends, asking, Are you okay? and What happened?? and Where are you??? Looking, Melissa knew, for information to pass on.

Messages from Chris, coming like clockwork every couple of hours.

Those were the only texts she didn't read.

There was a store down the path, the convenience store Jake had told her about. Melissa didn't know how long they were going to stay here or where they were going next, but they needed food.

She made her way down the path, water to one side, forest on the other. Jake had told her it was a half mile to the store, and now that evening was settling in, the weather was colder and windier than she'd expected.

The store turned out to be closer to a mile away—at six feet, Jake had a much longer and faster stride than she did at five two (and a half, she always added)—and when Melissa finally reached it, she was happy to push open the heavy glass door and step out of the cold and into the light. A dozen aisles of snacks, auto supplies, drinks, and various odds and ends occupied the middle. A refrigerated section along one wall held cold drinks and food opposite a sleepy teen at a register. Melissa walked over to a rotating stand of sweaters with either "Chesapeake" or "Maryland" scrawled across the front. Pulled out one in her size, another in Jake's.

Ten minutes later she headed to the counter, arms full of food, the two sweaters slung around her shoulders. The cashier, a tall, orange-haired kid, kept glancing up at her as he scanned her items.

Melissa was used to men eyeing her, but her paranoia gave his glances a sense of danger. She hadn't checked the news and wondered if the incident at the diner had already been reported, their faces everywhere.

She pulled out her burner, scanned TikTok, searched for her name. Jake's name. The Heartbreak Diner.

Nothing turned up.

The unread messages from Chris were like a door Melissa was scared to open, but she had to read them. As unlikely as it was that Chris had changed his mind and accepted that she was gone, there was still room for hope. Sometimes he'd surprised her.

Melissa opened up the most recent text Chris had sent.

After the first few words, she numbly put her phone back in her purse and handed over some of her dwindling cash.

She slowed her breathing, took out her phone again.

> im goin to cut you open from your

"Miss?"

Melissa hadn't realized she'd taken a few steps away from the counter, away from the orange-haired kid and her grocery items, now stuffed in plastic shopping bags.

"Are you okay?"

Melissa couldn't manage even a slight nod.

She'd never heard Chris like this.

"You're really pretty," the cashier blurted out. He bit his lip. "I'm sorry. I shouldn't have said that."

Melissa's normal response would have been to apologetically smile, to excuse the man from his own clumsy words, but she was too distracted. "I'm sorry. I just have a lot on my mind."

"It's okay."

At this response, his quick acquiescence, something unexpected hit Melissa, a longing. There was a longing for the stereotyped rurality in this store and town and in this shy boy's awkwardness that suddenly washed over her.

Melissa wished she lived here, had grown up here, spent her life in a small house with the wind whipping outside and the lapping of the bay and maybe falling in love with a boy like this and having nothing but each other—no danger and no fights—just a long, quiet life and simple happiness. A garden without snakes.

"But thank you for saying that," Melissa told him.

The boy nodded, still looking down, and said something else. His voice was too low for Melissa to understand him.

"What?"

Slightly louder. "Do you want to go in back?"

"In back?"

"I heard Mexican girls like that stuff."

Melissa gathered her bags and left.

The walk back to the warehouse was quick, despite the heaviness of the shopping bags. Melissa walked resolutely, warmer in the sweatshirt she'd bought, carrying supplies, and, with each step, a growing determination as she strode through the cold night.

For years her life had been out of her control. Chris was always in charge of their relationship, leading her in whatever direction he wanted. Jake was different, beautifully different, similarly following a path but without the inclination to shape it. He was content to let Melissa make choices.

This wasn't a position she'd ever been in.

She was used to reacting to everything, especially to the men in her life, and Melissa knew now that she couldn't continue that way. Not if she and Jake were to survive.

A plan formed. She and Jake could hide in the warehouse for a few days, just long enough to befriend Harold, gain his trust, enough so he wouldn't turn them in after they let him go. There was a nice sentiment in that notion, the chance to win someone's trust again, to prove that they were more than simply selfish lovers. She and Jake would find a new place to run, somewhere beyond the reach of the Winterses, maybe out west where they could hide in anonymity. Put dozens of states between them and Chris, a home hidden in the deserts of Arizona or lost in the plains of Kansas or nestled in the Colorado mountains.

It was possible, provided they didn't make more mistakes.

Melissa reached the warehouse and walked around back to the broken window.

"Hey."

Jake emerged from the woods.

"What are you doing?" Melissa asked. "Where's Harold?"

"He's inside. And he has our gun."

Chapter Seven

Jake

Jake couldn't tell if Melissa was angry, bewildered, or both. And he was too embarrassed to meet her eyes and figure out which. Instead, he gazed up at the dark shadows of trees, their bare branches like ancient writing scrawled on the night sky.

"I'm not a great guard," he admitted.

"No?"

A slight mocking tone in Melissa's voice. He blindly lifted his camera and took a picture in the general direction of her face.

But even as Jake snapped the photo, he kept looking up. As if, should he stare hard enough at those branches, he would decipher their writing.

"So what happened?" Melissa asked.

"I had to use the bathroom. And I left the gun on the other side of the room from Harold, and I thought that would be okay. But when I came back, Harold had knocked his chair to the floor and dragged himself over to the gun."

The wind through those branches was a whisper, a chant or prayer.

"You walked back into the room," Melissa asked, "and Harold was on the floor with our gun?"

"Yeah. Then I walked back out."

Melissa rubbed her forehead.

"But at least he's still tied up," Jake added helpfully.

A rustling sound within the warehouse.

"Maybe not so much anymore."

Jake was trying to be glib, but he hated this feeling. This sense of failure returning, a bruise he'd borne since childhood. The idea that everything Jake did led to helplessness, the sense that he was never good enough.

He remembered his high school counselor's face, the resignation when she'd told Jake he didn't have the grades to graduate.

The way that experienced photographer had stared down at Jake's portfolio, dismissively flipping through the pages.

His mother sitting quietly on the couch when Jake closed the door to her house, when he'd left despite her admonishments and warnings. The last time he'd ever seen her and the pain he felt after that door shut. He was abandoning her . . . even if he'd felt that, long ago, she'd left him for alcohol and depression.

It was this futility that plagued Jake in everything in life, including photography. Art offered an escape, but it also provided a challenge unlike anything he'd ever faced, a difficulty that struck soul deep. Jake's art, the rare times he'd shared it, only seemed to make his limitations more pronounced. When someone looked at his photographs, Jake felt like they were looking at him in a way that went beyond a physical or even emotional understanding; it was like standing before God, his soul weighed.

Those doubts drove him, kept him staring into his camera or monitor for hours, working relentlessly, retouching a photo until the exact image he wanted was realized. And this despite the very real and extremely likely chance that none of his efforts would amount to anything. Jake didn't use social media, even though it had worked well for other photographers. Something about those platforms seemed poisonous to him, desperate and, most damaging, identical to everyone else. Jake didn't like how those sites compressed photos, losing the minute details and heartbreaking colors he savored, the resonance he'd discovered in whatever inspiration had driven him to this particular photo and that he'd spent days or weeks or, when he'd first started, even months developing.

It had started with a book, a collection of black-and-white photographs from Margaret Bourke-White he'd found in his high school's library. A photo of African Americans in the early twentieth century waiting in line, underneath a poster of a beaming white family next to the words "There's no way like the American Way." Even at his young age, Jake found the contrast overstated, but that wasn't what drew him to the photo. It was the expressions of the waiting men and women, resolute and disappointed, a few of them glancing doubtfully at the camera, others glumly staring forward, as if they'd been waiting lifetimes and there was no end in sight. Jake stared at the image for almost the entire lunch hour, noticing small details about each person, the way one man clutched a bucket, the way another stared warily behind himself. Jake returned the next day and wanted to lose himself in the photo again, the way someone might repeatedly listen to a song, but instead he flipped through the book, his hand trembling, and saw Bourke-White's other photographs. Industrial images hopelessly darkened by gray smoke. Scenes of nature, but as if they'd been taken abruptly and on the verge of nature changing, wilting plants, melting snow. Grim people, often working, toiling with a sense of inescapability and despair. These photos left Jake with so many questions about the subjects and their lives—and, strangely, he felt that if he only examined the photos closer, he'd discover the answers.

Jake did have hopes for his own book someday, a long, flat book with protective covers and soft pages and quiet text on the sides or underneath his pictures: title, date, and location. An introduction by a master of the field in the beginning, an index at the end. A photo of Jake on the back, a self-portrait taken somewhere like Baltimore's Patterson Park, just below the famed Japanese Pagoda, Jake smiling with his arms outstretched.

He'd never told anyone about this fantasy, even Eric, despite everything his friendship with Eric had given him. Only Eric had understood him, and only Eric had seen most of his work. He wanted to, would look at Jake's photographs with the type of rapt attention and curiosity Jake was too embarrassed to admit he craved. Eric understood Jake's work, and so Eric understood him.

And Jake knew what he offered his friend in return. Eric's mother's death had haunted him; his abrupt departure to South Carolina, where he'd grown up after her loss, had left him isolated, the only half-Asian kid in his school, seemingly in the entire state. Jake would listen to Eric's stories, absorb them because, somehow, on some distant level, he empathized.

The two of them had a relationship they needed and cherished, and Jake had never had anything else like that until he'd met Melissa. She and Eric had liked each other immediately, despite Eric's trepidation about her relationship with Chris Winters and the danger that she brought.

He remembered when Melissa and Eric had first met, and the two of them had talked about Jake's photography, about his reluctance to share it.

"Don't you ever want to show it?" Melissa had asked. "Wouldn't that make you happy?"

He hadn't known how to reply. And so he hadn't.

"Jake," she'd said, crestfallen, "don't you think you deserve happiness?"

"It's okay," Melissa said now, and, as always, her words burned away whatever bad feelings were inside him. "We'll figure this out."

The warmth Jake felt toward her at that moment was like heat seeping through a man who had nearly frozen. He didn't feel dumb or judged.

Just loved.

As if her words had translated that message in the night sky.

"What are you smiling at?" Melissa asked.

Jake blinked, reality resurfacing. "I was just thinking about how much I love you."

"Cute. But do you think we should do something about that angry old guy who has our gun?"

"We really should."

"Got any ideas?"

"I really don't."

"Hey!" Harold's voice from inside the warehouse, but close. "I'm coming out!"

They stepped away from the window.

"He sounds scared," Jake whispered.

"He sounds angry," she whispered back.

Harold sounded both angry and scared. "I'd better not see either of you!"

Jake and Melissa moved farther away from the window.

"We need to let him go," Jake said quietly. "But we should leave first. Get the car and go."

She didn't respond.

"Melissa?"

"He'll tell people about us," Melissa said. "He knows too much. We can't just let him leave."

The resolve in her voice worried Jake.

"But what do we do?" he asked. "He has our gun."

"When he comes outside, you need to flash him."

Jake stared at her, then down at his zipper. "Sorry?"

"Flash him *with the camera*. And then we'll grab the gun."

"That's crazy," he said, but when he looked at Melissa's face, even in the dark, Jake saw defiance. The commitment to whatever they needed to do next.

The same expression just before she'd driven that knife.

That was something in her that Jake admired and envied and feared. He saw the fighter inside her, the kind of ancient warrior who would run into battle. She was Achilles standing over Hector, Hannibal staring up at the Alps, Joan of Arc glaring as flames rose.

"You'd best not let me see you," Harold said, his voice just on the other side of the window. His fingers appeared on the sill, straining. Jake heard scrabbling on the other side of the wall.

Melissa touched Jake's arm.

Harold's head appeared next, his eyes wide and wild behind his glasses, peering vainly. More scrabbling, and his upper body suddenly filled the window, leaning awkwardly, his arms flailing for balance. No gun in sight.

"Jake," Melissa urged him.

Harold landed with a thud on the ground. Rolled to his back and panted.

Melissa took a step toward him.

Harold reached behind himself, whipped out the gun. Pulled himself up and sat against the wall and wheezed.

Melissa looked back at Jake. He knew what she wanted but couldn't bring himself to lift the camera.

Jake tried to tell himself it was because of Harold's gun, that he couldn't risk Melissa getting shot . . . and that was part of it but not all of it. The truth was, he couldn't welcome violence. This was the passivity within himself Jake often resented, timidity and cowardice. It was why he'd lain still as Chris knelt over him, pummeling him. Jake's own fear of striking back, of provoking an even greater anger.

Don't you think you deserve happiness?

"There are people looking for us," Melissa told Harold, urgently. "If they find out we're here, they'll come for us and kill everyone in their way. You can't tell anyone about us, Harold."

"So what were you planning to do here?" Harold asked, and Jake thought this was a fair question. "Keep me here forever? Kill me when you figure out your next move?"

"We didn't know what to do," Melissa said.

"I won't tell anyone," Harold said intently. "No one." He tried to lift himself up and grunted. Slipped back down, the gun in the dirt.

Melissa looked back at Jake, and there was something in her expression that finally spurred him to act.

Not the defiance he saw earlier; it was the opposite. A moment of pity, of knowing he was incapable of helping.

Jake lifted the camera, and the world was suddenly on fire.

The flash was so sudden and bright that, even though Jake knew it was coming, he was still blinded. It was more than a light in darkness, it was an X-ray, showing Harold's surprise, his eyes and mouth wide. Melissa in slow motion, running toward him, reaching out. Jake following her, unsure what he was doing.

And then he slipped, and his face was pressed against Harold's chest, buried against his shirt, Jake's shoes helplessly digging into the dirt, his left knee wet from the ground. Melissa shouting something Jake didn't understand. Harold screaming like a siren, the same sound over and over.

The camera flashed again and again. Spots of light like winking stars. Jake's hands covered Harold's. The gun swung toward Melissa, and she stared at it, frozen, like this was fate.

Strength, mystical strength. Jake bent the other man's will, bent the will of nature itself as the gun pointed away from Melissa and pressed between their bodies.

"Please," Jake said, his cheek against Harold's forehead, Harold still screaming, Jake kneeling above him. The gunshot sounded like splintering wood.

CHAPTER EIGHT

LUCKY

"Nice to see you again," Lucky said. "Your son's about to die. Can I come in?"

Ruby Smith stared at him from her doorway.

"Jake?" she asked.

It was just one word, but it was enough to remind Lucky of the hitch in Ruby Smith's voice, the way a single sound stretched into a pair of syllables.

"Yes." Lucky glanced up and down the street. Ruby lived in a rambler, and the houses were spread apart, separated by long lawns and lines of trees. Within the triangle of DC, Maryland, and Virginia, houses and businesses were in close proximity, and concrete was everywhere, developers overtaking nature. Here, on the outskirts of Winchester, Virginia, just an hour away from DC, it was the opposite. Distant mountains were like storm clouds, roads disappeared into woods, the air held a slow quiet.

"You'd better come in," Ruby said.

Lucky followed her inside, closed the door behind himself. The entrance led immediately into the living room, a squat couch in front of a muted television showing *Wheel of Fortune*, doors leading to other rooms. A painting of Jesus on the wall, long brown hair and demure eyes, hand over his heart.

Very little resale value, which was a shame because outlying towns like Winchester were growing in popularity, spurred by the revolution in remote work and families taking the opportunity to find safer communities with lower costs of living. But any family interested in this aged house would be better served by tearing it down. Building on ashes.

Ruby sat on the couch. "Who's looking for Jake? The cops?"

"Not just the cops."

"You too?"

"Yes."

Ruby's shoulders slumped.

Lucky intently studied her without appearing like he was intently studying her. He couldn't read anything in his old friend's face.

"Of all the people to get involved with . . ." Ruby sighed. "You'd think he'd know better."

"You'd think we all would."

She grunted in reply.

Lucky hadn't seen or spoken to Ruby for years, but there was something in her that hadn't changed, violence underneath a placid surface, a shark about to erupt from calm waters. This even despite her sadness, the way everything about Ruby was resigned: her squarish stomach; slumped shoulders; small blue eyes; unbrushed, dyed orange hair.

"Did you hear about that mess at the diner the other night?" Lucky went on. "Over in Maryland?"

A shrug.

Lucky wasn't surprised. The story had already disappeared from the media, stolen by the Winterses or lost in the news cycle. "The paper said a guy named Bruce Parks was after two people. Not sure if you remember him from your time. A pair of customers got shot and killed, and two people escaped and are on the run. That was Jake and this girl, Melissa."

Ruby took a slow breath before she spoke again. "But Jake's okay?"

"So far."

Lucky wasn't supposed to meet Ruby back when they worked together. She was just the voice on the phone, telling him about jobs, giving details in clues. But there came a night when Lucky was sitting in his car, waiting for the lights to go off in a house across the street, and someone rapped on the passenger side window.

He lowered the window.

"This is the wrong house," Ruby had told him.

"I wish you'd told me that five minutes ago."

Even in the night, he saw her pale.

"Kidding."

Relief took her over. She smiled.

The job was postponed, and she had sat with him in his car, and they talked. Their encounter and the ensuing conversation was probably against some rule the Winterses had, and they indulged in the illicit experience. An hour passed and easily could have slipped into two, but when a neighbor walking a dog stared at Lucky's car, they decided it was time to leave.

And their friendship remained even after Ruby left the Winterses.

Repentance for her actions had left Ruby desperate to disappear, to change her appearance and name and address, to move to a different city. Lucky had helped her hide, found the house in Winchester for her and her young son. He kept an eye out, and, eventually, the Winterses stopped searching.

"You look exactly the same," Ruby said.

Lucky hadn't realized she was examining him as well, but Ruby never missed anything. Those small scanning eyes.

"How's Marybeth? Almost done with high school, right?"

"Almost."

A small smile. "How are you handling that?"

"Barely."

Ruby squinted past Lucky, at the television set behind him. Slid over on the couch to the end table, picked up the remote, and turned it off.

Lucky stayed still.

"So I take it you're still doing the family man thing?" she asked. "Selling houses during the day, working for the Winterses at night?"

"Why, is Kim Flowers looking to sell?"

"You remember."

"I should. I was the one who came up with your new name."

Ruby's elbow perched on the edge of the couch, her hand dangling near the drawer of an end table.

"We had some good times," Ruby said.

"It'd be a shame to ruin those memories by going for the gun in that drawer."

Ruby glanced at the end table, as if surprised. "You think there's a gun in here?"

"I do."

"There isn't."

Lucky had already calculated the distance, knew he'd made an error. There was no chance he could reach the table before she pulled out the gun, even if Ruby was half as fast as she used to be. He'd be better served by running through the doorway to his left. He wasn't sure where it led, but at least it'd give him time to pull his own weapon.

"This doesn't have to go the way you're thinking," Ruby said.

"Then why's your hand next to that table?"

"To distract you."

Ruby pulled out a small pistol from between the couch cushions with her other hand.

"Told you nothing was in the drawer," she said. "Now tell me about my son."

◆ ◆ ◆

"Oh, Jake." Ruby sighed.

She was sitting opposite Lucky at her small round kitchen table. Chipped white cupboards over laminate countertops and a linoleum floor. Lucky considered outdated kitchens an almost personal affront, but he kept his annoyance inside, his desire to replace the counters and appliances and entirely remove the wall separating the kitchen from the dining room.

Instead he distracted himself by looking out the window into a square backyard of splotchy grass and dirt.

Ruby's gun was on the table between them, but closer to her.

"It was always going to be some girl," she told him. "You know I used to get jealous of them? The girls, I mean. They'd come over, and Jake was so naive, and girls grow up so much faster. I knew what they were doing. What they wanted." Her voice turned bitter. "He had no idea, of course. Boys are so blind. Then they grow up into stupid men."

Lucky didn't necessarily disagree. "You never met Melissa?" he asked.

Ruby shook her head. "I haven't seen Jake in years. We got into an awful fight, and he left."

"You were drinking back then?"

She regarded him evenly. "I was."

"What about now?"

"It's been eight hundred and nine days. But who's counting?"

"Where are you working?"

She unscrewed the top of a plastic bottle of water, took a drink. "With a pair of bankruptcy attorneys. Over in town."

"You're a lawyer?"

"Office manager."

"Ah."

Ruby frowned at him. "You don't seem like yourself, Lucky."

He felt like he couldn't hide a thing from her.

"Family ages a person," he offered.

"Want to talk about it?"

Lucky was tempted, but he worried emotion would again overwhelm him. "I came here to tell you that your son is being hunted down, and you're asking me about my marriage?"

"I didn't say your marriage." A half smile. "I guess I can't help it. It's what I do now. Help people. I have found the Lord."

"Oh no. Are you going to ask me to pray with you?"

"Do you want me to pray with you?"

"No."

"Then I won't," Ruby said easily. "The thing with the Lord, Lucky, is that we can only help people who want help. It's like the bankruptcy office. If people don't walk through the door, then we can't do anything for them."

Lucky thought about what Ruby was saying, remembered breaking down the day before in front of Chris Winters and Marley.

"Who do you think killed Victor Winters?" Lucky asked.

"The Devil struck him down."

"I'd say you're looking in the wrong direction."

"There's only one direction," Ruby replied. "There is the Lord, and He is God, and He is the Devil, and He is us. And we are sin, and we are blessed."

Lucky thought for a moment.

"I'm not following any of that."

"And you couldn't. It is beyond our comprehension."

"You don't want to just say, maybe, it was some other bad guys who killed Victor?"

"Whatever killed Victor Winters had a power that went beyond bad or humanity, even his own reaches. The only thing that could have killed Victor was something belonging to death. Assassins more dangerous than anyone we know."

Ruby's words and steady gaze shook something in Lucky, and he had a distinct urge to stand and leave and return home, ensconced within family.

But there was no peace with his family.

Not with Renee, working at her school right now, William McKenna teaching some class down the hall from the administrator office. Renee walking down the hall, glancing through the window of his classroom door. William looking back, and the two of them meeting eyes and smiling. Department meetings where they sat at the same crowded table, maybe occasionally next to each other, their legs pressed together without anyone's knowledge. Sudden dalliances in her office, the door closing and him sweeping her up in a rough, quick kiss or more, Renee fixing her hair and adjusting her clothes after he left, that flushed excitement in her cheeks.

"Lucky?"

Ruby's gun was aimed at him.

Lucky had been reaching into his pocket but stopped. "I'm just getting my phone."

"Stand up and let me watch you do it."

He stood slowly, reached into his jacket pocket. Pulled out his phone.

Ruby lowered her arm.

Lucky opened WatchFull and checked the camera outside William McKenna's house. He hadn't received a notification but had a distinct feeling, one of those moments of sudden instinct or superstition, that he would see Renee's car parked outside.

The driveway was empty.

He slipped his phone back inside. Sat down.

"I'm surprised you still have the gun I gave you."

"Why?" Ruby set the gun back on the table, close to her.

"Because, Jesus?"

A shadow passed through those piercing blue eyes.

"There's a bar down the street," Ruby said. "Right around the corner. I drive past it every day to and from work. And I always look at it. Always. I look at the entrance, and I think about how I didn't go in and how some days I want to. Some days I come here, and it's just me and my memory, and that bar is around the corner, and nothing's lonelier than that."

"Sounds like you need to move. We should do something about this kitchen, though."

"But what helps me," Ruby went on as if Lucky hadn't spoken, "is what's around the corner, on the other side of this street. A church. Sometimes, at the beginning, I'd go there crying, almost crawling, every single night. That's the place I'd go when I wanted a drink. When I was alone."

"One addiction traded for another."

"Maybe," Ruby agreed. "You're probably right. And I could probably do something about that. See a shrink who figures out why I'm so needy and sad. But you and I both know there's no way I can tell anyone what plagues me."

Lucky didn't say anything. Ruby just watched him. He looked out the window, at the weeds in her backyard.

"I'm going to find Jake," he told her. "Or someone else is. It's not just me looking."

"I know."

"He and this girl aren't going to make it."

"Is that what you want?"

"It doesn't matter what I want."

Ruby took another sip of water. "It's been a long time since he made his choice."

"What choice?"

"Jake doesn't want to come home, Lucky. He's not going to walk through that door. I told you, I can't help someone who doesn't want help."

◆ ◆ ◆

On the way to his house, Lucky almost hit a deer, a dark shape that suddenly bounded in front of his car and frantically raced into the woods. His neighborhood in Annandale was full of wildlife—deer and foxes and squirrels and raccoons. The deer, in particular, swarmed the neighborhood in spring, and then hunters were hired by the city to kill them, armed with bows and crossbows to avoid the sounds of gunfire ringing through the woods. Sometimes Lucky would take walks at night or early in the morning and see the hunters perched in trees, steam rising from a drink as they waited.

He pulled his black Jeep Grand Cherokee into his garage, checked both phones. No calls on either.

He walked into an argument between his wife and daughter.

"I don't really care!" Renee's voice had reached a pitch Lucky knew well, a point beyond compromise. "You're not going!"

"But Mom!" Marybeth pressed. "I'm telling you about it! What the hell?"

"*Do not* talk to me that way!"

Lucky strolled into the kitchen, and the two women started talking to him at the same time, Renee angry, Marybeth indignant.

"Mom's not letting me go to a party next weekend!" Marybeth said. "Even though I told her about it and my friends are going."

"The boy she likes is there," Renee said. "And he's older."

"How much older?" Lucky asked.

He looked at Marybeth, not Renee.

Lucky desperately wanted to look at Renee, to see if there was anything to catch in her expression, the utter hypocrisy of forbidding their daughter from an illicit relationship.

But anger and sadness prevented him.

"Does it matter?" Marybeth asked. "He's not in high school, and that's what Mom's freaking out about."

"It's not okay," Renee said tersely.

"Him being older makes him more responsible than high school boys."

Despite everything, Lucky couldn't help laughing at that. Renee joined in.

"You can't date an older guy," Lucky said.

"But he understands me!" Every word from Marybeth was like it was being wrung out, forced from some tortuous depths. "Not like boys in high school."

"It's a no," Renee said.

"But Dad . . ."

"Goddammit stop!"

Lucky's tone silenced the room like a smack. Both women flinched, as if this was something they were used to. Or something they had dreaded.

Marybeth rushed out of the kitchen, up the stairs, slammed her bedroom door.

"That was a little harsh," Renee commented.

Lucky walked over to the fridge. Popped open a can of Coke, felt the acid bubbling down his throat. His insides were shaky, and he wasn't sure caffeine was the best idea, but he felt uncertain, directionless, a need to do something without a clear idea of what exactly that thing was.

It reminded him of the first person he'd been paid to kill. How, afterward when the man was lying on his bedroom floor, bleeding from a bullet hole that had sloppily landed on the side of his head, Lucky had walked around the house, glanced into the rooms. Gone to his kitchen (nice—stainless steel, marble), turned on the television, and stared blankly at *House Hunters*.

"I don't know how we can stop her," Renee was saying. "She asked to go to this party even though we just talked with her about this! Can you believe that?"

"She'll find a way. Liars always do."

A pause in the conversation.

"Is everything okay with you?" Renee asked.

Lucky heard fear in her voice.

Or maybe guilt.

He pulled out his phone, opened WatchFull. "How was work?"

"Fine?"

Lucky stared at the front of William's house, the doorway faintly illuminated by a streetlamp.

If Renee took a step toward him, one single small step, she'd see the image. And everything would change in that one moment, the curtain flung aside, the book skipped ahead to the last page.

But he wasn't ready for that.

"Lucky?"

Lucky was lost, imagining himself walking to William's doorstep, ringing the bell. Pulling William out, dragging him into the night. One hand over his mouth, the other digging a knife into the side of his neck. Working the knife like a corkscrew.

"Lucky?" Renee asked again.

This was where Lucky's path was going, toward that house. To confronting and killing William. There was no peace otherwise, and it would never be found until he went through that door.

"Look what I have," Renee said, and she held a magazine out to him. "I went ahead and opened your special package."

Lucky closed his phone and took the magazine from her. Stared down at the cover of the annual Lemax Christmas Village catalog.

This year's cover photo was impossibly bright and cozy, a warm brown blanket draped over a red recliner, blurred orange flames from a fireplace. And in front of this pleasantly designed nostalgia were small houses and shops—this year's newest additions to their Christmas Village. A tiny coffee shop and dog-grooming salon, a cupcake store with an illuminated baker in the window, figurines of children and parents strolling through, a tiny train wrapped around the town.

"I know you like to open it yourself," Renee said, happiness in her voice. "But your face is really cute when you first see it. I wanted to be there."

Lucky was already on page six. "They have a truffle factory this year. With a little moving conveyor belt!"

"Marybeth and I saw that! You should get it."

Every year Lucky and Renee and Marybeth spent an entire weekend in early December decorating the house for Christmas. His wife and daughter would place ornaments on the tree, Renee carefully unwrapping each one and remarking on when and where they'd first obtained it, while Marybeth hung tinsel and candy canes. Lucky, of course, was in charge of the village, and it had grown in size to occupy both their fireplace hearth and their living room table, like two neighboring towns.

There was a certain precision to the village that Lucky enjoyed, everything from where the houses intersected with the stores to the placement of the trees and signs. And the lights were similarly planned, so that when the living room lamps were off, the entire village was lovingly illuminated. Sometimes Lucky would sit in the darkness and stare at the village, the way the light pressed the shadows away.

He knew better than most how romanticized this idea was, how unrealistic, how likely it was that a scene such as this had never lasted longer than a moment. But that was what he loved about it, this captured happiness, this tender, glowing image.

"We're decorating some more this weekend, right?" Renee asked.

Her voice brought him back. Lucky closed the catalog, gently.

"Maybe," he said. "I might have work."

He'd look through the catalog later, read every description and caption, study each joyful image. But first, he had to find Jake and Melissa.

He had another lead.

And after he found Jake and Melissa, Lucky wanted to murder William as brutally as possible.

Then he and Renee and Marybeth could get back to decorating.

Lucky headed out to his backyard office to research his new lead. He still hadn't looked at Renee's face.

Chapter Nine

Ruby

Lucky had left, but his message remained. Ruby sat at her kitchen table and bit her thumbnail.

What she'd started to suspect was true: she'd sent assassins after her own son.

She'd ordered Jake's murder.

Ruby had always been able to find some sort of distance between herself and her errors. And when her conscience refused to allow her remorse, she'd turn to the Lord.

But at the thought of Jake, a terrible darkness welled.

Ruby needed to think, to clear her head, to leave this silent house, empty except for her memories of Jake, those moments she savored: she asleep at the table or on the couch or in bed, his timid "Mom?"

This house a silent companion, watchful and unspeaking.

Ruby abruptly stood, grabbed her handbag and keys.

She hurried down the road, hands clenching and unclenching, wondering if it was exertion that was causing her to breathe hard as she walked. She didn't know where she was going and was surprised to find herself, after two blocks, behind the liquor store.

Ruby had no idea what had brought her here, what she was doing in this clean little alley as if someone from the Winterses would be here, Joe returned with another message and a few minutes of conversation, Frank watching her through his yellow glasses.

And if either of them were miraculously there and waiting for her, Ruby would fall on her knees before these figures who could save Jake with a few well-placed words, kings whose casual decisions shaped or slaughtered lives. *Give me your message,* Ruby would tell them, *and I will pass it to the world.*

I only ask for this.

But there was no one there; the alley quiet.

Ruby wanted to scream, to run and find someone who could help her, a stranger she could beg to save her son. She hadn't felt such utter helplessness since Jake left her, walked out of their home that summer after finishing high school, after he'd learned the truth of who she was.

Learned what she had done.

Ruby's mind frantically cast back, the way it had that night after Jake slammed the front door, after she'd confessed the truth about Tiffany. A truth her son couldn't accept.

Even if it was a secret he was willing to keep.

And then her mind went further back, to her father, the failure father, the meek man she barely remembered who had been unable to control her raging, alcoholic mom, who spent most of his time at his job and was home in the evenings, timidly entering the apartment after Ruby's mother was passed out, then quietly preparing a dinner for himself and eating alone in the kitchen, his thin body huddled as if anticipating a blow.

Ruby had so hated his weakness that she was surprised when he simply disappeared one day when she was seven, surprised he'd even had the strength to leave. She'd lain sideways on the floor of the living room and watched *The Price Is Right* while her drunk mother screamed and smashed glasses in the kitchen.

That led to the darkest times, months of her mother drinking beyond reason, sitting curled on a chair on the couch, a blanket over her, crying, missing so much work Ruby thought she must have lost her job at the call center.

And then there was Ray.

At first Ruby thought he was just one of the men her mother had started bringing home, her mother dreamy eyed and demure, laughing too loud at everything he said, touching his arm constantly, glaring red-painted lips, her voice too slurred to be seductive. Ruby didn't expect to see Ray again, but he returned a couple of nights later, her mother leading him proudly through the door, as if excited to prove to her nine-year-old daughter that this was more than a one-night stand.

He kept returning. Ruby was diffident toward him in the way she was with all the men her mother brought home. Some of the men stared at Ruby in a way that made her uncomfortable, and she felt like she could sense their gaze through the wall between her bedroom and her mother's, and she would lock her door.

Ray was different. He was friendly to her, but not overly friendly, not like he was luring her. He crouched on the floor opposite her, commented on the castle she was coloring,

"I could color better than that," Ray said.

"No you couldn't," Ruby replied.

He grinned, stood when her mother grasped his arm and pulled him to the bedroom.

Ray started coming by during the days, would bring a sandwich and chocolate milk for Ruby whenever he stopped in. He'd sit on the floor while she sat on the couch, the two of them laughing at cartoons while her mother slept in her bedroom. Ruby noticed that her mother stopped bringing over other men. It was just Ray. Ruby liked that.

She carefully watched her mother with him, the way she flirted and said things designed to have Ray react in the way she wanted, and Ruby realized something disquieting: she and her mother liked the same thing about Ray. There was something withdrawn about him, reclusive. He had a secret. That secret drew them to him, moths fluttering around a light.

And she felt the same happiness her mother did when Ray started moving in, the night he showed up with a pair of duffel bags, one in each hand, answering Ruby's questioning glance with "Might as well keep some clothes here, right?" Her mother jumped and clapped her hands. Ruby felt the same happiness, although she restrained a smile.

Ruby didn't want to let herself grow too attached. She knew the devil inside her mother would soon emerge, rip through her body, and turn her into the violent, profane creature that had made her father cower. And it did, a few nights after Ray brought those bags. Ruby could sense it emerging as the three of them ate dinner in front of the television, her mother growing quiet during *Wheel of Fortune*, her lips small and narrowing. The tension in Ruby's back felt like it was going to snap her spine in half, and she was almost relieved when her mother abruptly stood, knocking her TV tray to the floor.

But Ray stood up as well, fast as a striking snake, a finger in her mother's face.

"Pick that up," he said, his voice cement. "And sit down."

To Ruby's astonishment, her mother did. As meekly as her father used to. Knelt on the floor and picked up the spilled food, carried it to the kitchen. Returned and sat on the couch, tears on her face, but quiet.

This was a new side to her mother, one Ruby had never seen. But the devil still emerged when she and Ruby were alone. Then her mother was worse than she'd ever been, as if she'd held her anger somewhere deep inside and finally allowed it to erupt. That was when she started hitting and kicking Ruby, in places Ray would never see—Ruby's stomach and back and thighs. And when Ray returned and Ruby's body ached, she hid her pain. Didn't want to risk Ray leaving, losing the side of her mother that only he was able to bring out.

Ruby could only remember one time when her mother stood up to Ray. Once when Ruby was moving his jacket from the table, and she saw a gun underneath it.

"Whoops," Ray told her, but he didn't seem alarmed.

"That yours?"

He nodded.

"Want to hold it?" he asked.

"Okay."

Ruby had just touched the gun, the textured rubber grip, when she heard her mom's voice.

"Ruby!"

Ruby's hand shot back as if she'd been stung.

Her mother marched into the room, picked up the gun, handed it to Ray.

"Maybe when you're older," he said easily.

Ruby was never entirely sure, as years passed, if her mother and Ray had married. At times they called each other husband and wife, often in a playfully exasperating tone, but Ruby never saw any evidence of a wedding, even a quick one. And Ray never fully lived with them. He was there a lot, but the house seemed more like a temporary base for him, a second life away from some other one.

Ruby was sure that other life had to do with his gun.

And so when she learned the truth, that terrible night she and her mother rushed to the hospital after Ray had been shot, the weeks after he'd come home from the hospital in a wheelchair and told sixteen-year-old Ruby who he worked for and what he'd done and how he and his men had lost some street war, Ruby wasn't entirely surprised by the revelation. He was crying, shattered, hitting his limp legs over and over as they dangled off his chair, her mother ashen and terrified.

"No one's coming after me!" he shouted at her mother, after she'd asked over and over if she was in danger, implored him for the truth.

But Ruby stayed awake that night, holding his gun in the closet by the front door, waiting for men to enter their apartment. An unseen danger, a power she'd never encountered, had ripped through their tiny apartment like a tornado, torn apart the base supporting their family. Ruby was used to her mother's rage, understood its parameters . . . but this was something different, dangerous, outside the realm of her imagination, something she could only understand through an otherworldly lens.

Something she could only hope to fight back with the power of a gun, that instantaneous way guns had of suddenly ending or forever altering the course of a life.

Sitting in that dark closet, Ruby felt safer the tighter she gripped the handle.

Ray was right. No one came. And this only seemed to dispirit him further. He wasn't in danger of going to jail or facing reprisal. Ray was forgotten, spending days and nights sitting in front of the television, morosely wheeling himself to the kitchen and bathroom. Sometimes Ruby would sit with him, watching whatever he wanted; sometimes she would realize he was crying, and she would join him, the two of them indulging in depression while her mother drank or slept in the bedroom. It was strange to Ruby how natural this depression seemed. She didn't even necessarily feel sad about anything in particular; it was just a familiar sense of dejection, like a coat she put on, winter after winter.

Her mother was the one who found Ray's body later that year, the gun in his hand and a hole in the back of his head, slumped off his wheelchair, his body blocking the bathroom door. She didn't seem, to Ruby, particularly sad—whatever hold Ray had had on her was gone, as if now that he was unable to take care of her in the way she needed, they had nothing left. It was an odd strength that, in some disquieting way, Ruby understood.

When Ruby thought about Ray, she remembered who he had been, his cheerful confidence as he sauntered into their apartment, the way he'd kept the devil in her mother at bay.

The way his secret sustained him until it was revealed.

And this unseen force that had crippled and then killed him, overthrown the natural order of the world with a gesture. Like a stone blocking the entrance of a cave shoved to the side, and what emerged was both true and incomprehensible, terrified witnesses falling to their knees, unable to rise as it stood before them.

Ruby stood uncertainly between the liquor store and the church and couldn't go to either, knew she wouldn't find refuge in a bottle or a pew.

Neither would save her son.

She didn't even have a way to contact the Winterses. All she ever received from them were burner phones with a few saved numbers and messages to remember. And the people she called were the ones with orders to kill. Yes, she had been the one to tell them, but the messages came from someplace higher, and if the Winterses knew her relation to Jake, then there was the chance they would use her to get to him.

And her death wouldn't save his life.

She couldn't turn to Lucky, not after she'd deceived him for so long, even though he'd helped Ruby when she'd decided to leave the Winterses, and Lucky had found a new home and life for her and Jake.

And then the Winterses had found her.

She'd thought Lucky had given her up, revealed her new location. But he hadn't; the men who came to her house one morning when Jake was at school told her how they'd found her—a camera at a gas station. And Ruby didn't reveal that Lucky had helped her attempt to leave. The men offered death to her and Jake, and Ruby begged to return instead, and somehow they accepted her offer. They gave her mercy, and because of that she wholly gave herself, tempering any regrets with alcohol.

She never told Lucky she was back, never betrayed that sense of hope he had that, perhaps, there was another life to which he could return. Sometimes he would check in on her, and Ruby never confessed that she hadn't escaped.

And when Jake left her and she left alcohol, Ruby found something else to turn toward, a church where she learned about a God who had struck down His enemies, who had drowned a world, and in this God Ruby understood everything she had ever witnessed.

There is the Lord, and He is God, and He is the Devil, and He is us. And we are sin, and we are blessed.

And she was His voice.

Evening was setting over Winchester, and the nights here were blacker than Ruby had ever experienced when she'd lived in Alexandria, the way that city's array of lights had silenced the stars. Ruby trudged back home.

Her nails bit into her palms as she desperately tried to figure out how she could save her son, wondering if she even should, until she felt a trickle of blood over her fingers.

Her phone buzzed.

Ruby stopped walking, slowly pulled it out of her pocket. Worried about what she would be told.

"Wharfside."

One single word, spoken by a voice she didn't recognize. But she understood the message.

Jake and Melissa were in the town of Wharfside. That was what she needed to convey to the assassins, to Lucky and the others.

But with that information, Ruby understood, there was a path ahead.

There is the Lord, and He is God, and He is the Devil, and He is us.

She pressed her bloody palms together, in plan and prayer.

Chapter Ten

Melissa

Morning came when Harold had finally stopped moaning and fell asleep. Melissa had cleaned his wound with bottled water, used a pair of shears Jake had found to cut away the cloth from Harold's pants. Tied and loosened a tourniquet throughout the night, all advice she and Jake had hurriedly read on their phones. Now she stared intently at the bullet wound just above his knee. It was still a mess of torn skin and bone fragments, but the wound had dried.

Melissa sat back heavily.

Harold was going to live.

She hoped so anyway.

Jake had been a panicked mess after they'd lifted Harold up and pushed him back through the window, Harold dropping inside the warehouse with a thud and a shriek. Jake and Melissa had dragged him back to the yacht and its lanterns, but Jake was unable to stop his hands from shaking as they tried to treat the older man. Eventually Melissa had asked him to hold Harold down.

"It wasn't your fault," Melissa had told him over Harold's moans. "He shot himself."

"We should have just let him go."

His words were too mired in self-loathing to sound like an accusation.

Besides, regardless of what had happened, even if Harold had died, Melissa knew letting him leave would have been a mistake.

She knew that as firmly as Jake believed the opposite.

And that impasse between her and Jake was apparent, even if unspoken. Their silence grew so thick it felt like a living thing between them. Eventually Jake had stalked off.

She'd let him go, staring down at Harold, wiping sweat away from his face. And had an odd thought.

Was she acting like Chris, and had Jake assumed her role?

Melissa remembered Chris perched over Jake, his fists thundering down, and the horror that had filled her. A horror at the shine in Chris, the luster in his anger.

And yet, somehow, she'd understood his actions. Not that she agreed with them, just that she expected them, in the way that a child awaits punishment. This was the order of the world she'd lived in for so long . . . and now Melissa realized she hadn't emerged from it unscathed.

Her perspective seemed ruined but necessary, the way her immediate impulse had been to shoot Harold when she'd looked down from the deck and seen Jake standing behind him, that brief hope in her during their struggle outside the warehouse that the gunshot had killed him.

How even now, treating him alone, she thought about slipping into the yacht and returning with a pillow, pressing it over Harold's face until his arms and legs stopped flailing.

She poured water on a paper towel, ran it over the blood on Harold's leg, careful not to press down on the wound.

Melissa had made her choice between Chris and Jake, between violence and retreat, but it was a choice she would need to keep making.

"Hey," Harold said weakly.

He didn't try to move from his supine position, lying down with his hand suspended as if waiting for someone to high-five him.

"Where's your man?" he asked.

"Out." Melissa ran a hand through her hair, already starting to feel where it was coarsening due to days without washing.

Harold wiped his face with his free sleeve. "My leg hurts. Can you call me a doctor?"

"I can't."

"Okay," Harold said quietly, resigned.

"Are you in a lot of pain?"

He nodded.

Melissa bent over him, touched his forehead.

"You're really hot," she said. "Maybe it's infected."

"There's a store up the way," Harold told her. "A mile away. Straight up River Bend. They sell some medicine stuff."

"That little convenience store?" Melissa thought back to the clerk who had hit on her. "I was there yesterday."

"Want me to go?" Jake asked, and Melissa turned, saw him behind her. He lifted his camera and snapped a picture of Harold.

"I'm not going to smile," Harold said grimly, and Jake laughed.

Jake seemed sure of himself, his confidence returning now that Harold was awake and showing resiliency.

"I'm sorry," Jake told her.

"Why?"

"I should have trusted you," he said. "Shouldn't have waited to flash him."

"What?" Harold asked.

"It's okay," Melissa replied. "We're figuring this out."

"And we'll be okay."

There was something contagious in Jake's confidence, hope and happiness stronger than she'd ever felt.

"You got a good photo, didn't you?" she guessed.

"I got a great photo! Those tree branches and the sky. Like ancient writing."

Warmth touched her chest, love. Melissa couldn't help it.

She'd make this choice over and over, until the end of time.

"Will you two stop staring at each other," Harold asked, "and get me some damn medicine?"

The walk to the store seemed shorter than it had yesterday, but today Melissa walked with urgency.

She'd looked up infections, learned that fevers were a worrisome sign. And Melissa didn't have the tools or expertise to treat Harold and didn't trust the articles she'd read online to provide guidance. He needed true medical attention.

And to get that medical attention, they needed to leave. Drive at least a state away and take Harold to a hospital. She didn't know if doctors would realize his wound came from a bullet, but she knew all gun injuries had to be reported to the police.

The only other option was to leave Harold to die.

She couldn't trust him. He'd already promised Melissa and Jake whatever they wanted, promised to keep them a secret, agreed to hide whatever he knew. But what if he didn't? Melissa knew that even the most innocent gossip could lead the Winterses to them. Chris used to boast how easily they found people who ran.

Melissa had always wondered if that was a warning.

She imagined Harold slowly dying in the warehouse. Calling for help, hoping his voice carried through that open window, praying someone happened to be walking by outside. The stark realization that no one was coming to save him, that Melissa and Jake had abandoned him. Tied to that metal ring, unable to free himself as hunger and thirst approached.

Melissa reached the store and hurried inside, grateful for the warmth after her walk through the December morning chill. She wandered through the aisles, glancing over snacks and automobile supplies until she reached a row with medicine. There wasn't much, certainly not as much as she'd hoped. Small containers of Tylenol and aspirin, toothbrushes and floss and mouthwash and condoms and Band-Aids.

A single dusty brown bottle of peroxide.

Melissa grabbed the bottle and a package of Tylenol. She thought of a lie to tell in case the clerk questioned her about the purchase: her friend had cut himself during a fishing accident, a harmless cut, but they needed to be careful. Maybe change the male friend to a female, to distance Jake's identity even further. She and some friends were in town for a lazy girls' trip. Not that she could ever imagine coming to Wharfside in December with her friends.

She set the medicine on the counter.

The clerk wasn't here.

Melissa hadn't seen him when she'd entered the store but had assumed he was in one of the aisles, sorting items. Or maybe in the office or storage room or bathroom or whatever room she could see behind the counter, that door halfway open.

"Hello?" she called.

There wasn't an answer.

A sensation seized Melissa, something terribly wrong.

"Hello?" she said again, her voice quieter.

No response.

That half-open door behind the counter.

"Hello?"

Again, nothing. She walked behind the counter, slowly pushed the door all the way open, peeked inside.

It was a small square bathroom with white tiles on the floor and a toilet and a sink. A paper towel dispenser hung next to the door. A guide to washing hands on the opposite wall.

The dead clerk in the corner, legs splayed.

There was such horror on his face.

Melissa was standing in his blood.

Chapter Eleven

Lucky

"But you don't know for sure your wife is seeing him," Heather Anders told Lucky. She shifted under the zip ties binding her to the folding lawn chair Lucky had found in the Anderses' garage. She wore pajamas, thin shorts, and a matching top, and the shorts had risen high on her thighs when Lucky had tied her down. He'd realized her fear when she struggled, how she pressed her legs together, and he'd placed a blanket over her lap.

Not that a blanket brought much comfort when you're woken by a stranger with a gun, separated from your husband, zip-tied and blindfolded.

And then asked to counsel the man who'd kidnapped you.

Lucky knew all this, but he couldn't pass up the opportunity to talk with a trained mental health professional.

"I saw her car parked in front of his house," he said. "I saw her go inside."

"Can you loosen these ropes?" Heather tried again to adjust her position. "They're cutting into me."

"They're zip ties, not ropes," Lucky said from his spot on the floor. He lay on his back, staring up at the ceiling, thinking about his wife and William. Much of his worry, he knew, was based solely on suspicion.

But he'd built his life around suspicion.

He explained that to Heather and played with the ski mask in his hands. Lucky rarely wore the mask, found it tended to creep up and block his vision. He'd immediately taken it off after blindfolding Heather and her husband.

"I just think," Heather told him, "you might be imagining something worse than what's actually happening."

"Really?"

"It's hard to give a diagnosis right now. But, sure."

There was something about Heather that Lucky liked. She'd been scared, of course, when he'd woken her and her husband at gunpoint, when Lucky forced her husband to bind and blindfold her, the heartbreaking way she'd cried out "Bill!" when Lucky led him to a different room to question each of them about the shoot-out at the diner. Bill and Heather Anders had been there that evening, according to the article:

"I'll never forget any of this," local resident Heather Anders stated. "Never."

Lucky had seen her series of framed degrees on the staircase when he'd broken into the Anderses' modest colonial, each degree rising in level as he ascended the steps from the tasteful living room—dual-tone design, black-and-white furniture, good square footage, slightly outdated window treatments—until he came across her doctorate in clinical psychology from the University of Pittsburgh.

Lucky hadn't expected to ask her for advice about his marriage, but he couldn't stop himself. He was just so desperate to soften the lump in his throat.

"Do your other patients," he asked, "sometimes imagine things so much that they believe them?"

"You're not my patient."

"Well . . ."

"But yes," she said. "That can happen, particularly if something is affecting them, like a stressful job."

From his back, Lucky tossed the ski mask into the air and caught it. "I've done this for something like twenty years. Why's it affecting me now?"

"Obviously the threat to your marriage, real or perceived, can shake you. But have you experienced any other major life changes?"

"I have a daughter," he said carefully. "She's in high school. And she went to a party with older guys. I didn't like that."

"Watching your children make their own decisions is hard," Heather said. And then her composure slipped, urgency filled her voice. "Bill and I have children, two girls in college. Their names are Patty and Paula. We love them very much. More than anything in the world."

"In college? How old are you?"

"I'm fifty-nine. Bill's sixty-six."

"I thought you were ten years younger," Lucky said.

She shifted under the blanket, and he realized the compliment only made Heather more uncomfortable.

"Sorry." Lucky sat up gingerly to ease his aching back, changed the subject. "Was it hard raising your kids, even as a psychologist?"

Heather nodded under her blindfold. "That just made it harder. I knew what to expect but knew I shouldn't always stop it." She took a breath. "It's important that people do the right thing. That people know what the right thing is."

"I know!" Lucky clapped his hands. "That's exactly how I feel with my daughter. Like I need to tell her the right thing, even force her to do it. But I can't, right? You can't stop someone when they really want something."

"I think you can," Heather said unsteadily. "I hope so."

Lucky frowned. "I think there's a subtext here that's more about the situation you and Bill are in, and not about me and my family. Can we focus on me?"

Another pause. "Have you always been able to separate your life from your work?"

"I've killed people and had dinner with my family an hour later."

A sharp intake of breath from Heather. Lucky saw her hands tremble.

"But you can't, you can't do that anymore?" she asked hopefully.

"No, I could. My work isn't cutting into my family; my family's cutting into my work. Like, right now, I should be questioning your husband in the other room, and instead I'm here with you. He's fine, by the way."

Tears streamed from under Heather's blindfold.

"He really is fine," Lucky added. "I promise."

"Can I see him?"

"No."

"That makes it very hard for me to help you. Do you understand that? I need you to help me, so I can help you."

Lucky didn't reply. Heather sighed.

"I don't think you can simply say that your work isn't interfering in your marriage," she said.

Lucky had noticed that she paused a lot, and he wondered if that was due to the current circumstances or if she was a thoughtful, deliberative speaker. He'd never seen a psychologist before but imagined this cadence was common.

"Your work requires deception," Heather went on. "You feel that lying to your family is a lie to yourself. It's filling you with self-loathing."

There were moments in Lucky's life when a simple answer had been the solution to a complicated question, Occam's gleaming razor. And he realized this was one of those moments, the lid to the box cleanly yanked away, and he was able to behold what had been inside.

It was the lies.

He couldn't live a life of lies any longer.

Perhaps that had been reinforced by Renee's infidelity, but lying to his family now struck him in a way it never had. It was as if the corruption he engaged in was affecting his soul.

Lucky stood slowly, so as not to strain his back further. "I'll be back," he told Heather. He lifted the ball gag from around her neck, placed it gently against her lips. Checked the blindfold over her eyes. Strands of her brown hair were caught in it, tugged down.

Lucky stepped out of the primary bedroom and into the hall. Passed a bathroom and headed to the guest room where Heather's husband, Bill, was similarly blindfolded, bound, and gagged.

"I'm back," Lucky told him and removed the gag. "And you're a lucky man. Your wife just gave me an epiphany! Does she help you a lot?"

Bill didn't respond.

Lucky had noticed the other set of framed certificates in the house, these in the guest bedroom that they'd converted to a small office. The certificates commemorated Bill's achievements in the military and, later, his work with the police force of Frederick, Maryland. Honors for his time in Iraq, promotions and awards for bravery in the line of duty.

Sometimes, Lucky knew, history mattered. Sometimes men had a résumé marked by violence, and every line of text was a layer of steel.

And sometimes that violence just left them broken.

It was a good thing, Lucky thought, that he and Bill had Heather to talk to.

"So you and Heather were in the Heartbreak Diner during the shooting," Lucky began. "You witnessed Melissa Cruz and Jake Smith get into an altercation with Bruce Parks, which led to the deaths of—"

"I told you that I don't know anything about that." Bill's voice was strained. "Where's my wife?"

"She's fine. And she'll stay that way if you keep talking. Did you see them leave?"

"Who are you?"

"Did you see them leave? See their car? Get the plates?"

No response from Bill. Unlike Heather, Bill hadn't needed to tamp down his fear. He'd been angry when Lucky had woken him with a gun pressed against his head. Scowled and refused to do anything.

Until Lucky had pointed his weapon at Heather.

Lucky took a knee next to Bill. "Heather's fine, and she's going to stay that way if you talk. I don't want to hurt her. But I will."

"I'll kill you."

Lucky nodded. "You're saying that because it gives you strength. But the truth is, Bill, you can't stop me from hurting her."

Bill flinched like Lucky had struck him.

"There's only one way to save Heather," Lucky went on. "Telling me what I want to know."

Lucky's personal phone buzzed.

"But I need to take this first."

He refastened the gag around Bill's mouth. Headed to the hallway, where he could keep an eye on the rooms Bill and Heather were in.

Lucky answered his phone, spoke low. "Hello?"

"Hi!" The voice sounded familiar, but Lucky couldn't place it. "I'm sorry for calling at this hour. Is this Lucky?"

"Yes . . . who's this?"

"This is James Forrester? My wife Jean and I visited the house on Saint Jude the other day? We wanted to know, have you received any offers?"

Now he recognized the voice.

The disinterested couple at the open house, the ones who hadn't even bothered to glance into the basement.

Lucky thought back to that couple, tried to remember anything about them, whatever he could use to motivate them. Young, white, church clothes. James in brown shoes and a suit, Jean in a long blue Sunday dress. Huge wedding ring. BMW.

"Right!" Lucky said with enthusiasm and frowned at a wet spot on his sleeve from Bill's saliva. Kidnapping Bill and Heather had gone smoothly until Bill lunged at him and Lucky choked him into unconsciousness. Afterward Lucky realized he'd strained a muscle in his lower back. "Good to hear from you. And, yes, it is still on the market. For now."

Muffled conversation on the other end of the line before James spoke.

"Are you available for a showing next Sunday?" James asked.

"What time?"

"Morning?"

"I can do 9:00 a.m." Lucky cupped his hand over the phone, lowered his voice. "And, of course, I'll let you know if I hear from the other party before that."

"The other party?"

"There may be other interest," Lucky lied.

More muffled conversation.

"Right." Hesitancy in James's voice. "Is there any chance you could show it earlier?"

Lucky thought back to his calendar. He was free, but, depending on what information he could pull out of Bill, there was a chance he could be heading even farther out of state to find Jake and Melissa.

"Saturday at eight?"

"Yes," James said immediately.

He and James exchanged pleasantries and goodbyes.

"You have a second job?" Heather asked when he returned to her.

Lucky thought back to his phone conversation, tried to remember if he'd said anything revealing. Couldn't think of anything that directly mentioned his identity. But, regardless, he was sharing more than he should. A daughter in high school. A weekend business meeting. An adulterous wife.

"Maybe," he said carefully. "Do you think that's part of the reason I'm sad?"

"Depressed."

"What?"

"You're not sad, you're depressed." Forcefulness in Heather's tone now.

"What's the difference?"

"Have you ever been this sad before? For weeks?"

Lucky didn't reply.

"That's the difference. We all get sad, but depression is different. Depression doesn't fade without treatment."

"Are you saying," Lucky asked hopefully, "you'll treat me?"

"My God no!" A slip in Heather's determination, fear stumbling through. "You kidnapped me and my husband, tied us up, and threatened to kill us."

"It's not the ideal start to our clinical relationship."

"If you let us live, if you let me and Bill go, I'll make a deal with you." Heather's voice was earnest now, insistent. "I'll find help for you. Someone you can talk to."

That lump ached in his throat. "I think I might like that."

"It would help you so much!" Heather said excitedly.

She thought saving him, Lucky realized, would save them.

"Is Bill really okay?" she asked. "Can I see him?"

"Soon."

The single word sounded foreboding, a hint to death. Lucky thought about correcting himself but decided to let it stand.

Heather's head dropped.

"I haven't hurt him," Lucky told her. He patted her shoulder. "Except when I strangled him into unconsciousness. But that's the only time."

Lucky dropped to his knees in front of the bound, blindfolded woman.

"I have one more question for you," he said intensely. "It's about something I saw downstairs. The picture of your daughters."

Heather's legs were trembling. Lucky placed his hands on her knees to calm her.

"Underneath that picture," he said softly, "on your fireplace mantel, there's a small Lemax fire station. Can you tell me where you purchased it?"

"What?"

"The Lemax fire station," Lucky went on. "It has a dalmatian looking out through a window, and you can see a fireman's pole inside through the open door. This model was introduced in the late nineties, and I've only seen it online. Once at PutzPo, but I didn't buy it at the time."

"I don't, I don't . . ."

"Heather, I need you to think."

"What's PutzPo?"

"Putz Exposition," Lucky clarified. "Christmas Village enthusiasts are called Putzers, a word that originated from Moravian culture. PutzPo is a convention held every two years."

"I don't know where we got it," Heather told him. "I think we found it in a box in my mom's house after she died. You can just take it!"

Lucky was offended. He removed his hands from her knees.

"I would never," he told her firmly, "take something from someone's home."

But those words, *Take something from someone's home*, reminded him again of William. He regagged Heather and checked the camera app for William's house. A gray night view of a quiet empty driveway. Lucky hadn't expected to see Renee's car there, but the fact that it wasn't made him feel better. She'd known he'd be away—Lucky had told her he was looking at a new development in central Virginia as a potential model for a site up north, and the trip would be overnight.

Which gave her a chance to see William.

Renee wouldn't bring him to the house, not with Marybeth there, but she could go to his.

And she hadn't.

"Hey, Bill," Lucky said as he entered the office and knelt before the other man and removed his gag. "Got anything for me?"

"No."

"You told me what happened during the shooting, that you'd left your gun at home. But what happened after it was over?"

"I tried to help the wounded," Bill replied grudgingly. "But they were already deceased."

"And you have no idea where Melissa and Jake went?"

"No."

"You said you and Heather go there all the time. But no other regulars were there that night? No one else you recognized?"

He didn't answer.

"Bill?" Lucky prodded.

"We used to go there all the time," Bill said softly.

Used to.

The small words stopped Lucky, the way the past tense was already assumed. Was it because Bill had heard the diner was going to be closed down after being the site of a double homicide? Was it because Bill and his wife had already decided that they could never revisit it?

Or because Bill thought he'd never see his wife alive again?

Guilt was a low throb in Lucky's chest, like the echoes of a hammer falling.

He wiped his eyes with the back of his sleeve.

"We can end this in two minutes," Lucky told him decisively. "You and Heather will go free. Just tell me something I can use about the diner."

"Heartbreak Diner was almost empty," Bill said. "But I know one of the people there, one who survived."

"Who?"

"Rodrigo," Bill said quietly. "He's the cook. I don't know his last name. Or maybe that is his last name." Bill's shoulders slumped. He shook his head sorrowfully. "That's all I know."

Lucky couldn't tell if Bill was acting, and he wasn't sure what other information he could gather. Nobody else in the article had been identified by name, not the other customers, not the investigating officer.

Lucky felt like he'd been asked to search a catacomb by candlelight and all these people—Bill, Heather, Rodrigo—were flickering shadows ahead of him.

Then again, there was always the reporter who wrote the story about the diner for the *Washington Post*. Lucky could question her, find out what she knew . . . but that was risky. Given Bruce Parks's involvement, there was already a potential connection to the Winterses. Questioning and killing a reporter might initiate a minor investigation. And she'd have to be killed.

Unless, Lucky considered, he tried a different approach with the reporter. Pretended to be a journalist for another paper, a small local one. Ask for information about the story, see if she'd be interested in sharing. Lucky knew she might not confirm any of the names of anyone in the diner, but he could get the name of the cop from her. Not that he wanted to go through the police, but "Rodrigo the Cook" wasn't much of a lead.

Then again, this route would take longer. A day or two to hear back from the reporter, a day or two to hear back from the cop.

And Jake and Melissa could already be a country away by then.

"Rodrigo is all I have for you," Bill said. "I swear it."

"I believe you," Lucky said, and he pulled out his knife from its sheath around his ankle.

"Is Heather really okay?" Bill asked.

Lucky pressed the knife into Bill's hand. "Count to one hundred and cut yourself free," Lucky told him. "Go ahead and call for your wife."

Lucky left the bedroom, loosened Heather's gag. Heard Bill calling "Heather" as he walked down the stairs. Heard Heather calling back. Such relief in their voices, Lucky thought.

Such love.

◆ ◆ ◆

Lucky drove for an hour after leaving Bill and Heather Anders. He checked into a motel room just outside DC, unlocked the door to his room.

He lay on the bed and wept.

Maybe it was the decrepit room or the unreturned message he'd left with Renee, but Lucky suddenly felt terribly, heartbreakingly, lonely.

He hadn't felt this alone since the army, Lucky's mind turning to his last days in the service, when he'd stood outside a building in a small village named Arzo. The Afghan villagers behind the line of his fellow soldiers, all of them in a heavy silence after the deafening sounds of gunfire.

Lucky undressed in the middle of a circle of dumbfounded stares. He was always hot during the day, the sun shining off sand and stone, the dryness in his mouth, the way his lips tightened. He unstrapped his helmet and removed it, ran his hands through the ring of sweat around his head, his wet hair. He was sweating more than he had since his very first patrol months earlier, when he returned to the barracks and found his T-shirt drenched.

Lucky let his jacket drop down over the rifle he'd laid on the ground. Sat down and untied his boots, the laces that traced up his shins. Pulled off his socks and rubbed the soles of his feet into the hot dirt. This entire country was dirt. Closed his eyes and turned his face to the sky.

No one said anything.

And no one entered the building from which Lucky had emerged, the house where a pair of brothers lived, brothers suspected of sheltering Taliban soldiers. Lucky's unit had come to Arzo to interrogate them, found the brothers with their families, the house filled with men—uncles and cousins who'd maintained taut silence while Lucky's patrol questioned them.

No answers had been given, and Lucky's patrol had walked out. There was a restlessness in the unit, the emotional preparation for battle, and then that exhausted relief that it hadn't happened.

Lucky was tired from the exhaustion, of the suspicious way the Afghans regarded him, the secrets he knew those men were keeping. He'd been the last to leave and the first to return, to steal away from his unit and return to that house, to the quiet defiance.

There had been nine men in that house when he raised his rifle and asked them for information.

No one had any, and no one was left alive.

Lucky was sent back to the United States, and he expected to be placed in a military prison. Instead he was met at the plane by a large man, bald and white with hands the size of adult human skulls.

That man walked Lucky to a car at the other end of the tarmac. The military police didn't stop them.

His name was Victor Winters, and he'd heard that Lucky had a talent for killing and a lack of remorse. And those were two traits he valued. He had a proposition for Lucky: come work for him or go to prison.

And so Lucky was under his control, and he remained that way, even after Victor's death, nearly twenty years later.

But now he was finally close to leaving.

Everything inside him wanted to break his cover story and leave this room and hop in his car and drive to his house and climb into bed with Renee and hold her. Fall asleep with her in his arms, her leg draped over his waist, her hair on his shoulder.

His phone buzzed, and excitement rushed over him, one of those coincidences that seem nearly cinematic, a loving answer found in the darkest moment of despair. Renee reaching out to him.

But it was the wrong phone.

"Lucky Wilson?"

One of those faceless female voices from the Winterses.

"Yes."

"We talked yesterday about a property for sale?"

"I remember."

"I heard one of the other buyers made an offer. Might be near closing."

One of the other assassins.

They'd found Melissa and Jake. The job was almost over.

"Okay," Lucky said. "I understand."

"The buyers still may be open to other offers. But everyone's having a hard time reaching them."

Lucky softly exhaled. They might have found where Melissa and Jake were hiding but hadn't been able to bring them in.

"I can try," Lucky said. "What's the phone number?"

"Four one oh, four seven three, seven two four nine."

Lucky wrote the numbers down on a pad of motel stationary.

"Remember the offer we made earlier. It's still good."

He could still be free.

Lucky hung up and deciphered the numbers he'd written. The first three digits were an area code used throughout Maryland, the remaining were a numerical code indicating the town where Melissa and Jake were.

I-S-F-R-A-H-W

He reversed it. W-H-A-R-F-S-I . . .

Wharfside.

The phone call had dried Lucky's tears, but that grief was still inside him, aching, as if his ribs were a cage a wild animal had thrown itself against.

There was no other way out, nothing Heather had been able to advise, although Lucky very much wanted to seek counsel with her again and wondered if there was a way that was possible. He doubted it.

Besides, he didn't think his new therapist would agree with his plans.

Kill Jake and Melissa to free himself from the Winterses.

Murder William McKenna to save his family.

Slaughter everyone standing in the way of his happiness.

Chapter Twelve

Jake

Harold sat against the boat, balefully glaring at Jake.

"Have you been shot before?" Jake asked.

"Can't say I have."

"You're handling it really well." Jake glanced at Harold's bare leg, the pants leg cut away. His leg was surprisingly small and thin and starkly white, like wispy smoke.

Jake lifted his camera, the strap around his neck and under his arm, aimed it at Harold's thigh. The torn skin resembled brittle fall leaves, the dried blood a burnt auburn.

"What do you take all those pictures for anyway?" Harold asked. "Who sees them?"

"Nobody yet."

"You think someone's going to want to see my hurt leg someday?"

"It's not your leg." Jake lifted the camera, gazed through the viewfinder. "It's something else."

"Son, it's still a bullet wound," he heard Harold say. "No matter how you look at it."

"I meant it's not just that." Jake lowered himself to his elbows, looked past the wounded flesh in front of him, the edges like torn pages.

Jake snapped the photograph, examined it in the Lumix's display. He thought about showing it to Harold but doubted the older man would care. Subjects never responded the way he wanted. Instead, they often criticized Jake's photos, asked for a retake or a different angle.

As if they thought the image belonged to them.

"You worried about Melissa?" Harold asked.

Jake looked up from the camera guiltily. He'd been staring so intently at the photo that he'd momentarily forgotten Melissa had left.

"No offense," Harold went on, "but I don't think you're the kind of man to keep her safe. You barely took me down, and I'm not exactly Charles Atlas."

"I don't know who that is."

"Just can't see how you'll protect her."

Harold's words hung in the air.

Jake rose, picked up the gun from the floor. He didn't like holding the weapon, its heaviness or the way he felt that, at any moment, the gun might fire. He hated violence, how it permeated every instance of culture, seemed destined to affect every American. Jake knew the notion sounded hopelessly naive, but he often wondered if a peaceful country was even possible. He rarely watched the news, but when something flashed across his phone, a school shooting or a politician spewing hate, Jake felt such uneasiness and despair, as if the country was coming apart, different factions pulling it to the right and left until violence irreparably tore it in two. And violence would beget violence.

"You're right," Jake told Harold. "I can't protect her. But she and I can protect each other."

"What does that mean?"

"I don't know. Honestly, it sounded better in my head."

It *had* been a while since Melissa left. Jake walked around the back of the boat, reached the broken window, a dark stain of Harold's blood from where the older man had fallen. Jake gazed out into the day.

He didn't see Melissa. Didn't see anyone, just the fan of trees and the sound of unseen water lapping behind them, like an animal at a water bowl in a distant room.

Jake lifted his camera and heard Harold ask, alarmed, "Who are you?"

A response, low and indecipherable.

Fear filled Jake like light.

Whoever was talking to Harold must have climbed through the window and walked around the opposite side of the boat. He and Jake had inadvertently circled each other.

"Jake was just here," Harold said plaintively. And there was another low response Jake couldn't understand.

He wanted to climb out the window and run off.

He wanted to hide until whatever was going to happen happened.

He wanted to crawl forward on his knees and beg for his life.

Jake was afraid, violently afraid.

"I told you," Harold said urgently. "I don't know where they went."

Jake's hands were on the windowsill, shards of glass pressed into his palms.

He let go of the window. Quietly walked back toward Harold, like Harold's pleading voice was a siren, luring him to danger. Or a shipwrecked sailor, calling for help.

Jake carried the gun in one hand and the camera in the other, pressed against his chest. He crouched between the bows of two large speedboats, where he could hide and watch. Peered around the corner.

Jake could only see the interrogator's back, wide under a black duster and dark jeans and boots. He was bent over Harold, saying something too low for Jake to understand.

The shears Melissa had found and used to cut Harold's jeans were behind the stranger.

"I'm not ready," Harold said. "Please."

The man stood, and Jake saw the back of his neck and the side of his cheek. Scars everywhere, burn marks like a busy road map of some congested city. Despite his fear, Jake lifted his camera.

The man reached into a backpack and pulled out a bottle, squinted at the label, twisted off the cap.

He poured the contents of the bottle over Harold's body.

Jake smelled gasoline.

Saw the small yellow gleam of a match.

Jake hadn't planned on rising and running, wasn't exactly sure what he was going to do when he reached the man. He thought about abruptly changing course and turning in the other direction, and Jake actually liked that idea very much, but his body wouldn't obey his mind.

He simply couldn't stop himself from running over and grabbing the man's scarred wrist and snuffing out the match.

The man looked at Jake with surprise. He tried to pull his wrist free, but Jake grimly hung on.

What happened to my gun? Jake thought.

Oh no.

He had no idea where the gun was. Still in his hand? No, Jake's hands were wrapped around the other man's wrists, vainly hanging on.

Had he dropped it before he charged?

Maybe.

Strange how calm his mind was as he struggled, as the other man finally pulled one of his hands free.

"Get out!" Jake screamed.

Well, that scream wasn't very calm, Jake thought, still with that weird disassociation. It was like a version of him was fixed on escaping, another was determined to help Harold, a third was losing this fight, and a fourth was dismally watching everything happen.

"Go!" Jake screamed. He grabbed the man's free arm again, hanging on like he was dangling from a branch that protruded from just below a cliff's edge.

He wasn't even sure who he was screaming at, Harold or the stranger or himself. All of them. Begging everyone to leave this situation, for the violence to end.

An accidental kick sent the shears sliding toward Harold. The older man quickly cut himself loose, and, for a hopeful second, Jake thought Harold might help him. But Harold just stood and hurriedly limped away.

The gasoline seemed to be everywhere, in Jake's clothes and nose and hair and mouth. The other man again pulled a hand free, and Jake suddenly felt his fist. The punch was like finding out a car had run over your dog, so powerful it was emotional, and knocked Jake to the floor, a punch so transcendental it took all those versions of Jake and sent them flying back into his body.

He lay flat in the pool of gasoline, stunned.

I sure get punched a lot, Jake thought distantly.

The scarred man stood over him and glowered down. Jake lifted a hand as the other man lifted his lighter.

Chapter Thirteen

Melissa

Melissa remembered the control she'd felt that long night when Harold kept waking up in pain, a night that had left her sleepless but far from exhausted. There was something about that situation, the stress and strain, that energized her. Given her a newfound rush of being needed, and with need came something close to power.

But that feeling was gone. Ever since stumbling upon the clerk's body, Melissa had barely felt conscious. She ran back to the warehouse, crying and gasping, away from violence and death, like a dream from which she couldn't wake.

Melissa reached a bend in the path and stumbled off. Slipped into a small outcropping of trees near the water, collapsed to the dirt, tears clouding her vision. Panic thundered through her like raging horses.

That dying man on his knees at the diner.

The waitress crawling into death.

The murdered boy at the store.

Maybe someone other than the Winterses had killed him, Melissa thought, and she hated herself for that hope. But if it hadn't been the Winterses, then his death hadn't been her fault. It was possible some other criminal had strolled into the store.

Regardless, she needed to get back to Jake.

Melissa finally reached the broken window, grasped the frame where it was clear of glass. She wasn't sure what she and Jake could do or where they would go; she just knew they had to leave. Death was circling once again.

She saw something on the grass.

Blood, drops of blood, a red path like raindrops had fallen around the warehouse.

Voices inside.

Melissa climbed in, lowered herself softly to the floor, walked around the edges. Reached the other side of the warehouse and crept toward the yacht she and Jake were using. From the shadows of a catamaran, she saw a man standing over Jake, Jake pushing himself backward with one hand, his other raised defensively.

Melissa had never seen that man until this moment, but she recognized the scars from stories she'd heard.

Seth.

If men like Seth had been hired to find them, then Melissa knew she and Jake were in greater danger than she'd imagined.

Jake kept scooting backward, casting about desperately. Melissa spotted an open backpack on the ground holding several glass bottles filled with a yellowish-green liquid.

Again, that instinctual pull guided her, despite her fear. She stole forward, picked up one of the bottles.

Seth didn't see her. She knew Jake was glancing at her and trying not to.

That memory from days earlier, when she'd crept behind Chris with the wine bottle, the hit that had sent her on this path, a bloody christening like a bottle smashing against the side of a departing ship.

She raised her glass weapon over Seth's head.

Seth reached back and caught her hand before it lowered.

Suddenly Melissa was stumbling. He'd spun around so fast that she hadn't even seen his other hand move, just felt his fist slam into her cheek.

Melissa fell against one of the boats, a point from something hard pressed into her spine.

Jake stumbled toward Seth, his camera swinging.

Seth glanced over at Jake, almost casually, and grabbed him by the neck. Held him in place with one outstretched arm, squeezing as Jake dropped to his knees.

Seth's other hand snaked out, slapped the bottle out of Melissa's hand, grabbed her by the hair and pulled down.

Melissa couldn't break her fall as the ground rushed toward her. Her forehead smashed into the cement floor, nausea nearly overwhelming her. Patches of her hair felt like they'd been ripped out. His hand stayed on the back of her head, keeping her down, holding her in place as she struggled.

Seth held Melissa by the hair and Jake by the throat, Jake's face red and cheeks puffed and eyes wide as he choked. He began walking toward the front door, dragging Jake and Melissa with him.

Melissa's hands were over his, mitigating the pain from his grip but inadvertently holding his hand in place. Her feet scrabbled behind her, struggling to keep pace. Jake was on the other side as Seth grasped his throat, feet dragging, Jake's body bent backward like a spear's tip was pressed into his spine.

Seth threw them toward the giant steel door. Melissa felt herself carried as if by a merciless wind, then her palms and cheek slapping down, Jake collapsed next to her.

Seth removed a gun from his backpack and pointed it at her.

Her hands rose.

Melissa had long been fearful of men with guns, of the way men didn't respect their power, how they played with weapons as fantasy. Weapons were desire, and fear accompanied desire.

But Seth was different.

Until now, Melissa had never seen a man hold a gun who wasn't, in some way, scared.

Seth kicked the door leading to the small office up front. It took one kick for the door to splinter, another for it to fall open. He strode inside.

"I got Harold out," Jake told her, pushing himself next to her, his throat raspy. "This guy was going to kill him. Who is he?"

"Seth," Melissa said.

Chris had told her about him, in the same reverential tones usually reserved for Victor Winters and his murder. Chris had never believed his uncle had been killed by the cops or criminals. He thought a mysterious vigilante had done it, a masked mythical assailant who'd glided into Victor's house and coldly assassinated him and his girlfriend.

Melissa knew that story couldn't be true, but Chris wholeheartedly subscribed to it, the way people believed in bigfoot, or how children worried about monsters.

But Seth was real. A hired hit man for the Winterses, he was once set on fire by a woman he'd failed to kill. Probably the only person he'd ever failed to kill.

There was an unstated hierarchy in the Winterses' organization, and men like Seth were at the top. The pimps and dealers and traffickers were hard and scarred and violent and ruthless and wedded to brutality . . . but even they told hushed, admiring stories about Seth. For most of them, violence was a tool they employed. For Seth and the few like him—a pair of eastern European twins, a married couple in Baltimore, a father in the suburbs of northern Virginia—violence was like breathing. Killing has its rules, and those who navigate that world are the ones who make the rules. Something beyond men.

"The Winterses bring people like him in for important jobs," she told Jake.

"We're important?"

A rumbling sound as the large warehouse door behind them lifted.

Seth strode out of the office as the door loudly rose, clanged on completion. Melissa blinked into the sunlight, surprised at how bright the day was. As if she'd run from the store in a dense gray fog.

A small van was alone in the parking lot. Harold's old car, some type of aged Dodge, was gone.

"Get up," Seth said, the first words he'd spoken, quiet and direct.

She and Jake unsteadily rose to their feet and walked outside, clutching each other like an elderly couple. Jake wheezed as he walked. Melissa thought he was having problems breathing but realized he was whispering. Saying something to himself.

Jake abruptly stopped and turned toward Seth.

"Keep walking," Seth said, a hint of weariness in his voice.

"What if you just take me?" Jake asked. "And let Melissa go?"

"No. Walk."

Jake removed his camera from around his neck. Held it delicately, his thumb rubbing the black plastic.

"You can have my camera," he said solemnly.

"Jake," Melissa told him. "No."

"This is a Lumix D C dash F Z eighty," Jake went on. "It's not that expensive, but some bloggers think it's going to be a discontinued model." He wiped a spot of blood from the side of his head. "In a few years this little camera will be worth a lot. And right now, it's a great model for beginners."

Seth didn't say anything.

"It just has the one lens," Jake continued, "and that can't be removed, but you might not want to. It can even see the craters on the moon. I do want the memory card, but I have a spare in the car. I'll give it to you, and I'll even throw in a travel bag . . . although we'd have to stop by my apartment. You can have the camera, the memory card, and the travel bag, and all you have to do is bring me to the Winterses instead of Melissa. I know they'll still come after her, but this gives her a head start. That's all I want. Melissa to have another chance."

"No," Melissa said to Seth. "Don't listen to him."

Jake turned toward her. "Melissa," he said urgently. "They can take me, but they can't take both of us. I can survive if I know you're alive. They can't kill me as long as I know you're out there and okay. Do you understand that?"

She couldn't respond.

"Why don't I just take both of you *and* the stupid little camera?" Seth suggested.

"Well," Jake said after a moment, "you could do that."

Suddenly there was a flash, and Seth stepped back, hands over his eyes, the gun pressed against his forehead.

Jake grabbed Melissa's hand, and they turned and started to run.

They reached the edge of the parking lot, and Melissa wondered why she hadn't heard a shot yet, wondered if Seth was still blinded from the camera, if his handgun had malfunctioned. Jake must have had the same thought because he stopped, turned, and that's when she heard a crack.

They looked at each other, confused. And then a blossom of blood flowered near Jake's neck.

He let go of her hand and sank to his knees.

Jake's legs kicked as he was dragged and then shoved into the van, his hands over the wound, blood filling the spaces between his fingers. His mouth opened and closed, soundlessly, like he was underwater and drowning.

Melissa's fingers were shaking, her throat hoarse and raw. She wondered if she was screaming, emitting any sounds whatsoever. She felt her tears, dizziness, that rising panic.

Seth pushed her toward the van. She climbed inside numbly, dumbly, knelt next to Jake. Held his hand as he kicked.

Seth was saying something, distinctly, but it was like Melissa had forgotten words. Some small sentence in a threatening tone. He repeated himself, his voice raised.

And then there was another explosion.

But this sound was different from a gunshot.

Seth shouted. Melissa turned. Through the van doors she saw a car veer into the parking lot, gravel flying out from under its tires as it skidded and swerved.

The car, an old white sedan, stopped about fifty feet away.

The engine roared, and the car rushed forward. Seth fired and the windshield cracked and he kept firing, calmly stepped to the side of the van doors, outside Melissa's sight.

The car just missed the van's swinging open door as it rocketed past.

Melissa heard the sound of the car hitting Seth, like soup splattering.

And she heard the car dig into the gravel again. The engine revved, and the car screeched and stopped outside the van door. The front passenger window rolled down.

Melissa protectively knelt in front of Jake.

A woman she had never seen peered over from the driver's seat.

"Where's my son?"

Chapter Fourteen

Lucky

The setting afternoon sun brought an early evening excitement, one that reminded Lucky of the twilit summer nights in his neighborhood, back when Marybeth had been either ten or eleven, the age right before her teenage distance set in seemingly overnight. Renee relaxed and lovely as she talked to someone's wife, sitting in a lawn chair with her legs lazily crossed, a glass of wine in hand. Lucky standing in a circle of men, as he was expected to, but their conversations distant to him, lost in the evening, lost in Lucky's quiet observations of his wife and daughter.

But those evenings hadn't been lit by police cars.

Lucky walked back toward the cordoned off parking lot from the warehouse, toward a pair of cops standing apart from the investigation, mounted lights illuminating every inch of torn gravel and spilled blood.

His phone buzzed.

Lucky pulled it halfway out of his pocket, glanced at the screen.

A notification from the WatchFull app.

He pushed the phone back into his pocket, tried to focus on the cops' efforts to reconstruct what had happened. Towns like Wharfside didn't often come across this level of violence. He'd overheard that a CSI team from Baltimore was on the way to investigate the blood throughout the warehouse and parking lot, as well as the murder at a nearby convenience store. Lucky had gone to that store first but hadn't been able to get inside. Even so, he'd learned that the only corpse there belonged to the clerk. Not anyone he was looking for.

And there was little chance the cops would learn who'd killed him. Lucky knew the nearby Baltimore cops were too busy to offer much help, and a town this small lacked the resources to conduct an effective investigation on its own. Especially when the criminal knew what he was doing.

Law enforcement was stretched too thin. If you kept a low profile and hid your crimes with even a slight degree of competence, no one could catch you.

It was so easy to be corrupt in America that it barely felt like living a lie.

"When's building management getting here?" Lucky heard a nearby cop ask another.

"On the way," the other cop replied, "but coming from DC. Going to take a few hours."

"Who are you with? Waiting for your team?"

Those questions were directed to Lucky.

"Team?" Lucky asked.

"News team."

"I'm not media. PI." He showed the disinterested cops his badge; they didn't even glance at it. "Hired by a family searching for their son. I heard a rumor he might be in Wharfside."

"What's the kid's name?"

Another notification.

"Jake Smith," Lucky replied, ignoring the phone vibrating in his pocket. "About six feet, twenty-four, white. Curly brown hair, brown eyes."

"Haven't seen him."

"No worries. Better for his family that he wasn't here."

Lucky and the two cops watched an investigator measure the distance between drops of blood.

"You serve before?" one of the cops asked.

Strange, Lucky reflected, how distant he was from that question. Never compelled to mention his brief time in the military.

"I was San Diego police," Lucky lied.

"You ever work with ICE?"

"All the time."

The cop nodded approvingly. It was a lie Lucky had told before, claiming prior police work to help himself slip into crime scenes or gather information. Years ago, at his request, the Winterses had mocked up a fake badge for him, and he'd used that badge countless times. It was a gold oval with "POLICE OFFICER SAN DIEGO" written on it in blue, San Diego chosen since it was too far and large to easily verify.

Not that, after Lucky showed someone the badge, he ever stayed around long enough to answer questions.

"Is the pay good as a PI?" one of the cops asked.

"Not according to my wife."

The cops snorted and laughed. This was something Lucky had always been good at, easing his way into any group of men. He knew what men wanted, what they trusted. Men will believe anything if it has a sense of superiority to it. For some it was wealth, for others, strength. But the key was for that trait to be held aloft and superior. Men treasured that approach, mistook it as admirable.

"You two work out of this town?" Lucky asked.

"Nah, we're Salisbury. Wharfside doesn't have its own PD. Jim Carver. This is Derrek Lough."

"Lucky Wilson." Lucky shook each of their hands.

"You heard Harold's in the hospital?" Lough asked Carver.

"I heard."

"Harold?" Lucky asked.

"Harold Thompson," Carter replied. "Old local and part-time security, mostly as charity. Probably would have greeted customers at Target if Wharfside had one but kept an eye on the warehouse instead."

"Wrong place, wrong time?"

Another frustrating notification. Lucky reached into his pocket and silenced his phone. He was certain the camera was picking up a neighbor walking his dog or William checking the mail, not any incriminating evidence about William and Renee.

But, still, at the thought of them together . . .

Lucky forced those images away.

"Looks like Harold was out here," one of the cops was saying, "got dragged inside. Old Harold put up a fight, though. He's under right now, but they say he's going to pull through."

There was so much these cops didn't know, and so much they'd never know.

A call on the burner phone during Lucky's drive over had filled in these blanks ahead of time.

"Lucky? The buyers pulled out. Said they had a new job in a new city and couldn't commit. And their agent is going on vacation for a few days. They sent us a quick message that the property is wide open again."

This one was easy for Lucky to decipher.

Jake and Melissa had escaped and left town, and the person searching for them had been laid up, left with wounds that required medical care and a few days off.

The property is wide open.

The search for Jake and Melissa was still on.

Investigators were documenting everything inside, and Lucky had caught only a quick glance. But that had been enough. He'd seen the smashed window on the other side of the building, the broken door to an office, the bloody path from the center of the room.

The scent of gasoline.

The blood might have seemed like one of the most prominent clues in the investigation, but the real clue, Lucky knew, was the gas.

The man who had spilled it was named Seth Yates. Lucky had trained him.

A few years ago he'd been asked by the Winterses to take Seth under his tutelage. He'd thought the young man would be impetuous and flamboyant, like most dumb, immature criminals, but instead Lucky met someone hardened and serious. Saw that Seth was driven by anger and revenge, hatred of the scars a fire had mapped over his face and body.

Lucky channeled that rage, taught Seth the importance of death over desire. The Winterses were never interested in sending a message or torturing someone to prove a point. Death was the most effective message there was. Particularly when the death appeared natural or as the result of an accident. None of their methods caused attention, and that was the precise outcome the Winterses wanted.

Seth chose fire. Houses set ablaze, offices burned to the ground, a corpse found unconscious in a smoke-filled kitchen. He studied the science of fire, even considered being trained as a volunteer firefighter, but Lucky quickly dissuaded him of that notion. He knew that if these fires were ever investigated, those with training would be suspect: Seth's scars and demeanor made him memorable. Instead it was Lucky who took the training—a few weekend classes offered by the local FD focused on what to do if a fire occurred in different situations. Lucky took careful notes and gave his findings to Seth.

And then, after a few months, they parted ways.

Seth seemed confused by this, as if he'd expected Lucky to remain a mentor to him, to keep in contact as friends, but that was the final lesson Lucky wanted to teach.

Never mix your professional and personal lives. The only person Lucky had ever trusted with the Winterses was Ruby, and he forever had the knowledge that she could betray him. He'd helped her escape, and if she was found, he had no assurance that she wouldn't turn on him.

It would have been better to have never trusted anyone.

"If you don't mind me asking," Carver asked, "how much money are we talking?"

Lucky blinked back to the conversation.

"I hope that's not personal," Carver added. Lough's head was tilted as he listened to the radio mic on his shoulder. "Just curious."

"Depends how successful you are," Lucky said. This was a question he'd been asked before, one he'd researched. "Starting out, you might make in the twenties. Once you get established, maybe three times that."

"That's it?"

"Sorry."

"Damn."

"Hey," Lough said. "We need to look at the tracks. They're thinking we could have multiple victims."

"Okay." Carver didn't seem particularly motivated to look into the case. "So, what? You get your license and go right to work? Or did you work with someone first? I heard you have to apprentice."

Lucky could have continued this conversation, kept on fabricating a story that he'd told before, but his phone buzzed again and he finally gave in. Pulled it out, glanced at the WatchFull notification.

"One second," Lucky said, and he lifted his phone. "I need to take this."

He walked away from Carver and Lough, away from the conversations occasionally punctuated by laughter in the warehouse. Over to his car at the end of the lot, a few spaces away from the police automobiles. A younger cop was back there, vaping and staring down into his phone. Lucky strode past him, opened his own car door, climbed inside.

Shut and locked it.

Closed his eyes tight.

Realized he was gripping the phone so hard he was in danger of shattering the screen.

Lucky stared out the windshield at the dark night. At the silhouettes of trees, like sentries waiting to be told what to do.

Lucky swiped open his phone.

Tapped the app.

He pressed it too long, and an option appeared to delete it, the app trembling on his screen with a small *X* in the corner. Lucky briefly considered the idea, the bliss of ignorance from not knowing what was on the camera.

Instead he opened the camera to its live view.

Renee's car was parked in William's driveway.

Lucky didn't even wipe the tears off his cheeks. Just stared down at the phone.

He watched the door to the house open. Saw William McKenna standing in the doorway. Lucky squinted and imagined he could see the smile on William's face.

The car door opened, but it wasn't Renee who stepped out.

Lucky watched his daughter run over to William McKenna, watched her disappear into his embrace and then pull back and kiss him. William made a laughing sound the camera picked up, held Marybeth away, glanced up and down the street. Then he took her hand and pulled her inside and closed the door.

His daughter.

His seventeen-year-old daughter.

The screen cracked under Lucky's thumbs.

Part Two

You belong to your father, the devil, and you want to carry out your father's desires. He was a murderer from the beginning, not holding to the truth, for there is no truth in him. When he lies, he speaks his native language, for he is a liar and the father of lies.

John 8:44

Chapter Fifteen

Melissa

"I like that," Jake told her. "It gives you something different. Something special. Don't smile."

They sat on a grassy hill after he took that first set of photos, a sunny day in Baltimore's Patterson Park, the summer still too young for Baltimore's brutal humidity. A boy and his father kicked a soccer ball back and forth. Another couple was on a blanket to their right, the woman sitting up and the man lying on his back.

"Can I see the pictures?" Melissa asked. She slid next to Jake, pulled her dyed red-brown hair over her shoulder. Peered down at the camera.

She'd never had pictures taken by a professional photographer. The photo shoot had been Chris's idea, inspired by the photos of a friend's wife. Lately Chris had always seemed inspired this way; what someone else had, he wanted.

The friend's wife—Janet or Janice, Melissa wasn't sure which and, because she'd already met her, was too embarrassed to ask—had shown her own photos to Melissa and a group of wives and girlfriends a few weekends before, black-and-white pictures she was getting framed. "You probably saw them when I posted them on Insta a month or so ago," Janet/Janice told them, and the other women assented they had.

Melissa had been surprised to discover, over the rest of that afternoon, that the photos actually changed how she regarded Janet/Janice. Melissa had only met her that day and had seen her as somewhat shallow, empty, the kind of woman Chris's friends tended to date or marry and, she was certain, no different from how they saw her. But the pictures changed that impression, particularly one where Janet/Janice was glancing down, eyes away from the camera, conveying a sadness Melissa would never have suspected.

She showed that picture to Chris before they left.

"You like that?" he asked. "You want some old photos of you too?"

"I just think they're so pretty."

And now Melissa looked at the photos Jake had taken, one where she was staring at the camera, unsmiling but with a gleam in her eye. An excitement Jake had somehow spotted and captured. Melissa didn't recognize herself.

It wasn't just how she looked—something else about the picture drew her. How Jake saw her.

"I don't know where I am," Melissa said.

Jake's mother sat next to her, slumped with her hands wrapped around the back of her neck. She didn't look up as she spoke.

"We're at Steve Debko's. He's a friend and a doctor."

"I don't remember you telling me that."

"That's because you're still in shock." Ruby kept staring down at the floor. "You asked me where we were going three times on the way here."

"Dr. Steve, your friend, he can help Jake?" Melissa asked.

Ruby didn't answer. Melissa stood and walked over to the kitchen window and stared out at the neglected lawn, fading from green to gray, the bright colors of day changing to a black-and-white evening.

"You knew who he was," Ruby said softly, as if to herself.

Melissa didn't know how to respond.

"You knew who he was," Ruby said again. "You were with Chris Winters; you knew the kind of danger Jake would be in. This is your fault."

◆ ◆ ◆

Melissa remembered the day after that long first photo shoot in Baltimore, the text from Jake thanking her for her time, the way she relentlessly analyzed the closing words: . . . *and I loved your sunset eyes.*

She'd told Chris about the photo shoot, how Jake had taken her to different parts of Baltimore she hadn't yet seen. Highlandtown's Patterson Park. The tree-filled neighborhoods of Bolton Hill. The quirky, festive goofiness of Hampden. She'd lived near the city with Chris for years and felt like she had never seen any of it.

"So you had fun," Chris replied.

Melissa wondered, suddenly, if she was too excited, talking too much about another man. But Chris was staring down into his phone, pressing the screen with alternating thumbs, the slow way he texted. Melissa often wondered if that was why her texts with girlfriends were so much more detailed, their fingers smaller and nimble. Or maybe men were always more reserved.

"I did," she said and then added brightly, to make what she was saying about Chris, "I think you'll really like the pictures."

"Cool."

She wondered who Chris was texting. Melissa knew a lot of what Chris was involved with couldn't be discussed. She understood that, had grown used to it long ago—the way someone might accept their partner's drinking, a cautious eye toward excess, without realizing excess was already upon them.

Like the gun collection that had proliferated in the closet. The quiet men who came by late at night, whom Chris led to that room in the basement. Even the video she'd seen of that man being killed. The images that she'd forced herself not to think about.

What wouldn't she accept?

Melissa had been so terrified the night after she'd seen that video over Chris's shoulder. She'd lain awake afterward, alone in bed, tears wetting her pillow. And then she somehow fell into a deep, dreamless sleep and woke the next morning with Chris gone, the sun out, the video a memory that glaringly returned.

But it was easier hours later, a morning later. That dread in her, the fear rock, was smaller. There was a city outside her window, and it moved and lived and breathed, and so there was something else she was part of.

Melissa thought about the pictures Jake had taken, how he'd talked to her. How they'd walked through Baltimore together.

And she longed to see him again.

How she longed to see him again. To hear his voice. For Dr. Steve to walk up the stairs and tell her and Ruby that Jake was going to recover.

But there was no sound from the stairs or basement. Nothing but silence after Ruby's accusation.

"We knew we were in trouble," Melissa told Ruby. "Jake and I tried to stop seeing each other. But I loved him and—"

"But it's so small now, isn't it?" Ruby interrupted her. "The bad things we do are always small, compared to their consequence. The Lord will repay you for your sins."

Melissa quickly accepted when Jake invited her out for drinks. She was determined to prove this was casual, that she was only making a new friend, even quietly telling herself as she applied eyeliner in the bathroom, *This doesn't mean anything.*

"What'd you say?" Chris was lying on their bed in his boxers, watching men fight each other in a cage on his laptop.

"Nothing."

She and Jake met at night, for what she told herself wasn't a date. That was reaffirmed when she saw what he was wearing—jeans and an old faded T-shirt—which stood in sharp contrast to her short olive-green romper with a diving neckline and black platform heels that laced around her calves.

It wasn't a date, Melissa told herself. She just loved dressing up.

She wouldn't go on a date with another man. She let those words drum into her mind.

"Wow," Jake said when he saw her. "I should have dressed up."

"It's okay." *Because this wasn't a date.*

His gaze kept darting to her legs, and she suddenly felt uncomfortable.

"You carry that everywhere?" Melissa pointed at the camera on his chest.

Jake looked surprised, then touched the camera.

"Pretty much," he said. "It's kind of like my best friend."

Melissa thought that was cute, and then she was curious.

"But your phone has a camera, right?"

"Yeah," Jake said, suddenly serious, "but you lose so much with a phone. The sensors just don't compare, and that affects the number of pixels, and it destroys the light in your work. You can't really tell when you view most phone photos on their screens, but if you blow them up, the elements get blurred or distorted. The biggest problem for me, though, is the lack of lenses. I have a decent stable of lenses that I can use with this camera, and they all offer different—"

"Basically," Melissa interrupted, "you like using that camera more?"

He blinked, smiled that cute smile again. "Basically, yeah."

"I'm sorry," she said. "Was that rude?"

"Nah. Even I was losing me."

Jake and Melissa walked around the harbor. National Harbor sat near the borders of DC, Maryland, and Virginia, a recent development of shops and restaurants and hotels that the local business community hoped would bring the capitol's relentless flock of tourists outside the city. *The Awakening*, a sculpture famous to DC residents, had been taken from Hains Point and moved here, a giant stone arm and hand and head straining to emerge from the water's edge. A Ferris wheel slowly spun, offering a view of Washington's landmarks from its highest location. A singer sang on a street corner, accompanied by a guitarist, collecting change from pedestrians passing by.

"This is nice," he told her.

Melissa agreed.

"But why are we here?" he asked. "Is this a date?"

No, she should have replied.

Yes, she wanted to tell him.

"I don't know," Melissa said.

◆ ◆ ◆

"Why are we here?" she asked.

"You forgot again?" Ruby snapped.

"No. I'm sorry." Melissa felt too broken to do anything but apologize. "I mean, can we go to a hospital? Jake should be in a hospital." An urgency rose, the thought that Jake might die. "He should be in a hospital!"

"He'd never get out. You know that. Bullet wounds bring the police. And the police bring the Winterses."

Noises from downstairs. Melissa looked to the door in the kitchen that led to the basement where, hours earlier, she and Ruby and Dr. Steve had half carried, half dragged Jake. Jake bleeding and crying out in pain, Melissa numbly watching while Dr. Steve hurriedly placed a cover on a pool table in the center of the room, and then the three of them lifted Jake onto it. Dr. Steve told them to wait upstairs, but Melissa had been unable to move, and then Dr. Steve shouted, and Ruby's hand was suddenly on her arm, pulling her backward. Melissa wanted Jake to look at her, wanted to see promise in his eyes, hear strength in his voice. Wanted to know that, if she left him in this basement with Dr. Steve, she could return to him later. If she stayed with him, Melissa felt, he'd live. Jake would live, and he might never be the same, but he'd live. Melissa knew the effects of bullet wounds, had heard stories from Chris about people he'd known who'd been shot, and she had a friend whose cousin had been shopping in a mall in Maryland when a pair of young men with rifles had stalked through, casually firing into stores, killing over a dozen and wounding three times that many, and a bullet in her friend's cousin's gut had left her forever limping, resigned to a colostomy bag, her insides tattered. But she'd lived. Melissa would accept that, of course, patiently stay by Jake's side as he recovered, this penance for their lust.

The Lord repaying her for their sins.

"He's asleep," Dr. Steve had said, the only time he'd left Jake and come upstairs. "I had to put him out. He was moving too much, losing too much blood."

Neither Ruby nor Melissa said anything.

"The bullet is lodged in his clavicle," Dr. Steve went on. "After I cleaned up the wound, I could even see it protruding. But he's lucky. The subclavian artery is close to the entry, but it's safe. Jake's alive, but he'll only stay alive if you take him to the hospital."

"No," Ruby said.

"I know you can't. And I also know you can't stay here for long." Dr. Steve's words were heavy. "So the next option is to remove the bullet."

"You can do that?" Melissa asked.

"I don't have a choice. If that bullet stays there, there's a chance of infection, of rupture, of death, particularly if he's going to be moving a lot. And chances are, he's going to be moving a lot. I'm going to keep him under until he has the surgery, but there will be a couple of times you can speak with him."

"Thank you so much," Melissa said, and she heard the emotion in her voice. She couldn't help it, the combination of fear and gratefulness and deference.

Dr. Steve went back downstairs.

"Steve's a real doctor," Ruby told her. "Not a vet or chiropractor or something else."

"How do you know him?"

"I saved him from the Winterses."

Melissa thought about that.

"Jake told me a little about you," Melissa said to Ruby. "But he never said what you did for them."

"That's because he never knew."

Melissa gathered Ruby didn't want to talk. She didn't press her further. Just stood and paced. And thought relentlessly about Jake.

Love was relentless and inevitable, like Melissa's life had been a wasteland of snow, and love was summer and sun and children joyfully shouting.

Jake dared her, texting her that he was outside her house, asking her to step out for just a kiss, a quick touch. And his desire sparked hers. "Where are you going?" Chris would ask as he cleaned a gun, the now familiar smell of polish and metal, and Melissa would tell him she'd forgotten her phone in the car. And hope on her way out the door that Chris didn't realize she was actually holding her phone.

Melissa would step outside—no, she'd fly outside—not even conscious of the steps from the front door and then rush around back to the yard where Jake waited. His lips against hers, the rough brush of his whiskers against her cheek.

Melissa was in a place she'd never been, drunk off desire, as boy crazy as she'd ever felt. A love full throated and raw and obsessive, placed before everything and putting everything else as secondary in importance. She obsessed over him, ached in response to his words.

And Jake seemed to realize this with an almost unconscious coolness. Or maybe she was just that affected, his smile seeming to hold secrets. The way he looked at her, how she could almost feel his gaze on her body.

They made games of teasing each other, sly kisses in the back seat of his car, parked around the corner from her house, daring the other to go farther, his hands under her shirt, her tugging his belt. She'd return home to Chris, worried that the scruff on Jake's cheek had left her face red, worried he would somehow sense or smell the other man on her. And maybe, a year earlier, Chris would have.

But then again, a year earlier, maybe she wouldn't have turned to someone else.

Melissa often wondered if that was the case, if Jake would have remained just a photographer Chris had hired. She tried to separate the two, didn't want her attraction to Jake to be nothing but a result of her failing relationship with Chris. She still would have been attracted, Melissa imagined, but she wouldn't have acted on it.

Just been left wondering how happy she could have been.

◆ ◆ ◆

"You should come downstairs."

Melissa hadn't heard the door leading to the steps open, had no idea Dr. Steve was behind her.

"He's awake?" Ruby asked uncertainly, her voice young and confused, like a young girl's.

But Dr. Steve had already left.

Melissa turned, and she and Ruby glanced at each other, just long enough for each woman to notice the fear in the other's eyes, not long enough to hold a gaze, not long enough for comfort.

Melissa followed Dr. Steve down, one hand on the railing and the other on the wall of the narrow stairway.

Ruby stayed in the kitchen.

◆ ◆ ◆

"We can just leave," Jake told her.

They'd spent days together in Jake's apartment. Chris was out of town. He'd told her that he needed to visit family in upstate New York and would be gone a week, and Melissa had only returned to their house to feed his pet fish and change clothes.

The rest of her time was with Jake in his apartment, laughing and lost, immersed in embraces, their bodies rarely not touching.

"Leave?" Melissa asked. "Like, the city?"

"Leave him," Jake urged her. "Go to your place, pack a bag."

And there was that power, that suggestion of choice she'd never seriously considered before, the idea of hope. Why not leave? Why not leave Chris and this life of fear?

Melissa thought about it through the evening, staring at some home-renovation show in Spanish while, next to her in bed, Jake peered into his camera.

To Melissa, this wasn't a small thing, watching a television show in Spanish while Jake was with her. Like Chris, Jake barely paid attention to her show. Chris would have played *Candy Crush* on his phone, and Jake was scanning photographs, but there was a visible annoyance in Chris whenever Melissa watched something in Spanish or spoke the language to her friends or relatives or talked about visiting her birth country again. She wondered if it was jealousy, this connection he couldn't experience. Or maybe it was suspicion, the way paranoia had stolen over Chris the closer he'd grown to his family.

But Jake had the opposite reaction. He liked when Melissa spoke Spanish, even if he barely understood it. He asked her to teach him, to tell him the names of furniture in a room, the things they viewed from his bedroom window on the street below. The parts of her body she wanted him to kiss.

Melissa hadn't realized how much this side of her had been silenced.

"I'm going to pack tomorrow," Melissa announced.

Jake smiled as he stared into his camera.

That night, like every night that week, they were lost in love. Falling asleep together, waking together, not caring that there was a chance that they might die for each other. The covers a tangled rope wrapped around their bodies.

Melissa waited at the bottom of the stairs before entering the large basement rec room where they'd carried Jake.

She couldn't turn the corner.

Seeing him meant realizing his fate. He could be sitting up, an exhausted smile on his face, white bandages wrapped around his shoulder and chest.

Or he could be lying down on the table, eyes looking at nothing.

Melissa was too frightened. She went back up the stairs and didn't even make it to her chair. She sank to the kitchen floor, arms wrapped around herself.

Jake had never been to the house, and Melissa hadn't realized how large Chris's home was compared to Jake's apartment. Or Melissa had realized it but hadn't considered how it would look from Jake's perspective. How small it might make him feel.

"It's not legal," she told him, calling from the bedroom as she carried dresses from the closet to the bed. "None of this is."

"Yeah," he called back to her wryly. "That's a shame."

Instinctively Melissa had started analyzing her clothes, matching outfits as she brought them out of the closet, rather than doing what she'd imagined and simply throwing all her clothes into suitcases and sorting them later. She couldn't take everything in one trip, of course, but she could take enough to last her for a week or two, enough to get her started before she decided on the next step.

She closed the first suitcase, dragged it off the bed, wincing at the sound when it landed heavily on the floor. There was no way she could carry it out to the car, so she went to find Jake.

He was sitting in the dining room, his hands flat on his knees.

Chris stood next to him, holding a handgun.

Melissa suddenly realized how wrong she'd been, how easily she'd naively assumed everything would go. Her relationship with Chris had, for all intents, already ended.

But now she understood that Chris hadn't seen it that way, whatsoever.

"Who's this?" Chris asked, anger in his voice, hurt across his face.

Jake and Melissa both flinched when Chris pointed at Jake with his gun.

"Don't hurt him," Melissa said, and as she spoke, she realized her second mistake.

Now Chris knew Jake mattered to her.

His expression and hands both tightened, and Melissa knew her life was destined to change forever. And only for the worse.

◆ ◆ ◆

"Is he alive?" Ruby asked.

"I don't know," Melissa told her. "I couldn't make myself go into the room."

"You're the reason he's here." Ruby didn't soften her glare. "So get down there and find out what you did."

"I. . . I can't."

"Whore," Ruby said, breathing the word out.

Melissa's back tightened like a whip had lashed it.

"Get down there, whore." Ruby's voice rose; she began to scream. "Get down there! Get down there! Descend thee into hell!"

Chapter Sixteen

Lucky

Lucky glanced at the text on his burner.

> Respond.

The coy codes from the Winterses were gone.

He shoved the phone into his pocket.

All his thoughts were on Marybeth and William McKenna, his daughter's happy, youthful bounce into William's spread arms, his waiting smile.

Lucky held the steering wheel so tightly that his hands felt like they were going to rip it apart. His mind was a spinning compass, refusing to stop in any certain direction.

Lucky pushed open his car door, staggered up the walkway to his home.

He'd never been shot but imagined this was what it must feel like. A gaping pain in his side, so intense that he pressed his palm against it. Difficulty breathing, couldn't stand straight. Eyes blurred by pain.

"Hey Dad!"

So muddled that he hadn't even heard the car pulling up and parking on the street behind him, the car door closing, Marybeth approaching from behind.

He turned toward her.

"Jesus," Marybeth said. "Are you okay?"

Lucky wanted to yell at her, grab her, hold her, sob. Her insolence shook him—asking if he was okay even though she knew she was ruining his life.

He looked away. "Just some bad news about work."

"Kay." Marybeth walked past him to the door.

He watched his daughter, stared into the back of her head as she fumbled with the house key. Sadness at the memory of her head when she was a baby and then a little girl, when he'd marveled at how small she was. A little person, full of emotions and attitude and intelligence, part Renee and part Lucky and part something else, something entirely unexpected. Uniquely, uncontrollably Marybeth.

He followed his daughter into their house.

"Aren't you home a little late?" Lucky asked.

"Dad," Marybeth said, her voice full of that teenage annoyance of having to deal with the stupidest person in the world. "Mom sent me to the drugstore. She has a migraine."

"She does?"

"Yes." Marybeth held up a brown paper bag with "CVS" printed on the front. Pulled out a box of Excedrin Migraine, shook it, headed into the kitchen.

Lucky rubbed his eyes and he thought about William's open arms and Marybeth, and he again remembered her as a baby, the way Lucky had held her tight in his own arms, his lips pressing the top of her head, her soft wisps of hair.

He heard himself whimper.

Lucky covered his mouth with his hands and wondered, very calmly, if he was losing his mind.

Recently it was something Lucky had considered. He used to have the ease of compartmentalization. Lucky was able to be two different people, and they may have bled into each other on occasion, but he could separate them. The man who worked for the Winterses was a completely different person than the Putzer who loved his family and sold real estate.

But something about that dividing line had blurred, still visible but barely, like an erased pencil line in Marybeth's homework when she was in elementary school.

Lucky wondered if one was affecting the other, the violence invading the love like a neighboring country attacking.

And the more he invested into his family, the less real his other life seemed. Sometimes Lucky imagined himself strapped to a bed in a mental hospital, only imagining his life, the reality of his existence appearing in flickers. He could almost feel the straps around his wrists and ankles, biting into his skin, gnawing into bone until Lucky shook his head, forced those thoughts away, retreated back into reality.

He walked into the kitchen and reached for the counter, felt the marble under his fingers, cold and hard and real.

Marybeth was filling a glass with water from the fridge, the determined hum of the dispenser, the *s* sound of water rising.

Lucky waited until she finished, and then he pulled out a glass and filled one for himself. Drank greedily. He hadn't realized how thirsty he was.

"How was your trip?" Marybeth asked. She was struggling to twist off the Excedrin cap.

Lucky held out his hand, and she gave him the medicine. He squeezed it open, handed it back.

"Fine."

"Sell anything?"

"It wasn't that kind of trip."

He could tell that his daughter had already lost interest. "Oh, Dad, I wanted to ask you. Is it okay if I stay over at Elena's this weekend?"

"Elena?"

"We have this project due for biology, and we were going to work on it this weekend. And then she said I should just spend the night."

Lucky was certain Marybeth was lying.

She wanted to spend the night with William.

She'd probably already arranged it with Elena, one of her friends that Lucky knew well, the girl's parents a pair of lawyers who had live-in help for Elena and their two younger twins. Elena had spent the night at their house before, she and Marybeth lost in either giggles or their phones, that change in Marybeth, the indifference whenever she was around a girlfriend, *"Okay, Dad."*

"Why doesn't she just stay here?" Lucky offered grimly. "We could order pizza."

"You know Elena doesn't eat bread," Marybeth told him. "And she already asked. Plus they have a nicer place."

Marybeth's offhand remark was like a slap. Heat stirred within him, indignation at her casual contempt. The house he and Renee had bought and the life they'd provided and the money they'd sacrificed all for Marybeth, and she had the audacity to dismiss it simply because their house (admittedly, Lucky knew) wasn't as nice as her friend's parents'. That was a cruelty of children Lucky had long ago accepted, one every parent knew. The lengthily prepared meal met with groans. The mocking of older fashion. The realization that your young children prefer to spend more time with their friends than with you. But those instances were eventual, dreaded but expected.

Marybeth was old enough to know better. She knew she was hurting him.

Lucky didn't want to say anything else, didn't want to continue this conversation.

"I can take those to your mother." He pointed at the two pills in her hand.

"Mom always gets these headaches whenever you go away. Love, right?"

"Right."

Marybeth pulled out her phone—Lucky was surprised she'd gone that long without it in her hand—and he left his daughter in the kitchen. There was such an urge in him to grab the phone, see who she was texting, find messages between her and William, and reveal that he knew the truth of what was happening.

But that was something, Lucky consoled himself, he could do soon.

First he had to talk with Renee.

Lucky was halfway up the stairs when the burner buzzed again. He glanced at the message.

Now.

Lucky opened the bedroom door, peeked inside. Renee was sleeping. He let her sleep, pocketed the pills, headed back down the stairs.

Moments later he was in his backyard office, securely locking the door behind himself. He pulled out the phone, dialed a number. He'd memorized this number years ago, but this was the first time he'd ever called it.

"Okay," Lucky said.

There was an audible click, and the line immediately disconnected. Within seconds his phone buzzed with an incoming call.

"They want to know where you went." One of the unseen women.

He noticed the language she used. Still shadowy, cagey, not using that cryptic messaging but also not direct. *They.*

"Are you still working?" she asked.

"I am."

"Someone picked them up."

Lucky wasn't entirely sure what that meant, wondered if another assassin had captured Jake and Melissa. "It's over?"

"No." A pause as she sought a way to clarify her clue. "Someone was working with them."

Lucky thought back to the warehouse. There hadn't been any indication that anyone besides Jake, Melissa, or Seth was involved. "Any idea who?"

"No."

But clearly someone had rescued Jake and Melissa and hidden them away. And overpowered Seth and disappeared.

"The job is more important now. Are you working?" the woman asked again.

"I told you I was."

"You're at your house. We need you working."

Lucky sighed, and the sigh surprised him. He wasn't given to displays of emotion.

For a moment he was reminded of Marybeth and her insolence.

"Hello?"

The woman's insistence brought him back. "Yes, I'm still working," Lucky said. "I'll find them."

A pause. "The boy is hurt."

The boy is hurt.

Jake Smith is wounded.

Seth must have told them that, although clearly, he hadn't told them much. Jake was wounded and, along with Melissa, had been rescued. But not taken to the hospital.

"We don't have a lot of time," the woman said. "And we don't know where they went."

Lucky stayed silent.

"Do you know where they might have gone?"

"No." But he was lying.

◆ ◆ ◆

Lucky softly pushed open the door and headed into the dark bedroom. He didn't turn on the lights as he walked over to the bed and set the pills on Renee's nightstand, next to a copy of some book she was reading. She always read at night, before bed, novels that she immersed herself in, telling Lucky about the characters as if she'd made friends with them, excited or exasperated with their decisions.

"I'm awake," Renee said.

"Got a headache?" he asked.

Renee moved in the dark to the pills, swallowed them dry, disregarding the glass of water. Lucky watched her outline, her hands pressed against her forehead.

"Had a migraine, but it's getting better. I don't want to die anymore, so yay?"

Lucky had spent the last month relentlessly wondering about Renee's infidelity, about the sanctity of their marriage, his fears about its dissolution . . . and now all that angst was gone. Despite the crushing weight of Marybeth's relationship with William, there was a small sliver of relief for Lucky. As if he'd been buried under a pile of rocks but, through a crack, saw the sun.

Renee lay back, fists on her forehead.

"We need to talk," she said.

"We do?" Not surprise in his voice, Lucky realized, but hope.

Perhaps they knew the same thing about Marybeth.

"I know you didn't go look at some property down in Virginia the other night," Renee told him.

"What?"

Renee's voice in the dark, not tethered by pain, but anger. "You're lying to me."

Lucky took a step back. He felt like he was standing near some type of vortex, a swirling black hole behind him that was about to send him somewhere else, turn him into a different person in a different relationship in a different world.

"Who is she?" Renee asked.

"She?"

"Who are you seeing, Lucky? Who is she?"

"I'm not seeing anyone."

Renee reached over to the nightstand, snapped on the lamp. Her brown curled hair, tinged with gray, framed her face on the pillow. The lines around her eyes were pronounced. She looked hurt and sad.

Whenever Lucky looked at her for more than a few moments, his heart ached. And he felt like months had passed since he'd last seen her.

"I'm not with anyone else." Lucky could almost feel that vortex swirling, like the time he and Renee and Marybeth had gone white water rafting, and they'd heard thundering water around the corner of a bend. The way that the water had pulled them toward it, the fear that their paddles would prove useless, that nature was stronger than anything they could realize.

"Really?" Hate and sarcasm in Renee's tone. "Then where were you? Why'd I get a notification about a charge on our credit card from a hotel in DC?"

He'd used the wrong credit card.

"I promise, I've never cheated on you."

"What were you doing?"

He had to give her an honest answer, even if the answer would tear their lives in half.

But Lucky didn't want to lie anymore.

"Come with me to the office out back," he told her. "I'll show you."

Chapter Seventeen
Ruby

"He's asleep," Melissa said brokenly. "Dr. Steve said that's okay." She didn't say anything after that, just stood in the corner by the window, crying.

Ruby hated her.

She hated Melissa's tears, her helplessness, the way Melissa's flesh had failed her and her heart had followed. Her dislike was so intense that Ruby knew it was unnatural. She'd lost control when she'd screamed at Melissa, and now she felt like she had to force herself to stay on steady ground.

She tried to analyze her hate. Perhaps it was some latent jealousy, a maternal longing because her son had chosen another woman.

But Ruby didn't think so. More likely it was how Melissa let everything happen to her, did nothing to control her fate.

Melissa looked at her, her eyes wide with worry.

Ruby scowled back.

Melissa looked away.

Ruby remembered how she used to come back to her apartment past midnight and find Jake sleeping on the couch, five years old and under a blanket with the television on and his Pull-Up heavy with pee.

She'd carry him to his bed and change him and lie behind him, her arms over his thin body, his hand in hers, fingers wet from where he'd nervously chewed his nails until he'd fallen asleep.

"Dr. Steve says it's better for Jake to go to a hospital somewhere," Melissa was telling her, hands wringing.

"He worries," Ruby said. She'd seen another side of Steve, when she and Lucky had met with him at midnight at his old house, a giant home in Bethesda where Debko lived alone. He'd been waiting for them outside, carrying suitcases, fear like a rash on his face. For years he'd secretly healed gunshot gangsters and stitched up stab wounds, making money to do this work and keep it a secret.

Until the day he healed a woman named Blake, a woman Ruby had met and was fond of and who had nearly been beaten to death by her boyfriend, a member of the Winterses. Debko saved her, did what he could to heal her bruises, put her in touch with a women's rescue organization that spirited her away. But it didn't take long for the Winterses to find Blake. And then they found out Debko had helped her. Ruby owed him for helping Blake, and she had talked to Lucky, and the two of them had secretly worked out a plan to save him.

Steve Debko had left behind his home, his name, and his practice. But he lived.

"I just want to do what's best for him," Melissa said.

Ruby supposed she could see why Jake liked her. Melissa was pretty even in distress. Dark hair and wide deer-brown eyes, sun-dipped skin, her body filled with that effortless youth that seemed it would last forever.

"You know how they found you?" Ruby asked. Her voice ached from screaming earlier.

"I don't know. I thought we were really careful."

"Careful, like at the diner?"

"That was . . . I mean, after the diner, we were careful."

Ruby wondered what her relationship with Melissa would have been like had she traditionally met her son's girlfriend. Jake bringing her to her home one night, Melissa sitting next to him, nervous on the couch while Jake cracked jokes.

She still wouldn't have liked her.

"So you didn't go out?" Ruby asked. "When you were at the boat place?"

"I went to a store, a couple of times. The second time the guy who worked there had been killed. That's when I knew they'd come." Melissa looked away. "Maybe that's how they found us. Maybe that clerk told someone?"

"Maybe," Ruby allowed. "Or maybe you two did something else." Ruby heard it in her voice, a sense of blame she wanted to assign, guilt needing to be placed. A shark captured in a net, the ocean water churning as it searches for an escape.

"I don't think Jake and I did anything wrong," Melissa said.

Ruby kept her emotions in check, stopped herself from yelling, from grabbing the younger woman by the shoulders and shaking her until her neck snapped.

Human anger, Ruby reminded herself, *does not give what the Lord desires.*

"How'd you get involved with Jake?" she asked instead, irritation filling her words.

"He was taking pictures of me. I mean, we hired him to take pictures of me. My ex-boyfriend wanted them. Chris Winters." Melissa looked away. "He wasn't great."

That was all that needed to be said. That communication unique to women, where something wrong is conveyed in a short understated phrase.

"How did you find us?" Melissa asked.

"A man stopped by my place," Ruby said. "He was looking for the two of you. And then, later, he called and told me where you were. He's a friend."

"Was he with the Winterses? Or the cops?"

"If he was with the cops, then he's with the Winterses," Ruby reminded Melissa. "But he's not a cop. He was gathering information on you. Said he'd been hired to find you and bring you back. His name is Lucky Wilson."

"I never heard of him."

"He's one of their killers. Like Seth."

"Oh." The word faint, as if it came from someone lost inside a cave.

"They're going to find you again," Ruby warned her. "Soon."

"But we can't go anywhere right now. Jake needs to recover."

"He's not going to unless we get ahead of them. That's why I need to know who else saw you. Who knew where you were? Someone must have slipped up."

Melissa was shaking her head helplessly, and then she slowly stopped. Ruby saw realization spread across the younger woman's expression.

"Eric. Eric Liu. Jake called him when we were there."

"Eric's back?"

"He's been back for years. You knew him?"

"I knew his mom. They used to be our neighbors." The short sentence unintentionally weighed the air. "But they moved away."

"I don't know about that. I just know he's Jake's best friend. Jake called him, and I think he told him where we were hiding."

"Where's Eric living now?"

"He's at Highland Towers, in Alexandria."

Of course, he is, Ruby thought.

She stood, grabbed her purse. Hunted for her keys and remembered she'd left them on a table in the hall, after cleaning Seth's blood off her car.

"Are you going?" Melissa asked, panic in her voice. "What about Jake?"

Ruby left Melissa in the kitchen.

Ever since hearing Eric Liu's name, it was as if Ruby's hearing had lessened until it was a dull roar, like rushing wind, and she heard the voice of the Lord.

Urging her to rid the world of its evil.

CHAPTER EIGHTEEN

LUCKY

For some reason, Lucky couldn't remember which of his keys opened the door to his backyard office. It didn't help that Renee was standing behind him, cold and impatient, wearing a long coat over the shorts and T-shirt she wore to bed, her feet in an old pair of boots she used for gardening.

Lucky tried another key but had trouble fitting it into the lock.

"You've used keys before, right?" Renee asked.

He kept wondering if he'd left anything revealing in the office. Lucky was fastidious about putting everything away and, even if his wife or daughter had come inside, that anything incriminating was hidden. A Glock 22, box of bullets, stiletto dagger, and Taser were under a loose floorboard, and that floorboard was under a rug. Everything else in the small single-room office was a mix of real estate folders and files intended to bore anyone snooping around.

He had another hiding spot in the house, a pair of duffel bags filled with similar supplies buried in attic insulation. The attic was accessed through the closet in his primary bedroom, and as far as Lucky knew, neither Renee nor Marybeth had ever been inside.

He tried another key, his mouth dry at the thought of what they were about to discuss.

The doorknob turned.

"I felt this conversation was better to have here," Lucky told her. "I didn't want to talk in the house."

"I figured you were stalling to come up with a good story."

Renee walked in and immediately stopped.

"Where did you get that coatrack?"

"From a diner."

"I like it." Renee sat in his chair, gave it a slight spin. Rubbed her arms together and crossed her legs, her entire body huddled from the cold and, Lucky realized, from him. Tense as a trap, and poised to snap if he came close.

Lucky pulled out his phone, opened the camera app, found the video from earlier that evening.

He handed the phone to his wife.

He'd left his other phone inside the house and turned off. It had been constantly buzzing with messages from the Winterses, but Lucky was too heartsick to even think about the search for Jake and Melissa.

"What's this video?" Renee asked. "And what happened to your screen?"

Lucky ignored her second question. "It's Marybeth."

He watched Renee's face as the video played, concern overtaking her expression.

"Where'd you get this?"

"I thought it was you," Lucky said instead of answering. "I thought you were having an affair. I thought you were the one seeing William. I had no idea it was her."

"Where did you get this?" Renee asked again. "Did you hire someone?"

"I saw his address in our maps app and I was so worried." Lucky's arms were wrapped around his chest, as if he was holding himself together. "I saw your car in his driveway and thought it was you. I thought you were leaving me."

Lucky distantly realized he'd never been this honest with his wife before.

"William went to DC one night," he lied. "I followed him to this hotel and thought you were there, but I couldn't find him. I was so sad . . . I stayed overnight. I couldn't come home."

"Oh, Lucky," Renee said. "It wasn't me. Why would you think that?"

"I think work is getting to me. It's been on my mind a lot. I feel like . . ."

Lucky paused, that sense of need growing in him like wildfire, the way he'd helplessly broken down in front of Chris Winters and his man Marley, the desperate hope for help from Heather Anders. Sadness eating his soul.

Renee looked small and miserable, sitting on the chair opposite him, knees pulled to her chest.

"I can't believe this is her," Renee said, and she glanced around the room, as if searching for a distraction. Looking at the walls, his desk, the floor, anywhere but at Lucky. As if she was mad at him, the way she would avoid his eyes and face during one of their rare fights.

Her palms pressed into her forehead.

"How could Bill do this?"

Lucky sidled over next to her and pulled her to the floor, and she leaned into him and cried.

For a few minutes, that's all that happened. Her tears and sobs and his arm heavily over her shoulders. Lucky wondered, as he always did during Renee's moments of sadness, if he was helping. There was something in Renee that seemed as if she didn't fully need him . . . or she did, and he was only providing a basic level of comfort. Lucky wanted to be more for her. He wanted to offer her solace and intimacy, but he always felt as if there was some sort of emotional chasm, a part of her he could never reach.

"It's not your fault," Lucky said. "Or my fault. It's his."

"When did you find out?"

"About Marybeth? Hours ago."

"We can figure this out," Renee said, as if she was only speaking to herself. "This happens more than people realize. I mean, *I* was with an older man when I was younger."

"You were?"

The hurt in Lucky's voice surprised him.

She nodded. "When I was sixteen. He was twenty-six. Or, at least, he said he was. He might have been older."

Renee had never told Lucky any of this.

"He was my first," she added.

Lucky's own jealousy surprised him. He withdrew his hands from hers.

"I'm sorry," he said lamely. "I think I'm . . . I'm sorry."

Renee touched his knee.

Leaned forward and caressed his face.

No words were said, but everything was understood.

And that small moment of affection was one of the most intimate Lucky had ever felt.

"I know what Marybeth's going through," Renee said. "I know what it's like to think you're in love, or be in love, with someone older. I can talk about this with her. And then I'll let the school know. We can figure this out. I bet it's him she's been meeting up with. The 'older' guy."

Lucky imagined staying out here with Renee the entire night, coming up with different plans on a dry-erase board, writing and wiping away terms like *strangulation* and *gunshot* and *ice pick. It has to look like an accident,* Renee would tell him, and Lucky would be impressed by her insight. *You know,* he'd reply shyly, *I've actually done this before.*

"Lucky?"

Lucky blinked. "Yes?"

"What are you doing? You're just sitting there smiling." Renee paused. "I'm angry, but Marybeth can't feel isolated from us right now. We need to tell her she can't see William, even if she won't understand why. She won't understand that being with a man so much older isn't a healthy relationship . . . because he's not a healthy person. And this can affect her later in life; it can completely destroy her view of relationships and trust."

Cold's coming, Renee said in his mind. *So we pour water down William's driveway at night. Let it freeze and turn icy. When he walks down the driveway, one of us pushes him down, and the other speeds by and runs him over. Blammo.*

I've never heard you say blammo.

I'm just trying so many new things!

"If you yell at Marybeth and forbid her from seeing him," Renee continued, "then you're putting our daughter down this path forever. She'll try and find what she lost in someone else. And it won't be someone her age."

What about this? imaginary Renee asked. *We drug his food. Sneak into his house and put poison in his dinner.*

If he's eating sausage, Lucky would say, *we'll poison it and walk in and tell him, as he's dying, William, you're the wurst.*

Imaginary Renee laughed. *Lucky, when did you get so funny?*

"We can tell her we're mad," Renee said. "Honestly, I don't think that's something we'll be able to hide. Neither of us are that good with keeping secrets. But we can't give her something to push back against. She's going to be looking for that, something that seems unfair because, trust me, Marybeth's going to want to justify it. And if she can justify it, then she'll keep doing it."

We shoot him in the back of the head, imaginary Renee suggested. *Stab him in the stomach. Slit his throat. Hit him in the chest with a hammer until his ribs pierce his heart. Tape up his mouth and pour water up his nostrils until he drowns.*

"Lucky?"

Renee, honey, good news. I've done all this before.

"We need to do this together," Renee said. "Marybeth has to know we're on the same page, but, instead of us angry with her, she has to realize we're worried about her. That'll get through. It won't be overnight, but it will happen."

"Okay."

Renee pulled him toward her, and he lay down on the office's hard floor, his head in her soft lap, her hand stroking his hair. "A lot of young girls have stories like this. That's the problem. And it's wrong. It's disgusting how these men take advantage of young girls. It was wrong what happened to me. Men need to be adults, and they need to be held accountable. William needs to be held accountable."

"I promise you," Lucky said grimly, "he will be."

"Well, I mean, Jesus, Lucky," Renee replied, as she absentmindedly ran her fingers through his hair. "Let's not kill him."

Chapter Nineteen

Ruby

"Are you working with the Winterses?"

Eric Liu stared at Ruby, shocked to see her, one hand still on the front door that he had just opened.

"Jake's mom?" he asked.

Ruby didn't wait for an invite. Pushed past him into his apartment.

"I saw one of their cars down the street." Ruby closed the door. "Lexus with DC plates, tinted windows. The kind of car that would definitely get stolen in DC, except everyone knows not to touch it. So, let me ask you again, are you working with the Winterses?"

Eric stayed by the front door, as if unsure what to do.

"What happened to Jake?" Eric asked. "Is he okay?"

Ruby stared hard at him. "So you did talk to them."

"Yes." Eric's voice dropped to a whisper. She hadn't seen Eric since he was a child, but he was the same reed-thin boy she remembered, shaggy brown hair that always looked unkempt and too big for his face. Strange how men only have two or three hairstyles through their entire lives.

"They made me."

"Made you," she said with derision. "How?"

Eric lifted his shorts, showed her his thighs. The insides were dotted with reddish-black circles close to his groin. Cigarette burns.

"Don't tell Jake," Eric said. "He'll feel terrible."

And he looked down at the burns, his chin pressed into his chest like a little boy.

Only those who seek the Lord, Ruby thought, *understand justice.*

She glanced away from Eric, around the apartment. The layout was the same as she remembered from the last time she'd been here, years and years ago. Highland Towers, her first home after she'd left her mother.

"They shot Jake," Ruby said. "He's with a doctor now."

"Jake was shot, and you're not with him?"

His surprise was an accusation.

"I'm *here*," Ruby told Eric, "because I need to know exactly what you said to the Winterses. Because that's why Jake got shot."

Tears had swum up to Eric's eyes. "Is he okay?"

Somehow, Ruby hadn't expected to see this sadness. Love always surprised her.

"He's going to be."

"I told them Jake and Melissa were in Wharfside," Eric said softly. "That's what Jake said when he called. After the diner."

"Who talked to you?" Ruby asked, trying to refocus. "Was it a big man? Covered in scars?"

"Yeah. Two women, these twins, came by the day earlier. Then he showed up."

The Rusu twins and then Seth. Ruby remembered the impact of the car slamming into Seth, the reverberation, his head smacking down on her hood, and Seth stumbling back, collapsing. Lying so still Ruby had thought he was dead until Seth started crawling toward her, one of his legs dragging uselessly. His face a mask being torn off.

"I didn't want anything to happen to him and Melissa," Eric said.

Ruby still didn't want to look at Eric, so she turned her attention elsewhere. Glanced at a framed picture next to the TV. Eric with his mother, his arms wrapped around her waist, his head only as high as her chest, beaming proudly.

Tiffany.

Ruby had been pressed by memories of Tiffany from the moment she'd slipped back into this apartment building. And she didn't want to think about her, desperately didn't.

But Ruby couldn't stop herself from remembering.

Ruby couldn't stop herself from crying. She was in the throes of exhaustion, Jake's constant wailing frustrating her. Jake's father, James, had taken a job working construction in Minnesota, ostensibly because the pay was too good to turn down, and he'd never returned.

Ruby hadn't been entirely surprised. Her pregnancy had been unplanned, and she'd suspected that James wasn't as infatuated with her as she was with him. They'd been dating for half a year but in secret. He only came over at night, a booty call joke they both laughed at but, privately to her, seemed exactly what their relationship was. James never wanted to go out, content to order food and have it delivered, watch movies on her couch, stay at her place and never take her to his.

He was embarrassed of her, Ruby gradually realized.

But she liked James so much and spending time with him was so nice that she didn't care. She wondered if spending more time together would change how he felt about her. Sometimes she wondered what he saw in her. She wasn't thin, didn't have the delicate, cultivated features of other young women—glowing skin, effortlessly tossed hair, a sensuous appeal to the curves of her lips and cheeks.

Instead, Ruby had always been overweight, with big hair meant to distract from her face, a face full of round features, cheeks pressed into her mouth, small eyes. She'd never had a serious boyfriend, and she didn't want to call James one either. At least not to his face.

But she couldn't help thinking of him that way.

He wasn't pleased by her sudden pregnancy. A week of unsettling stops by her apartment and, once, an angry visit to her job at the DMV. Loud accusations of her getting pregnant on purpose. Pushing her toward an abortion that she couldn't bring herself to do. His disbelief that this could have happened, even though James despised condoms, and she'd never insisted. Urges for her to test herself over and over, sometimes while James watched, the humiliation of urinating in front of him while he glared.

When he told her about the new job and his move across country, Ruby wasn't surprised.

Or, by then, disappointed.

And so Ruby found herself alone and overwhelmed, living in this building, her small apartment filled with unwashed clothes and boxes of cheap diapers and small plastic bottles and containers with mismatched tops. James sent money for the first two months. But he never met his son, and the money soon stopped.

Ruby was holding the framed photo of Eric with his mother, one of her thumbs absentmindedly rubbing a smudge off the glass over Tiffany's face.

She quickly placed the frame back.

Eric was saying something.

"You're not going to tell me where Jake is?" he asked desperately. "You won't take me there? I need to see him!"

"I can't," Ruby said. But she wasn't sure if he heard her.

The situation had changed. She was no longer in control, emotionally or morally.

Sins carry more weight than wounds.

◆ ◆ ◆

She was at the breaking point, crying every day, lying in bed while five-month-old Jake screamed in the living room, when she heard someone walk into her apartment.

"Hello?" a woman asked.

Ruby dried her eyes.

"Do you need help?"

Ruby pulled herself out of bed, peered into the living room. A woman she didn't know, but recognized, stood in the doorway. Jake had stopped crying and was grabbing the bars of his crib and staring at the stranger.

"I'm Tiffany," the woman said, "from down the hall. I heard crying."

"Mine or his?"

Tiffany smiled, but it hadn't been a joke. "May I?" she asked and pointed at Jake.

"Okay."

Tiffany held Jake, and he quieted. A few whimpers, but the screams were gone.

Tiffany had a child as well, a one-year-old named Eric, which seemed to Ruby a wondrous distance from having an infant. The two women became instant friends, constants in each other's apartments. Both women were single mothers of only children. Both were under thirty—Tiffany, twenty-five and Ruby, twenty-three. Both had been left by the fathers of their children. Tiffany's family lived down south and was well off and sent her money, enough so Tiffany could be a full-time caregiver to her child while they begged her to return home.

But they'd never accepted her boyfriend, Tiffany explained. Couldn't abide her having a child with someone Asian and had really only started talking with her after he left. Ruby could see her resentment, although she couldn't help but notice that Tiffany still accepted the money they sent.

Not that she judged her for it. Ruby wished she had family.

Except for Jake, she'd been completely alone since James had vanished.

But with Tiffany, Ruby was able to manage stress without feeling overwhelmed. Able to enjoy motherhood, despite its complications. Able to do it without being alone.

The two women made a habit of sharing a bottle of wine in the evening after the babies were in bed, sitting on one of their couches, watching some reality television show and trash-talking all the people on it. Even when they weren't together, they talked on the phone or texted, Ruby automatically smiling whenever a message from Tiffany appeared.

Ruby got Tiffany a job at the DMV, and, although the work was drudgery—standing at counter number eleven for eight hours a day, helping angry people with their license issues—Tiffany was delighted, grateful for the opportunity to do something other than parent. And Ruby was excited to spend even more time with her friend.

"I remember asking Mom why you two never talked. Why Jake and I could play together, and you never once saw each other. She said she was mad at you. She said you broke her heart."

"It was mutual."

Eric's eyes flashed. "So you're saying it was her fault?"

"No." Ruby took a moment, forced herself to look away from Eric. She stared down into her hands.

"How did Jake end up involved with the Winterses?" she asked.

"It was a coincidence."

"No such thing."

"It was! He was taking photos, and this woman started talking to him. She loved his work, told him she was looking for someone to take a picture of her for her husband. Her husband was connected, but Jake didn't know that." Eric rubbed the back of his neck. "Melissa saw the photos and contacted him."

"He should have known better."

"You mean like you should have known better when you got my mom involved?"

That wasn't what had happened, but Ruby didn't correct him.

◆ ◆ ◆

"This is Gabe," Tiffany told her one day during lunch at the DMV.

He was charming, and Ruby appreciated that he at least acted interested in meeting her, smiled warmly, gave her a quick hug that she wasn't expecting but didn't mind. He told Ruby that he worked in finance. He dressed nicely, a slim suit and a sizable watch glinting on his wrist, shiny shoes and belt. Tiffany was infatuated, touching his arm and laughing too much at his jokes, a constant smile on her face.

"So finance?" Ruby asked. "Like, in a bank?"

"Not exactly. I work for the Winters Corporation."

How had it started? Ruby really didn't know, couldn't remember exactly how she and Tiffany ended up printing fake IDs from their apartments for Gabe. Was it her or Tiffany who seemed to have the idea once Gabe brought it up one night, somewhere along the three-month mark of his relationship with Tiffany? She remembered Gabe saying something about a struggling undocumented family who needed papers, or they were going to be deported.

"You know," Gabe said casually, "you can get a lot of money by making fake IDs. I know someone who'd pay a lot. And it's not even that risky."

Ruby and Tiffany looked at each other.

"How much money?" Ruby asked.

A night later he showed up with two laminating machines, small printers, specialized paper, a pair of razors, and walked Ruby and Tiffany through the process. When people came to the DMV to renew their driver's licenses, they would keep the old ones. They'd bring those old IDs to their apartments and remove the security hologram with the razors. Then they'd fill out the new IDs with personal information and photos he'd provide, print it out on the thick stock, and carefully seal the old hologram to it. Run the fake ID through the laminator and let Gabe know when the batch was complete.

"These are for good people," he said earnestly. Ruby didn't believe him, but she also didn't care.

The day after she and Tiffany had each created ten licenses, Gabe showed up at her door with a thick roll of twenty-dollar bills, and Ruby felt a deep excitement stir in her. It was the money, but it was more than that; it was her own lack of remorse. There was no difference to her about how the money had been obtained. It felt right for her to have it.

The money mattered and, over the next few years, mattered more than almost anything. Ruby had always lived just above her means but without extravagance. Every last dime she made went into the essentials for her and Jake to survive. Rent, clothes, food, a sitter for the days she had to work late, and, even then, she didn't have enough money to cover any other expenses. She had a pair of credit cards that were close to the max, and she knew any unexpected expense could push her permanently, irreparably, into poverty.

But now, with the money Gabe gave her, Ruby finally made enough to pay a little on each of her credit cards; to buy better, healthier food at the grocery store; to make the repairs on her Toyota that had lingered for years; to buy her and Jake clothes from somewhere other than the consignment store.

And all she had to do was make a few dozen fake driver's licenses every week.

"She was a better person than you were. You ruined her."

◆ ◆ ◆

"Should we stop doing this?" Tiffany asked.

"Why would we?" Ruby asked, honestly surprised.

"I mean, I was talking to someone at work about this, and it's, like, a federal crime."

"You were talking about this with someone?"

Tiffany gestured with a bottle of water. Lately she'd been drinking less wine. "I didn't tell them about us. But someone down in Florida got arrested for doing the same thing. They're going to prison."

Ruby looked at her friend curiously. "Are you okay, Tiff?"

Tiffany stared uneasily into her lap. "I don't feel great about doing this anymore. Especially since that conversation. And we don't even need the money."

"Are you serious?"

"You told me you paid off your credit cards. Started putting money in the bank. We got raises at work. You're fine."

Ruby was silent for a moment.

"What?" Tiffany prodded.

"I don't think," Ruby said, choosing her words carefully, "we have the same deal with money."

"What's that mean?"

Ruby could hear Tiffany's emotions under her words. And she could sense the feelings stirring under her own. She took a sip of wine before she continued.

Lately she'd been drinking more wine.

"We're different," Ruby said. "That's all. You have your family supporting you. I don't."

Tiffany's cheeks pinked. "I need to work. I need a job."

Ruby doubted that was true. "Okay, but Jake and I don't have anyone to turn to. I was going broke before Gabe told us about this." Something occurred to her. "Do you want to stop doing this just because you and Gabe aren't seeing each other anymore? Is that why?"

Tiffany controlled her voice but bristled. "I told you, I don't care who Gabe's with now. I just don't see what the big deal is with stopping, or why you want me to keep breaking the law. If you want to keep doing this, you can do it alone."

"I don't care about being alone."

It felt like a long time before either woman spoke again.

"I should go," Tiffany eventually said, and she stood.

"You were never there for anyone but yourself."

"I was there for Jake. Always, even after he left."

"He didn't think so."

Ruby walked over to the front door, broken by the truth in Eric's words. It had been a mistake to come, to seek repentance without confession.

A few weeks later, Tiffany was assigned to a different DMV in Fairfax. Ruby heard she'd requested it.

They still lived doors away from each other, but Ruby took pains to avoid running into her. She knew Tiffany's routine intimately—when the other woman went to the store, when she dropped Eric off for day care.

Seeing Tiffany would break her heart.

Even if Ruby resented her. Tiffany had made Ruby choose something terrible: either be lonely or impoverished. And neither of those were things Tiffany could understand.

Still, sometimes, Ruby wanted to walk down the hall, knock on Tiffany's door, fall back into their old relationship.

But if she did, Tiffany probably would have asked if she was still working with Gabe.

And now Ruby was working for the people Gabe had worked for.

Gabe was gone, arrested and in prison somewhere. Ruby had found out when a man had come by her apartment that night, taken away the printer and lists of names. Asked her if she had any other materials relating to her work with the Winterses and, even after she told him no, ruthlessly searched her apartment, Jake staring as she stood by the door.

"And why are you even here?" Eric asked, staring at her as she stood by the door. "Jake's hurt, and you just abandoned him again? Shouldn't you be with him?"

"That's enough," Ruby told him abruptly, thunder in her tone. "I let you vent. But that's enough. We're not talking about that."

Ruby hadn't realized she was standing. Eric was taller than her, but, at this moment, she towered over him. His hands were up, shielding his face.

Had she struck him?

Ruby couldn't remember.

She just knew that she was shaking, breathing rasps.

A knock on her door. Ruby opened it and Tiffany stormed inside.

"They searched my apartment!" Tiffany told her. "I haven't worked with them for months, and they come in and search my apartment!"

Ruby had imagined talking to Tiffany so often that she was surprised how hard it was for her to speak. Her lost friend stood before her, eyes blazing.

"They had no right to do that!" Tiffany went on. "Eric was there!"

"Gabe got arrested. They're making sure, if he talks, there's no evidence the cops can find. It's keeping us safe."

"That's not what they're doing. They're covering their asses."

"I don't know."

Tiffany stopped fuming, seemed to gain a touch of control. She looked at Ruby, and Ruby almost cherished that moment, their eyes locked, the way they would when they shared something important about their past or laughed or the excitement they felt when they first saw each other.

But that moment ended when Tiffany asked, "How can you put Jake in this kind of danger?"

"I'm doing this for Jake," Ruby said.

"You're going to get him killed if you keep . . ."

"You don't understand!" Ruby's voice had risen and she didn't care. "You don't get to tell me how my life is wrong and evil and I'm hurting my son when you have a rich family. You played with the Winterses, and you don't understand that there are people who can't just play. At any moment you can go down south and have three meals and a bed, and I can't do that! I have to fight for it."

Tiffany trembled as she spoke. "I am going back home," she said slowly, each word like a driven nail. "And you should leave before I do."

"Why? What does that mean?"

But Ruby knew what that meant. Tiffany was going to the cops.

The next afternoon a car rushed down the street as Tiffany was unlocking her driver's side door, Eric sitting in the back seat. Ruby hadn't known what the Winterses were going to do, but she'd known they were going to do something.

She heard the car's impact. Shouts.

Ruby knelt and wept.

And wondered why she was weeping.

She'd done what was necessary. She'd kept Tiffany from getting her arrested, from separating Ruby from Jake.

They'd hurt her, and they'd helped her, these men.

These men who created and shaped the world in which Ruby lived.

A day later a man showed up, with money and a phone that he installed. Codes that he taught her.

"You good?" he asked her before he left.

◆ ◆ ◆

Ruby opened the door but stopped before she stepped through.

"I was wondering . . . ," she began and faltered, that thunder gone. "Before I go, can you tell me what Jake's like now?"

Eric took a moment to answer.

"He's a good man," he said. "Nothing like you."

Oh, Eric, there is no good. Or evil.

Only the sword.

My voice echoes through this winter wasteland, and with it I dispel shadows.

There is the Lord, and He is God, and He is the Devil, and He is us. And we are sin, and we are blessed.

And so none are pure.

I whisper my parables to the man with the sword, and he strikes down this world of sin, dragging his scythe through fields of dead wheat. I am the harbinger of death and this world is a tomb of bones.

And mine eyes have seen the true coming, the Lord standing on the edge of oceans, holding the bleeding spear that impaled His son.

And on that day men will run, and men will weep, and men will devour each other.

He will strike us all down.

And all that remains will be all that ever was.

The word and the sword.

Chapter Twenty

Lucky

Confronting Marybeth had gone, even in Lucky's most optimistic assessment, catastrophically wrong.

It was obvious that it wasn't going to go well from the moment Marybeth returned home from school to find Lucky and Renee waiting for her in the kitchen, presenting a united front. Lucky had started by showing her the video from the camera outside William's home.

"You're spying on me?" Marybeth asked, incredulous.

"Yeah, I wouldn't have opened with that," Renee murmured.

Lucky realized his mistake. This was the tactic he used when questioning people, presenting them with their guilt to throw them off-balance for the remainder of the interrogation.

That hadn't been the right approach with Marybeth.

"What the hell, Dad?" she'd asked and turned to Renee. "Did you know about this?"

"We were worried about you," Renee said. "When your father thought you might be seeing William, he put a camera outside his house to make sure."

"That's an invasion of privacy!"

"How?" Lucky asked.

"You can't just stalk someone!"

"It's legal to install a camera or any sort of nonintrusive monitoring device outside of a residential property," Lucky explained, "provided that a reasonable sense of privacy isn't inhibited."

"It's creepy that you know that," Marybeth replied, and she turned to Renee. "Right? That's creepy."

"A little," Renee admitted. "But that's not important. You can't keep seeing him."

"Mom!"

"I'm sorry."

"William and I weren't even doing anything!" Marybeth fumed. "Just hanging out. We never even . . . he wanted to take it slow."

"I don't believe that," Lucky said.

"Oh, fuck off, Dad."

Silence hit the room.

"You can't talk to us like that," Renee said incredulously.

Lucky could tell Marybeth wanted to relent, but she couldn't let herself apologize. "But it's okay for Dad to spy on me? To put a camera outside someone's house?"

Both Renee and Marybeth looked toward him, waiting for his response.

But Lucky didn't want to speak, didn't trust himself to say the right thing. He was offended, of course, but something else had been held in Marybeth's retort that was even more distressing. It was the maturity in the insult, her push away.

The loss of his child.

"Dad?"

Lucky left the kitchen. Kept walking as Renee called, "Lucky!" Headed out the front door.

He hadn't been sure where he was going to go when he climbed into his Grand Cherokee. He just wanted to drive.

Lucky kept the radio off as he drove out of Springfield, past Alexandria, past the National Harbor, each location jarring something from his memory. Springfield, where he'd driven Marybeth to day care every morning. Alexandria, where he and his daughter had walked around Mount Vernon one hot August afternoon when she'd had a week between summer camp and school, and he'd taken the day off from work to be with her. The National Harbor, where they'd ridden a giant Ferris wheel, and he'd pointed out the monuments of DC.

He was in Maryland now, and Lucky always found it peculiar how Virginia and Maryland were so closely connected, yet so foreign to each other. The neighboring states had a natural rivalry, and Lucky had sold enough homes to longtime residents of Virginia to know that most of them would never consider living in Maryland. And he knew the same was true of Marylanders. But Lucky secretly liked a lot about Virginia's sibling state. He drove past exits for Annapolis and Baltimore and had fond memories of trips his family had taken, wandering around Baltimore's wondrous aquarium and touristy inner harbor, visiting Annapolis once for the Fourth of July, Marybeth's face gazing up at fireworks. The cities seemed to have greater demarcation than northern Virginia's, separated by long forests and stretches of road until they finally appeared over a crest of highway, the glittering skylines. "That's where we're going!" Marybeth had declared, back when she was the age that merely being with him was exciting and fun for her.

Lucky rounded the road past Baltimore's exit, and another memory tugged at him. Not of Marybeth but Seth, the young killer he'd apprenticed. The day he'd finished training Seth, had taught him the importance of subtlety and silence, instilled in him the way the Winterses wanted death to appear natural. And Seth had asked Lucky if he was going to partner with him. Lucky had given one final lesson. "I need a moment," he'd said, and he'd left the young man sitting in that Baltimore coffee shop, slipped out the door and driven off.

Lucky already had a family.

He drove past the high-priced neighborhoods of Chevy Chase and Bethesda, towns that bordered the district of DC and were considered some of the wealthiest in the nation. Recent news reports claimed that the Winterses had family who lived in these cities, but that hadn't cast a pall over the area. If anything, like controversy always does, it lent a mystique to the region, particularly since those cities tended to be closed off and reserved, constantly and carefully guarding their secrets.

An hour and a half later, Lucky finished rounding the beltway, pulled back into his driveway, pressed the garage door opener. Drove his car inside and shut off the engine. Walked into the laundry room that, back when Marybeth played soccer, had also been used as a mudroom, every weekend the floor covered with her discarded dirty gear.

A woman waited for him in the kitchen.

"Hello, Lucky," she said.

Lucky stood still, kept his face impassive despite his surprise. But his mind was working fast. The gun hidden in the attic. The other one in the backyard office. The knife rack behind her. Her empty hands clasped in front of her. Renee and Marybeth.

But he didn't move, because he knew someone else was in the room.

"Bianca," Lucky said.

"She's not Bianca," the other woman behind him replied. Lucky could almost sense the gun in her hand. "I am."

"Adriana," Lucky corrected himself.

"All these years . . . ," Bianca Rusu said, walking around him, joining her twin sister on the other side of the kitchen counter.

". . . and you still get us confused," Adriana finished the sentence.

"Not like we spend a lot of time together," Lucky replied. Bianca stood next to her seated twin, her hand resting on the countertop. They each wore dark tops, thin hoodies, with their blonde hair pulled back into ponytails and pressed through the gaps in their black baseball caps.

"When did we meet you?" Adriana mused.

"And was it just once?" Bianca asked.

"It had to be."

"He's not very memorable."

Lucky remembered exactly when he'd met the twins. It had been almost a decade ago, when they'd first started working for the Winterses, and Lucky had been sent to clean up the bloody mess they'd left behind. Adriana and Bianca Rusu had come from some eastern European country—Bulgaria? Romania? Lucky could never remember—pretending to be sex-trafficked teens, but they were actually working for the traffickers to keep the other women with them in line. Upon meeting Victor Winters, they'd decided to kill the men they were working for and take over the operation themselves. But their tactics were excessive, even for the Winterses, and they'd instead been given a job as enforcers and then assassins.

Lucky had been called to a home in Annapolis—a large waterfront house with its own pool and a separate guesthouse, very nice—and that's where he'd found the man the Rusu twins had murdered. But they hadn't just murdered him. He was icily dismembered, his limbs spread throughout the property, head placed on a lawn chair looking out over the bay, a leg standing on its own in the kitchen, an arm on the bathroom floor, the thumb poised in an ironic thumbs-up gesture. There was a dichotomy that struck Lucky as unpleasantly as a raspy alarm, refusing to quiet. When he'd been called to clean up the mess the Winterses had assumed the twins left behind, Lucky had expected to see a sloppy murder, puddles of blood, the kind of inexperienced killing done in rage.

The casual ease of the assassination, the comfort with arranging such a grotesque display, brought a discomfiting sense to Lucky, something alien, occult.

He wondered if his distress was because the killers were young women, since women were rare in this line of work. Most killers were men, as were most criminals. The notion that women had begun to descend to this base violence was, in some ways, distasteful to Lucky.

Or perhaps he was bothered because the Winterses had assumed he could handle the crime scene, which Lucky had witnessed as he walked through the house.

Which meant he could understand it.

He didn't like thinking about that.

Lucky had met the twins on his last trip out of the house, lugging a plastic bag of towels and limbs, the sisters waiting by his car. He hadn't been surprised; for some reason, it was almost as if he'd expected them to show up.

"It was in Annapolis," Lucky said now. "Your first job."

"It wasn't our first."

"You have a nice house."

"We love the closets."

"And the finished basement."

Lucky knew what they were implying, understood the threat. They'd gone through every inch of his house, were aware of his secrets.

The Rusu twins were better at this than he was, Lucky grudgingly realized. They'd gotten the drop on him, kept him off-balance, were probably weighing his death as they spoke.

The rumor that infatuated most people about the killing of Victor Winters was the idea of a secret vigilante. Privately Lucky had always wondered if that vigilante had been the Rusu twins, one or both of them, dressed in some disguise, perhaps acting on behalf of someone else.

"I've always wanted to ask you," Lucky said in an effort to distract them, but also genuinely curious. "Do you know who murdered Victor Winters?"

For once the twins were silent.

"Some people say it was a vigilante," he went on. "And if it was, it would have to be someone good, someone who knew how to break into a house belonging to a dangerous person and surprise him."

"Was it you?" Adriana asked.

"Is that what you're saying?" Bianca went on.

Lucky was taken aback.

"I thought it was you," he said.

"Victor gave us our lives," Bianca replied.

Adriana shook her head as she spoke. "We'd never take his."

"It wasn't me," Lucky said.

"I don't like the idea of someone out there," Adriana said. "Someone who, I think . . ."

"Someone better than us," her sister finished quietly.

A disturbed silence, confidence shaken loose. Lucky didn't like thinking about that either.

"In your backyard office," Bianca said, and she cleared her throat, "there's a loose board in the floor."

"She's right," Adriana replied.

The twins were letting him know they'd gone through his backyard office, searched his entire house, found his weapons. Reasserting themselves.

"This house has all sorts of spots that need to be touched up," Lucky replied, hinting he had more weapons.

He hoped they couldn't tell he was exaggerating.

"The truth is," Adriana said, "we don't want to stay long."

"All we really need," from Bianca, "is an address."

"Whose?" Lucky asked, although he knew exactly what they wanted. He tried to keep his face blank, unexpressive, despite his worry that he had no weapon nearby. And despite how their shared cadence, like two smiling demons strumming a single harp, plucked his nerves.

"Your old friend. Ruby Smith. We found out Jake is her son."

Lucky nodded. "Lot of people looking for Ruby right now. I'm one of them."

Bianca's hand shifted behind the counter.

"We'd like to find her first," Adriana said.

"You heard about Seth?" Bianca asked her sister.

"He's in the hospital."

"Not expected to recover anytime soon."

"That means there's one less person looking."

"One less chance of someone taking our reward."

"Less is good."

The way they passed words back and forth was mesmerizing, drawing him in, sirens luring Lucky's ship toward submerged stones. Somehow, he had to change course.

"If Jake and Melissa are with Ruby, then Ruby could take them and disappear," Lucky said. "She already left the Winterses once. She could do it again."

"True."

"So?"

"So," Lucky went on, "the only other hope is that she reaches out to an old friend. And I was one of the oldest friends she had. You need me."

The twins glanced at each other.

"Do we?"

"I don't think we do."

"Ruby's probably going to contact me," Lucky bluffed. "When she does, I'll tell you."

"Why would you do that?"

"I don't think he would."

"We could just torture him."

"We could torture his family."

And, in an extraordinary moment of bad timing, that's when Lucky heard the garage door open.

◆ ◆ ◆

The sound of the garage door rising echoed through the kitchen.

The Rusu twins watched Lucky calmly, something close to a smile tugging each of their lips.

"Looks like we are going to meet the wife," Bianca said.

"How do I look?"

"Beautiful. Me?"

"Gorgeous."

"Weird," Lucky observed. "But you need to leave. Both of you."

"Do we?"

"I want to say hi."

He took a step toward them, and Bianca's hand rose.

She held a gun.

The door leading from the garage opened.

"I'll tell you when Ruby contacts me." He tried to make sure the desperation he felt didn't creep into his voice. "I promise."

"Lucky?"

Renee behind him.

He turned toward his wife, blocking Bianca's hands from Renee's view with his body. "Hey."

Renee curiously peered past him at the two women. "Is Marybeth here?"

"I thought she was with you."

"After you left, I . . ." Renee looked to the twins again. This time Lucky followed her gaze.

The gun was gone.

"Hello?" Renee asked.

"Lucky's selling our mother's home," Adriana said.

"She died earlier this year," Bianca added.

"Oh, I'm sorry." Lucky heard the apprehension in his wife's voice.

"We thought we'd have more time with her," Adriana said. "But when it happens, it happens faster than you expect."

"One second, she was there. The next second, gone."

"We didn't even get to say goodbye."

"I'm . . . sorry?" Renee offered again.

A moment passed.

"We'll be in touch, Lucky," Adriana said.

Lucky walked the twins to the door.

He kept his eyes focused on them until they drove away. He tried to think of his next move, of what the Rusu twins were going to do and how he could get ahead of them.

He knew the twins were going to try and find Ruby, and, failing that, they would return. But they wouldn't go after Lucky. Easier to break him if they went after someone else.

Lucky glanced into the living room, at the end table where their family pictures had been moved to make room for the Christmas decorations.

Marybeth's picture—his daughter in her high school soccer uniform, smiling with one knee balanced on a ball—was gone.

Lucky returned to the kitchen. "Where's Marybeth?" he asked.

"She left right after you did." Renee was staring down at her phone. "I told her she'd better not see William, but she probably went right there. Also, those women were weird."

"We need to find her."

"I know."

"Renee, we need to find her *now*."

Renee looked up from her phone, puzzled. "Why?"

Lucky paused, like a foot poised before stepping onto some new, uncertain land. "Because the women who were here are going to kill her."

Chapter Twenty-One

Melissa

"It's me," Melissa said.

She didn't expect Chris to respond right away, and he didn't. Melissa pictured him holding the phone away from his face, scowling at the unfamiliar number.

She waited through the silence, the phone pressed tight against her ear. Calling him wasn't something she'd done lightly; Melissa knew it was likely that there was no reasoning with Chris anymore.

But she was out of options, and her only hope left was that there was still some chance for a connection between the two of them. He'd never hurt her and, as far as Melissa knew, never cheated on her. Everything about Chris had grown corrupt except, seemingly, their relationship.

"Is Jake dead yet?" Chris asked.

No, she realized. *There is no chance.*

"I heard Seth shot your boyfriend." Chris went on. "Wish I'd been there to see it."

She knew what Chris was doing, heard the pain in his voice. The pain he wanted to drag her into.

And even though she knew what he was doing, it worked.

"Jake's going to live," Melissa said, her voice hot.

"Should have been you. A bullet right in your face."

Melissa had never felt hate like she did at this moment. But she knew she had to control her anger, push it down, refuse to let rage get the best of her. This was a sharper pain than she would have expected, injured love, the way you can never shake yourself entirely free from someone you once cared for.

"Let us go," she said.

A bark of laughter.

"You know what happened at the diner," Melissa went on. "Innocent people died, and your guy ended up arrested. It's better for everyone if you just let us go."

"Chris will burn down the world to find you," Chris said.

Christ, he's still doing that third person thing, Melissa thought, but something about Chris seemed different. It took Melissa a moment to realize what it was.

This was how he acted when other men were around.

She had to get him alone. Melissa tried to control her anger, tried to stop this fury from devouring her further. Searched for a way to convince Chris to change his mind, to find something in their relationship—old feelings, innocent memories, heartful love—something to which he clung.

"Chris," Melissa said. "Please."

A moment of silence, and then he offered an abrupt, "Hold on." She heard rustling.

He was walking away from the men.

She wondered where he was, if Chris was in their house, heading down the hall to their bedroom. Or walking into the small backyard, the high fence, the bushes of roses she'd planted. They were likely in their final bloom of the year, curled and blackened red.

She stared out the kitchen window at Dr. Steve's yard, uncared for and overrun by weeds. Melissa wondered if Dr. Steve spent time in the yard or if it was something he'd inherited when he'd moved in. Sometimes Melissa imagined herself working in a nursery, delicately planting seeds that would bloom into lovely flowers. Lilies with their long petals, stark whites and dramatic reds, straining pistils. Tender, tall yellow daffodils, bashful toward the sun, their long necks bent. Cups of tulips, insistently firm, their heads tightly wound together, as if they only released on their own terms, keeping their beauty to themselves.

It was like the brief fantasy she'd entertained in Wharfside of a quiet country life dominated by routine, the simplicity of happiness.

"Back."

The little word was a sharp reminder of Chris, how he always returned to a call or text with a quick "Back."

Chris sounded different now, and Melissa knew it was because he was alone. She was certain that ever since she'd left, Chris had spent all his time in the company of men. He hated being alone, which, at first, she'd found sweet, his desire to be with her. It wasn't possessive or overbearing, just an eagerness to share experiences, the way new relationships happily occupy the entirety of each partner's time.

But Melissa noticed after months had passed that there was something desperate to it. Once she took a trip to Florida to visit a cousin from Panama who had moved to Orlando, stayed for a week to help her get settled and adjusted to American life. Chris was miserable during the week, calling Melissa constantly, sometimes just sitting on the phone in silence. Especially when he detected her joy, the way she and her cousin couldn't stop laughing, how her cousin spoke in rapid Spanish, and Melissa was getting better at replying.

She'd wondered if his behavior had been motivated by some aggrieved sense of ownership or jealousy . . . or if Chris was just a deeply lonely man.

"You're not going to let us go, are you?"

"No."

"I'm sorry," she told him. "I'm sorry about everything happening the way it did. But I don't want anyone to get hurt anymore."

Chris made a weird sound, a mix of a laugh's surprise and the sarcasm of a snort.

"Sure. No one should get hurt."

"I'm serious."

"You have to be hiding out somewhere," Chris said, pondering out loud. "Seth said he put a bullet right in him, just before Ruby hit him with her car. You're not in a hospital. So where are you?"

His thought process made Melissa uneasy, worried he'd actually be able to reason out where they were hiding. She tried another tactic.

"I'm really sorry for leaving the way I did. It's just that last year, we were so different. And apart. I thought you . . . I thought you could tell."

"I thought you were happy."

"Happy? I was terrified! You'd changed so much."

"You're the one who changed. Left me for some photographer."

"I—"

"You broke my heart." Chris was whispering, either because he was trying to control his emotions or because he didn't want to be overheard. "Was Jake the first? Were there others?"

"There was never anyone else."

The words sounded as if she had never loved anyone but Jake. Melissa didn't know what to say to correct that and wasn't sure if she should.

"What does he . . ." Chris stopped speaking, his voice tight when he resumed. "What do you like about him?"

"I don't want to talk about him. I want to talk about us."

The latter sentence felt too intimate, as if there was still an *us* to return to.

"Maybe we were apart this last year," Chris went on as if he hadn't heard her. "Maybe I was becoming someone you weren't sure about. Maybe you were scared. I get that."

She waited for him to continue.

"But I was scared too. Why do you think I stayed away from my family back when we were first together? Why do you think it took me so long to join up with them?"

"I know."

"I needed you. Knowing you were there for me, knowing I had you in my life . . . my family was one side, but it couldn't be my only side. Do you understand that? I *needed* you, Mel."

"That part's still there," Melissa said. She stared at Dr. Steve's dead garden outside under the sinking sun. His home was so isolated, only one other house on the road, far in the distance, unseeable through the trees.

"I was so lonely back then, except for you." Chris's voice was filling with reproach. "And I knew there was distance between us. I knew we needed to circle back. And I wanted to, but then he was in my house. He was with you."

"I'm sorry."

"And now you call Chris and ask him to forgive you?"

Melissa looked at the dead garden.

"There's no saving you," Chris told her.

She hung up.

A hand on her shoulder.

Melissa turned, too shocked to make a sound, half expecting to see Chris behind her.

But it was Eric, a messenger bag slung over his shoulder. Ruby was behind him, standing in the kitchen doorway.

"How's Jake?" Eric asked, his voice breaking. Melissa saw his tears, felt them against her shoulder as she held him, as Eric apologized for what had happened to Jake and her, desperately apologized. Melissa held him and gazed at Ruby, trying to decipher the stoic, stony expression on the other woman's face. It was like peering into deep shadows, and wondering what was about to emerge.

Chapter Twenty-Two

Lucky

"What do you mean," Renee asked Lucky, "those women are going to kill Marybeth?"

Lucky and his wife stared at each other.

"Follow me." Lucky briskly walked out of the kitchen.

"Lucky?" Renee asked. But she followed him.

Lucky had a thousand thoughts swirling through his mind, like a pile of windblown leaves, but there was one he couldn't escape:

This was the end.

Everything was over. Every secret would be spilled, every element of his life changed. Everything he'd struggled to maintain would shatter.

But he felt happy. Euphoric, even.

"In a way," Lucky said as he and Renee hurried up the stairs from the living room and toward their bedroom, "this is a good thing."

"I'm sorry, what?"

The Rusu twins had left the hatch to the attic open, the retractable stairway unfolded. Lucky knew why. They wanted to complicate matters, hoped Renee would see the open stairs, discover his secrets.

And that was fine. It was time. He felt a wonderful sense of relief at the thought of unburdening himself. Lucky was reminded of a conversation years ago with a neighbor who had been recently laid off from his longtime job, and that man's strange sense of peace when he'd shared this news with Lucky and Renee. They'd assumed, discussing it later, that he'd been deep in denial.

But no, Lucky thought now. It was relief. Leaving a bad situation is always a good thing, regardless of the next uncertain step.

He climbed the ladder.

"Renee," Lucky began decisively, "I haven't felt right for a while. I was doing fine for so many years. It was like I had one secret part of my life, and you and Marybeth were another, and I kept them separate. Far away from each other. And that felt like the right thing to do."

He could see the removed patch in the insulation that the Rusu twins had yanked away, his duffel bag inside. Lucky pulled out the bag.

Of course, they'd taken his weapons. The Glock 22 was gone, as were the knife and Mace. All that remained were bullets. He placed the square of insulation back into the wall, walked to the other side of the attic.

"Kept us separate from what?" Renee asked from below. "Is this about William? Was one of those women married to him? Why are you in our attic?"

Lucky pulled his key chain from his pocket, unfolded the tiny Swiss Army knife blade attached to it, plunged it into the insulation, and cut it open.

Pulled out a second duffel bag. Unzipped it.

The Henry AR-7 rifle wasn't Lucky's ideal choice, but he was out of options. His only other hiding spot was in the outdoor office, and the Rusu twins had already gone through it. He used to keep an emergency bag of weapons hidden in the garage, but once Marybeth had learned to drive, he didn't trust that she wouldn't stumble upon it.

"This isn't about William," he said. "It's someone else."

"Who?"

The good thing about the AR-7 was that the rifle was small, lightweight, and easily assembled. It only took Lucky about a minute, kneeling on the floor, opening the stock pad to pull out the receiver, barrel, and magazines. He quickly inserted the receiver into the stock, screwed it in place. Threaded the barrel to the action, tightened it, and replaced the stock pad. Pushed in a magazine. Racked the bolt back.

Renee had climbed up the steps and was staring at him.

"Why do you have that gun?"

"It's a rifle," Lucky said and hooked a strap to it.

"Then why do you have that rifle?"

"We need to call Marybeth," Lucky said. "She needs to come meet us."

Panic overcame Renee's words. "Why do you have that rifle?"

Lucky slung the AR-7 over his shoulder. Lifted his pants leg and wrapped a sheath around his calf. Pulled out a steel-black Tanto knife from the duffel and slid it inside.

"Let's go," Lucky said.

Renee climbed down the attic stairway, clumsily, losing her grip and catching herself. Lucky jumped down after her, didn't bother with the ladder. He didn't land as smoothly as he'd hoped, stumbling on the floor, knees aching.

Renee was hurrying out of the closet. He caught her arm, turned her toward him.

"I told them I want to walk away," he said insistently, "and it felt *so* right, Renee. And they agreed. Even after all the years I've worked for them, they were just going to let me walk away after this job. But I'd have to give up an old friend of mine. And I don't want to do that to her. I don't want to lie anymore."

"Let me go."

"If I let you go, you'll run away. And they'll find you and Marybeth and kill you both."

"Who!" Renee stopped struggling.

"The Winterses."

"As in Victor Winters? Those people who were in the news?"

Lucky loosened his grip on her arm. And he noted that the more information he gave Renee, the less inclined she seemed to run.

"Grab some clothes," he said. "Take some for you and Marybeth. Enough for a week. You have ten minutes. And I'll explain everything."

Lucky heard her frantically rummaging upstairs as he walked into the living room. His Lemax Christmas Villages were sprawled out on the fireplace hearth and the living room table, and Lucky knelt between them. He tried not to have a favorite, but Lucky loved the village on the hearth. It had been built on three long tiers, each covered with blankets of fake snow, hiding the wires underneath.

There was another reason he was always fixated on this village. One of the pieces didn't belong to it. This misplaced figurine was similar to the others, plastic and about two inches tall, but it lacked the reddish cheeks, the stocking cap and scarf, the depicted cheer from assembling a snowman or tugging a sled. This piece had a grim countenance and a cape, and Lucky always kept it carefully hidden in the village, so that it wouldn't disrupt the tableau. He'd had this tiny superhero since he was a child, and Lucky had no idea what its name was or anything about it—his father had given it to him, and Lucky suspected it was a knockoff. But he'd kept this toy with him ever since, deep in his pocket or backpack during his school years, in his car's glove compartment after graduation, even tucked in the breast pocket of his rented tuxedo the day of his wedding.

Lucky debated taking this nameless superhero with him now.

But no, this was where he belonged.

Twenty minutes later he and Renee were driving out of their neighborhood, the afternoon sun dropping like a coin into a piggy bank when he spoke again.

"So there's obviously a part of me I've never told you about," Lucky said, his eyes everywhere on the road, scanning the cars parked on the side of the street, glancing back into the rearview mirror. "And it's never been a problem before."

Something caught his eye.

"Did you know the Petersons are selling?" he asked, pointing to a colonial with a Realtor sign in the front yard.

"You were selling houses for the Winterses?" Renee guessed.

"No."

She waited.

"I found people they wanted me to find."

"What?"

Lucky said nothing.

"And then what?"

Lucky still didn't reply.

"But these are bad people, right?" Renee asked in his mind. *"These are people who deserve it? I know this was a secret you kept from me, but I guess it was for the best. And I know we're in danger, but Marybeth and I will do whatever you say to keep us safe. Thank you, Lucky."*

Lucky shook his head.

Renee was screaming and her door was open and her right foot was outside and bouncing on the pavement.

"Wait!" Lucky shouted, and he swung the car to the side of the road. Renee unfastened her seat belt and ran into the golf course bordering their neighborhood. Lucky grabbed the rifle from the back seat and ran after her.

Renee was faster than he expected, although Lucky knew her speed was motivated by fear. He'd chased people down before, and, once their adrenaline left, once they'd fled a short distance, they dramatically slowed. Even trained runners found their energy emptied by fear, bent over, hands on their knees, saying variations of "please . . . please, just hold on," as Lucky approached.

Renee stopped at the edge of a man-made lake, now nearly black this late in the day, as if she was debating jumping in.

"Renee, that water's filthy."

She turned toward him. Lucky had never seen her eyes so wild.

"This is a joke," Renee said. "This is a joke, and you don't mean any of it."

Lucky didn't approach her, didn't respond.

She was staring at the rifle. Lucky lifted off the strap and set the weapon on the grass.

Renee took a step backward.

"Careful," Lucky warned her. "The lake's behind you."

How weird it would be, he thought, *if Renee accidentally fell in?* What an odd moment that would be in this surreal evening. Lucky imagined them discussing it years from now, laughing on the porch of a cabin. *"I fell right in!"* Renee would exclaim, and Lucky would tease her, and they'd laugh at her silliness.

"This isn't true, is it?" Renee asked.

He didn't respond.

"My God." Renee sat abruptly on the grass, her legs sticking out before her like roots that had been yanked from the ground.

"I'm not asking you to forgive me," Lucky said. "All you have to do is believe me."

"Why are they after you?"

"Like I said, those women think I have information about someone they're looking for."

"And do you?"

Lucky considered it. "Yes."

"So why not tell them, if you're putting us in danger? Why not just tell them?"

"Because they'll kill us if they don't need me. And because I can't do that to her."

"Her?"

Lucky detected the different note in Renee's voice, the one-word question that was on the verge of something deeper, like the tip of a spear protruding from a cave. And a part of him marveled that, even with what he was telling Renee and everything she was learning about him, his faithfulness to her still, in some way, mattered.

"I met her when I started working for them. And I helped her when she left, because no one escapes Win . . . I'm sorry, that's such a terrible slogan. She was a friend, nothing more. I've never cheated on you."

"I don't care about that right now," Renee said.

"I know where she is. And she probably knows how to find who they're looking for. When I came home today and found those two women in our house—"

"Those women broke into our house?"

"Then I knew I was out of time. Once the Winterses know I can find her, they're going to come after me. And not just me. You and Marybeth too."

Renee looked out over the darkening lake. But she didn't turn her face away completely. As if she had to keep watching him.

"I never wanted to hurt you," Lucky told her quietly. "I just wanted to lie to you."

"Ma'am, are you okay?"

A stranger's voice. A man's voice.

It came from somewhere behind him, Lucky guessed maybe twenty feet or so.

The rifle was lying on the grass in front of him.

The Henry AR-7 wasn't a very powerful rifle. It was mainly used for hunting small animals. Lucky kept it sentimentally; it had been one of the first weapons he'd trained on, shooting squirrels and sparrows in his backyard as a teen while his parents drank in the kitchen.

If Renee called out for help, if she suddenly let the panic edging into her face overcome her, then he'd have to turn and run down this man and use the knife strapped to his ankle. Lucky hoped the stranger didn't have a weapon of his own . . . but he probably did. This was the exact situation men craved. A woman in need of protection. A seemingly threatening assailant. And the advantage of starting a fight, so men have the time to summon their courage.

But Lucky knew what truly awaited this unseen person standing behind him.

Because sometimes a man opened a door and didn't realize what waited on the other side.

Lucky waited for Renee to respond to the stranger.

To open that door.

Chapter Twenty-Three

Jake

"Hey, Jake," Eric said, "Do you mind moving? I want to play pool."

There was a dryness to Jake's voice he hadn't expected when he laughed, the sound hoarse, scabbed. And the throbbing in his shoulder increased, threatened to break beyond his control. The pain was already close to something worse, like a sword was lodged in his shoulder, and too much movement would drive the blade through.

"I'm lying on a pool table?" he asked, weakly.

Melissa leaned down, holding back her hair in a gesture Jake found comforting, and gently kissed him.

"There's a huge board covering it," she told him. "But it still looks more comfortable than that mattress you had."

"I kept having these dreams," Jake said. "I couldn't wake up. I was here, in this room. And I could hear people talking. But I couldn't wake up."

"Jake," Eric said softly. "That sounds like the most boring dream."

"Yeah, I've had better."

"How do you feel now?" Melissa asked.

"Tired."

"I think Dr. Steve gave you a lot of meds," Melissa told Jake, "since he doesn't have anesthesia. He went to get more."

"What am I on?"

Eric and Melissa looked at each other.

"Morphine?" Melissa guessed.

"Helium?"

"We don't know drugs."

"Is my camera okay?"

No jokes now, Jake noticed. Just solemnity from Melissa and Eric. And something about their staid response saddened him. Guilt rose, so strong that the pain in his shoulder intensified, guilt that he'd demanded anything from the people he loved, including their devotion to his art.

"The bullet didn't hit it," Melissa said.

"Just you," Eric added, and that offhand humor he'd been trying to keep, that detachment, slipped. He blinked fast, touched his eyes.

"I'm glad you're here," Jake told him.

Eric looked like he wanted to say more, but stopped himself.

"How'd you find us?" Jake asked.

"I followed Ruby."

Jake's arm jerked, and pain and worry flooded him. "Ruby's here?" He tried to rise, but the injury to his shoulder and Melissa's hand on his wrist kept him in place.

"She came to see me," Eric said uncomfortably, "to ask about the Winterses. I told her what I told Melissa upstairs. That they made me talk, made me tell them about Wharfside. I'm sorry. I'm so sorry."

Jake didn't care about that. "Is Ruby here now?"

"She was," Melissa said. "I think she stepped out."

"We need to go. You can't trust her."

Melissa's hand hadn't left him. "She saved our lives."

"We are leaving," Eric told him. "Tomorrow. We're going to head south or west. Find a small town with a tiny hospital, get you patched up, and then figure out the best way to disappear from the Winterers."

"I think it's *Winterses*," Melissa said.

"I don't trust Ruby," Jake said flatly. "I don't. We need to go now."

Eric and Melissa stayed silent. The harshness of his words hung in the air.

"Well, we can't leave right now," Melissa told him. "Dr. Steve said he needs to take out the bullet. It's still in you. He's going to do it later today."

"He is?"

She nodded. "That's why he's getting more drugs."

Jake shifted, grimaced. "Watch Ruby until then," he urged. "Closely. Please."

"We will," Melissa said, and her eyes met his.

Jake couldn't look at Eric. He was too worried his expression might somehow reveal everything he knew, the truth he'd kept from his friend for years.

The next time Jake woke, the pain was deeper, jagged.

And Ruby was with him.

"Where's Melissa?" Jake asked, alarmed. He struggled to sit up, but his shoulder hurt too much to allow him even that freedom. "And Eric?"

"They're upstairs." Ruby was perched on the stool Melissa had been sitting on, peering at him curiously.

"Why are you here?" Jake's voice still held a rasp, but he didn't mind it now. It felt like spewing poison.

"Steve told me to come down. He said I should talk to you first."

"I'll be fine."

"You may not, Jake," Ruby told him, and now he noticed the redness in her eyes, the tightness around her mouth. "The bullet's close to an artery. Steve's worried."

Her words were like another weight on his chest, forcing him to stay in his place, and Jake hated this trapped feeling, impotency and agony that left him helpless on the table.

"But Steve's a good doctor," Ruby went on, as if she was trying to reassure both of them. "That's what Victor always said."

"I don't really care about Victor Winters's Yelp reviews."

Ruby smiled at that, and Jake suddenly remembered how he could sometimes make her smile.

"You should cut your hair." Ruby touched it, fingered a curl. "It's getting too long."

He flinched, and that imaginary blade in his shoulder cut deep. It took him a moment to say, "Don't touch me, Ruby."

She looked like she wanted to touch him again, but instead she brought her hand back to her lap. "They told you what I did? Saved you from Seth?"

There was something different in her tone now, far from what he remembered. "Are you still drinking?"

"I am not."

"So you waited till I left."

"When you left," Ruby said slowly, "that's when I knew I *had* to stop. I'd lost too much."

"I can't trust anything you tell me."

"I know why you're afraid." Ruby's voice dropped a tone. "You're worried I'll tell Eric what I did, and he'll find out you knew. All this time."

Jake didn't respond.

"I wouldn't do that to you."

"I had a dream," Jake said as a way of testing her. "A lot of dreams. And in one of them I heard you shouting. Was that real?"

"It was," Ruby assented. "I was calling Melissa a whore."

"She's not a whore."

"All people are sinners, Jake."

"Are you still working for them?"

Jake studied her closely, his gaze searching her face like a metal detector scanning the ground.

Her eyes met his. "I stopped years ago."

Their stares held, until Jake and Ruby simultaneously let out small sighs and turned away.

Jake was irritated that he'd had the same reaction as Ruby, even more annoyed that it seemed to make her happy.

"What?" he asked huffily.

Ruby quickly, gently, ran her fingertips over his face.

"You're still my boy," she told him.

And then she left. Jake watched her trudge up the stairs, like a heavy axe slowly being lifted.

Chapter Twenty-Four

Lucky

Lucky felt good.

No, he felt *wonderful.*

A burden was swept off his shoulders, and he hadn't realized its full weight.

Renee sat in the passenger seat, stoically staring forward.

She'd held her tongue on the golf course. *I'm fine,* she'd called back to the concerned man watching them. *We're just talking. He's my husband.* And Lucky had known, with those three short sentences, that there was a way forward for their relationship.

"How long has it been?" Renee suddenly asked. This was the first thing she'd said since they'd gotten back into the car, the hour-long drive from their neighborhood to the town of Front Royal.

"Since I've been working with them? Too long."

"Were we ever in danger?" she asked. "Marybeth and me?"

"No," Lucky lied firmly. "Not until now. Not until the Rusu twins realized they need information I have."

“But you’ve hurt people,” Renee said. There was a tremor in her voice, as if she was close to tears. Lucky wanted to pull over and talk with her but didn’t want to risk her running off again.

“I did, but I’m done with that,” Lucky told her earnestly. “I’ll never do it again.”

A quiet “Okay.”

This moment felt like a fresh start.

“I can get all this straightened out,” he assured her. “I’ll fix it and leave the Winterses. We can get back to normal.”

Renee didn’t respond.

They drove on in relative silence. Lucky tried to talk with her about Marybeth’s outburst, the anger he’d felt toward William McKenna, hoping to find ground on which they could commiserate. But Renee barely responded aside from an occasional murmur.

Lucky decided to stop talking and enjoy the drive. The sprawling suburbs of northern Virginia were left behind, and blue-gray mountains appeared in the distance, like rumpled bedcovers. They drove into Front Royal, the small town at the base of the Blue Ridge Mountains, a mix of homes and stores and stores fashioned from homes and ramshackle small buildings made up of weathered boards. The roads narrowed and curved, and Lucky had the same sensation he’d had last time he’d driven here, years ago: the feeling that he was approaching the mountains without realizing he was already in them.

They were close to the cabin when Lucky realized Renee was crying, and he pulled the Jeep over and tried to comfort her with an embrace, but Renee pushed away from him and screamed. Lucky lifted his hands, settled back into his seat.

“Okay okay,” he said and restarted the engine. “Not ready for a hug. I get it.”

But that was the only outburst, which Lucky considered a win. He had never known what would happen if Renee learned the truth of his other life, but he’d assumed it would take weeks, months, maybe years of work to repair their marriage. Two outbursts in an hour—both of which she'd calmed down from—were far better than he'd expected.

Lucky parked the car, hurried around to her door to open it, a chivalry he regretted not practicing more.

"You'll be safe here," Lucky told her. Renee stood behind him next to the cabin's door, looking around at the dusty furniture illuminated by faint sunlight through smudged windows. The cabin was small, nothing more than a rectangular living room, an adjoining room for a bedroom, another for a bath. "One of my clients had this place, and his daughter inherited it after he died. But the daughter is married and living in Europe, and she and her family never come here."

"Did you kill the owners and take it?"

"What?"

She just looked at him.

"No!"

Renee made a noncommittal sound, moved away. Touched the top of a couch.

"It's only a little dirty," Lucky assured her, "but you only need to stay here for a night or two. I texted Marybeth, and she's on her way. I'm going to fix everything. You'll see."

Renee nodded.

"When Marybeth comes, you can take the car to town to get food, but I wouldn't spend too much time in public. Don't use any credit cards, and delete all the apps with location tracking in your phones: social media, family trackers, all of it. This area is pretty empty this time of year, but you two still shouldn't be seen. If you do go into town, and you think you're being followed, make sure Marybeth is safe and try to lead the pursuer away. Do you want my gun . . . no? Okay, no gun, but once you lead the pursuer away, make a scene. Scream or yell. That will likely drive whoever it is off but *don't* stay around until the police arrive. Remember that the police work for them—not all the cops, but enough. If you're here with Marybeth, and you see someone approaching the cabin, make sure the doors and windows are locked. They'll break through the window, but there are knives in the kitchen. Stand by the side of the window, and, when they're trying to come in, use the knives to keep them out. If they do climb in, slash them and run for the door. Remember, you want to slash, not stab—it's too easy for a knife to get lodged in muscle or bone. Slashing has a better chance of severing an artery. Keep the lights off at night, the noise low in daytime, and the curtains always closed. Don't watch television together, because one of you needs to hear what's happening outside. At night don't look directly at a light because it's hard to see if you need to quickly look away. Always move quickly, inside and outside. Given the choice, a good assassin will wait for a target to be still, and the Rusu twins are good assassins. And remember, they're not going to want to kill you, because they want to find me. But don't ever assume they'll let you live."

"How do you know all this?"

"Because it's what someone should do if I was after them."

Lucky wasn't sure what else he should say after that. He nodded and started out the door.

"Be careful," Renee said faintly.

And those two words were enough to reassure Lucky that Renee was still there for him.

He patted the AR-7 on the passenger seat, content in a way he hadn't been for years, as Lucky drove off to find Ruby. To end this part of his life.

Chapter Twenty-Five

Melissa

Jake was sweating so much it worried Melissa, a wet sheen like wax over his sleeping face. There was a damp odor to his clothes, Jake's scent that Melissa faintly remembered from his pillows and sheets, but now that scent was sickly, gaseous and medicinal. She could smell it distinctly when she replaced the blood-reddened bandage on his shoulder from where Dr. Steve had removed the bullet.

Eric's voice was coarse when he spoke. "Ruby told me she had Dr. Steve put Jake under for a lot longer. He'll be out tonight, maybe even till tomorrow. Dr. Steve said the pain would be severe, and Ruby didn't want to see him hurting."

"I'm just glad he'll be okay," Melissa said. During the procedure, as she and Eric had waited upstairs, her anxiety had felt like rabid dogs nipping at her heels—so much so that, even in relief, her exhausted body ached.

Eric leaned back on the stool, looked over his shoulder at the stairs leading up from the basement.

"I don't trust her. Jake doesn't either. He never told me why, and I just thought it was because she was this terrible mother. But when she came to my place earlier, I felt like there was something else." He gazed at Melissa from under the hair dropping over his eyes. "What about you?"

"Well, she keeps calling me a whore, so that's not great."

"She blames you for Jake getting shot." Eric's words were somewhere between a statement and a question.

"She's got a point."

"How?"

"He almost died because of me," Melissa said, her voice small. "And he keeps getting beat up. I'm sort of thinking, maybe I'm not the right girl for him?"

Eric smiled at that, and he looked down warmly at Jake's bruised, sleeping face. "He can sure take a beating, though, right? One time this guy called me a . . . not-very-nice name for an Asian. I was going to ignore it, but Jake went over to the guy and told him to apologize. Of course, the guy wouldn't, so then Jake took his picture, and then the guy threatened to kick his ass. But Jake just wouldn't back down."

"What happened?"

"Oh, the guy knocked him out with one punch. Jake can't fight, not even when his life depends on it. But he does stand up for his people."

"He really does." Melissa picked up Jake's hand, held it, rubbed his thumb with hers. "How did you follow Ruby here?"

"The Winterers have been watching my place, but only the building's front door. I knew Ruby would leave through the back, so I did the same. Drove right behind her. I mean, she pulled over after, like, a mile, and I told her I wanted to see Jake. She didn't want me to come, but I think she felt like she owed me."

"Why?"

"She introduced my mom to the Winterers, got her involved with them."

"I didn't know that."

"Jake didn't tell you?"

"No."

Eric cleared his throat. "People make their choices, right? When I remember my mom, I remember this young woman who was always holding me, always smiling. And I know there's more to her; I know she wasn't just that person. The same way I know there's more to Ruby. It's just hard for me to accept that.

"I think Jake was right," he went on. "We can't trust her. And if I need to, I'll kill her."

Eric picked up the messenger bag by his feet, opened it, showed Melissa a gun inside.

"I don't think Jake would ever forgive you," Melissa told him as Eric closed the bag. "I know what he says about her, but she's still his mother. He won't understand."

"Killing her is protecting him."

"I don't think he sees it that way. And I don't think you'll be the same afterward."

"You don't think I could do it?"

Melissa had heard men threaten violence before, especially when she'd been with Chris. Most of the time it was braggadocio, the way men talked, how they craved scars.

But this was one of the times she believed it.

One of those times when violence was spoken with a sense of promise, a dog's bared teeth.

Movement upstairs before she could answer, rustling. Melissa and Eric looked at each other.

"I'll check on her," Melissa said.

Ruby was sitting at the small kitchen table, Melissa's handbag in front of her. She wondered if Ruby had gone through it.

"Where's Dr. Steve?" Melissa asked.

"He'll be here soon."

Something about Ruby's simple sentence sounded ominous, but Melissa couldn't figure out why.

"I don't know why I didn't abort him."

Melissa couldn't hide her surprise.

"It's not that I regret him." Ruby shrugged. "I just didn't fall in love right away. When I found out I was pregnant, Jake's dad didn't stick around. I spent nine months wondering if I should keep the baby, thinking about abortion, then adoption. But I was so terrified by the idea of regret that I couldn't do anything. Too scared."

Melissa noticed a similarity in Ruby and Jake, how they stared intently at her as they spoke, like they were studying her reactions.

"I was mad after he was born," Ruby went on. "Mad at Jake's dad for leaving like I thought he would, mad at myself for keeping Jake. I'd see these new mothers when I'd take him to the park across the street from our apartment talking softly to their babies. I never felt that same way.

"But there was this moment when Jake was doing tummy time. You put a baby on his stomach, and he's supposed to lift his neck to strengthen it. Jake was doing that, and I was watching him, and I heard this sound. I wasn't sure what it was. I leaned in close, and I heard him, and he was *grunting*. This little baby was struggling to raise his head and making this *uh* sound, and that was it. That's when I fell in love.

"Maybe it's because I fell in love when he was struggling, and I saw he needed help, but that was the moment he became an actual person to me. Not something invisible inside me, not some crying body I had to take care of, but an actual person with a soul. He wasn't causing me pain."

Melissa watched the way Ruby's thumb rubbed over her index finger as she spoke.

"I told myself I needed to make money," Ruby said. "And I did. That's the truth. The Winterses gave me that. I didn't have Jake's father sending me anything. I didn't have family. I needed what they gave me."

"What they gave you?"

"I'm not looking for forgiveness," Ruby said intensely. "Not from you. What I did for the Winterses, and what I did to myself and Jake with all those years of drinking—all that's on me, and all I have is the Lord. I have Him. And He hath me."

Ruby rose from the table, went to the window.

"Jake left and returned," she said. "The Lord teaches us to embrace the prodigal son, to vanquish ourselves of pride and accept. To even forgive ourselves of the sins we may commit on His behalf."

Ruby turned toward Melissa.

"They're here," she said.

"Who?" Melissa joined Ruby at the window.

A man was approaching the house. He held a rifle.

"How?" Melissa looked wildly around, as if she would find an answer.

Ruby was already heading downstairs.

Melissa wanted to scream, to run, to do something even if she had no idea what. She knew the basement was a bad idea, a place to be trapped, but Jake was there, and she wasn't going to leave him.

Melissa started down the stairs. Remembered her handbag with her phone on the kitchen table.

She ran back, grabbed her handbag, glanced out the window.

The man stood in the dead garden, watching her.

He lifted his rifle and fired.

Chapter Twenty-Six
Ruby

From the basement, Ruby heard the shot, and she heard Melissa shriek. She paused at the bottom of the stairs.

"What was that?" Eric was standing next to Jake's unconscious body, one of Jake's arms dangling off the pool table.

"The Winterses are here."

"What?" Eric hurried to the stairs, called up. "Melissa?"

No response.

Ruby switched places with Eric to stand next to her son, used her foot to push the bag Eric had been standing next to under the table. She lifted Jake's hand, gently laid it at his side. A day hadn't passed in the last four years when Ruby hadn't thought about him. She'd actually tried calling him once and received the melodic three-note notification that "this number is no longer in service." The sudden realization that she had no means of contacting him left her frightened, almost panicked.

And yet she'd resisted searching for him.

Ruby didn't know if it was pride, but if it was, now she understood the relation of pride to sin. Pride had kept Ruby from her son. Casting shadows in her mind, dispelling light.

Melissa emerged at the top of the stairs, one hand on the railing, turning and pulling the door closed. Wildly rushed down.

She ran into Eric, and he grabbed her, tried to calm her, ask what happened.

"I don't know," Melissa said.

The weight of Eric's bag against her foot surprised Ruby. She knelt, opened it, pulled out the gun. Eric didn't seem the type to use a gun. Like Jake, there was a softness to him, a grasp of childhood he refused to let go.

"What do we do?" Melissa was asking, and she turned toward Ruby. "Should we . . . ?"

She and Eric saw the gun in Ruby's hand.

And then Ruby slowly lifted her head, her eyes on the stairs.

"And it came to pass after these things," Ruby said.

"Eric?" Melissa turned toward him.

But Eric just watched Ruby, even as Melissa grabbed his arm, even as the door handle turned. Eric watched her like a patient listening to their doctor's diagnosis.

"Behold," Ruby whispered, "here I am."

"What are you saying?" Melissa asked desperately.

"Get thee into the land of Moriah."

"What are you doing?" Melissa asked. "We need to save Jake! They're coming!" Melissa was wild eyed and off-balance, as if she wanted to run but had no direction. "They're coming!"

The door leading to the basement opened.

Heavy footsteps on the stairs. Men's footsteps.

Marley walked into the recreation room, looked around at Jake's wounded body on the table, Melissa scared next to him, Eric silent beside her. Ruby standing with the gun.

"Ruby," Marley said. "Thank you."

Ruby didn't respond.

"What?" Melissa asked, her voice faint.

Two men followed Marley. One of them was gagged and blindfolded and bleeding. But even with the blindfold and bruises on his face, Ruby recognized Steve Debko.

The other man had a shaved head, calm disposition, the bearing of former or active military. Surety to his movement, the casual way an athlete steps onto a field or a priest wanders among his congregation. As if this was where he belonged.

He took Melissa by the arm, dragged her to the wall, forced her to the floor. Eric and Steve followed, albeit with less resistance. They were pushed down next to her.

Steve looked around the room after his blindfold was removed. His eyes landed on Ruby.

"You told them where I was," Steve said uncertainly, as if he couldn't believe what he was saying. "Your own son. You told them where we were."

"Her son will be fine," Marley said. "And so will she."

"And they came to the place which the Lord had told him of," Ruby said.

"Where's Chris?" Melissa asked desperately. "I want to talk to Chris."

"Chris doesn't need to talk to you again," Marley said.

"And there Abraham built an altar."

"Where's Chris?" Melissa asked again, as the bald military-looking man pulled a handgun out of his holster. He pointed it at Steve's head.

Ruby had forgotten how loud a gunshot was, like the Lord clapping His hands together.

Ruby heard Melissa's and Eric's screams after her hearing returned, faintly, like the screams were coming from another world, or a memory that had seeped into the present.

And Ruby heard her own voice as Melissa wept, as the bald man raised his weapon at Melissa, as Steve's blood spread.

"And they came to the place which the Lord had spake of, and Abraham laid the wood. And stretched his son upon the altar."

"You don't . . . ," Melissa was saying, her face blurry tears. "You don't."

The gun swung wildly, and it took Ruby a moment to realize Eric had grabbed the other man's arms. It was a hopeless fight. The bald man had been surprised but recovered quickly. He wrested the gun from Eric's grasp, spun it in his hand, whipped Eric's face with the handle.

Eric fell back to the floor, stunned. Melissa was breathing hard, scared breaths, animal breaths. Marley just watched.

The bald man pointed the gun at Eric.

"Do not lay a hand on the boy," Ruby said, but she knew they wouldn't listen to her.

Eric looked toward Ruby, and she gazed back, and she wondered if Eric knew, in this last moment of his life, what had happened to his mother. It was as if she and Eric had spoken some instinctual language, and the word "mother" was present between them, as real as if the word had been carved from stone. A scared look overtook Eric's expression, his eyes wet, and he seemed like he wanted to say something. He tried to stand, but it was as if he'd forgotten how.

"And Abraham stretched forth his hand," Ruby said, "and took the knife to slay his son."

The Lord clapped.

Ruby looked to the stairs as Eric's body slumped to the floor. Melissa was rushing up, a soul fleeing its body.

But Ruby knew there was no salvation waiting for her.

Chapter Twenty-Seven

Lucky

Lucky cheerfully parked his Jeep outside Steve Debko's house, stared at the AR-7 next to him. Decided to leave it in the car.

He wouldn't need a weapon for this.

He'd assumed Ruby had brought Jake and Melissa here, particularly once he'd heard Jake was injured. A local hospital would have been too dangerous, and Jake was probably too hurt to travel much farther.

He spotted Ruby's car parked down the street, the same old, faded silver Corolla he remembered.

Lucky's plan was to tell Ruby that she needed to leave—he was about to be questioned by the Winterses, and he'd have to give them some accurate information about her, enough to prove his loyalty. But he'd also help Ruby escape and leave bread crumbs for the Winterses to follow, although those crumbs would be scattered in different directions. His faith would be proved, Ruby and her son would be safe, and Lucky would be able to return to his waiting family.

A perfect plan.

The front door opened as Lucky approached.

His perfect plan shattered into a thousand pieces.

"Looks like you and I both knew the kids were here," Marley said.

Lucky wasn't sure how to respond. He tried not to stare at the silver-plated pistols holstered at Marley's waist.

"Come inside," Marley told him. "I have something to show you."

Lucky numbly followed Marley inside Debko's house. He hadn't been here for years, not since he'd helped Ruby find this place, a property that sat in the town of Cabin John, abandoned, too deep in disrepair to be attractive to anyone.

A man was assembling a handgun in the kitchen. Lucky didn't recognize him, but he had a different bearing than the men normally associated with the Winterses. Former or current cop. Maybe military.

"Lucky," Marley said, "meet Spence."

Spence didn't acknowledge Lucky.

"How'd you find Ruby?" Lucky asked Marley.

"She called Frank," Marley replied as he picked up his own gun, a chrome Beretta, and snapped in the clip. "Gave up the girl and Debko in exchange for her and her son."

"Where's Ruby now?"

"Gone with her son, but the girl escaped. Spence went looking for her. He's going back out soon."

Spence loaded his weapon with a snap.

"You knew Ruby, right?" Marley asked casually.

If Ruby had given up Melissa and Steve, Lucky wondered, had she also given him up? Had she betrayed him?

All this time Lucky had thought she'd left, that there was hope for him . . .

No one escapes.

He forced himself to stand still, fought the urge to lunge forward, to wrest the handgun free from Marley.

"I heard you two were tight," Marley went on.

Lucky wasn't sure how to respond. "This isn't the kind of business where you make friends," he said carefully.

Marley's eyes glinted. "It is if you're honest."

Spence reached below the counter, brought up a shotgun. Pumped the slide backward and forward. Something about the two clicks always reminded Lucky of a pause, the wait for a third.

"Do you want to know who else Ruby gave up?" Marley asked.

He knows.

Lucky didn't move.

"You didn't bring a gun, did you?" Marley went on, instead of waiting for Lucky to answer. He tapped the handle of one of his pistols. "Strange to come here and not bring a weapon."

Lucky was suddenly conscious of the closed pantry door behind him. He wondered if someone was inside, aiming a second shotgun at his back.

"Did you know Ruby helped Debko find this place?" Lucky couldn't tell if these were real questions or if Marley was simply goading him. "Hid him here from us. She owed him a favor, and he wanted out."

"Did she?" Lucky asked.

His throat was so dry it was difficult to speak.

"Like I told you, I always heard you and Ruby were close," Marley said.

"What are you trying to say, Marley?"

Marley studied him with sharp eyes. Spence had finished with his weapons and was watching both men.

"I think," Marley said, "you came here to warn Ruby."

Nobody said anything for a moment.

"But you should have figured we were already here," Marley went on. "Come on, Lucky. We know you and Ruby were tight. We figured she'd turn to you."

Lucky couldn't stop thinking about the closed door behind him. His back ached.

"What were you thinking?" Marley asked.

It was one motion.

Lucky bent and pulled the knife free from his ankle holster. Lifted his hand to bring the blade down on Spence.

Spence calmly stepped away.

Lucky's knife cut air. Nothing else.

He could see, out of the corner of his eye, Marley aiming one of his handguns at him, Spence raising his. Lucky turned sideways in between them, trying to keep an eye on both men. His heart was a wild dog trapped in a cage.

He'd been wrong about everything.

He'd imagined that Renee was going to wait for him to return, accept that her murderous husband had turned a new corner. Their lives could resume.

He'd imagined that the Winterses would allow him to walk away, let Lucky carry their secrets as casually as a knapsack slung over his shoulder.

Now Lucky knew, intrinsically knew, that Renee had reached out to Marybeth the moment he'd driven away from the cabin. Told her everything. They'd already run off, probably contacted the cops.

And Lucky knew Marley was right. The Winterses had completely controlled him, tricked him, seen through everything he'd said and done. Used him in the hopes of finding Ruby.

Everyone had known he couldn't be trusted.

"Sorry, Lucky," Marley said. "At least you'll go before your family will."

Lucky's world went dark.

◆ ◆ ◆

He lay on the kitchen floor.

Had he been shot? Was he his soul, rising from his body?

There'd been no sound after the lights flicked off and the gunfire, the two explosions boxing Lucky's ears after his desperate dive to the floor.

Shadows in the darkness. Someone saying something, Marley, his words becoming clearer.

"What happened to the lights? Who's there?"

A door closed from somewhere distant. A shadow moved. Lucky squinted uselessly in the dark. The shadow moved into a square of light from the window, and Lucky saw Spence looking elsewhere.

It was as if Marley and Spence had forgotten about Lucky after the power in the house had gone out.

Or they thought he was dead.

Lucky remembered a story he'd heard about a runner, on the verge of finishing a marathon, exhausted and barely conscious, who'd been shot in the back of the head during the last mile. The runner had been so tired that he hadn't even felt the bullet. He'd finished the race and then, when he realized the onlookers were staring at him as he crossed the finish line, touched the back of his head and felt blood.

Was he dying?

Lucky wanted to touch his head, his chest, search for a wound, but didn't dare move.

Spence walked over to Lucky, peered down, stared hard in the dark. "He still has the knife."

This time Lucky wasn't too slow.

He felt Spence's neck against his fist, the knife sunk to its handle.

Lucky rose, looking for Marley, but Marley was already rushing him, crashing into him. Marley climbed over Lucky, grabbed his ears.

The back of Lucky's head was slammed onto the kitchen floor.

Silence. Darkness. Pain coming but not yet present.

Lucky's body was moving independently of his dazed mind, still fighting. Trying to grab Marley's hands as the back of his head was driven into the floor again.

Something slashed his chin, and then came the pain, and then came nausea. A glint of light showed the gun in Marley's hand, lifted high, the handle wet from where it had whipped Lucky's face.

But that meant, Lucky thought groggily, the other gun was still at Marley's waist.

Lucky reached for it weakly, but Marley knocked Lucky's hands to the side. Pulled his second gun free.

Pointed both down.

"Your daughter's going to be first," Marley told him. "While your wife watches."

"Counterpoint," a woman said.

Marley was suddenly illuminated by a beam of light boring into his chest. He squinted into it as something whistled over Lucky, something black and hard crashing into Marley's right arm, that pistol skittering away.

Marley cried out, lifted the other pistol, and fired blindly into the light. The gunshot deafened Lucky, a quick exhale of orange light from the muzzle. Lucky saw a shadow by Marley's side, and that second gun was suddenly lifted, like a parent pulling a helpless child, and Marley's wrist was turned and his hand opened and the pistol bounced to the floor next to Lucky's head.

A boot kicked it away.

Marley turned over, reached for the metal rod that had struck him, but another boot slammed down on his hand, flattened his fingers to the floor. A gloved hand reached down, picked up the metal, and Lucky saw it smash across Marley's mouth, a tooth and blood flying away.

Marley listed to the side, fell out of the light.

A flashlight clicked on, beamed up and down Marley's body, then Spence's, then jerked over the room before settling on Lucky's face.

He squinted past the light, saw only one person standing behind it.
And he realized who it was.
"You saved me?" he asked.
The harsh beam of light didn't waver.
"It's too late to save anyone."

Part Three

It is mine to avenge; I will repay. In due time their foot will slip; their day of disaster is near and their doom rushes upon them.

Deuteronomy 32:35

Chapter Twenty-Eight

Melissa

Melissa remembered a time when, as a child of nine, she'd been at a hotel with her mother, and Melissa had gone down to the lobby to buy a Coke. She'd returned to the elevator in the lobby, pressed the button for her floor, but a hand caught the doors before they closed.

A man entered.

Melissa had a disquieting feeling, the fear of being alone with a stranger. That feeling overwhelmed her when, after the elevator had begun to rise, he'd pressed the "Stop" button.

The elevator jerked and froze.

Melissa couldn't speak. She just shrank into the corner.

The man stepped in front of her, her eyes level with his belt, and placed his hands on the wall. One on either side of her head.

"I'm sorry," she whispered.

And then, by some automated function or remote access or miracle, the elevator lurched to a start. Began to rise again.

The man stepped away as the doors opened. A trio of people stepped on board. Melissa ran past them and raced down the hall. The man stayed behind.

She didn't tell her mother what had happened. Never told anyone.

But she remembered it now, that feeling of helplessness. Her life at someone else's whim, someone stronger than her, and more dangerous, and desiring to take something from her.

Someone driven by a force so strong Melissa felt she had no choice but to surrender.

◆ ◆ ◆

Melissa stumbled away from Dr. Steve's house and down the street, blindly panicked. She turned a corner and ducked behind the only other house on the road. She sank to the ground, between a brick wall and the bare branches of a shrub. Tried to corral her thoughts.

Ruby had betrayed her, given her and Dr. Steve up to save herself and Jake.

They'd murdered Eric.

Was Jake safe?

Ruby was with Jake and those two men from the Winterses, and she'd do everything she could to keep Jake safe. Melissa was confident of that . . . but then she remembered Ruby's words: *Do not lay a hand on the boy.* A shiver rustled through her at the memory, the way the words came from somewhere ancient. And the men had blithely ignored her. The memory was madness.

Something caught her eye, a figure passing under a streetlamp. A man walking down the road, a hand plunged into his coat, the other shining a flashlight. One of the men from the basement.

Melissa pressed against the brick.

He looked in her direction.

Melissa had a fear that she was about to accidentally shake the shrub in front of her, slip from her knelt position, cough, something to arouse his attention.

But he turned and continued down the street, the flashlight's beam swinging left to right.

Melissa exhaled.

Her panic had almost left her dazed. She wanted to run around the side of this house, knock on the front door, beg for safety, for an ambulance, for the police. She wondered if the neighbors had heard the shots, if the cops had already been called. But the two houses on this street were separated by long lawns and clumps of trees, and the street was quiet, and the house lights were dark. There was no sign anyone had heard anything. Or that anyone was even home.

A car passed.

Melissa assumed it was more men with the Winterses. Her stomach tightened at the idea. Those men deciding what to do with Jake, Ruby powerless to stop them. Men soon spider-webbing into the streets, flashlights in one hand and weapons in the other, lights and bullets finding Melissa wherever she hid.

She stayed crouched until her legs ached, scared to leave the safety of the shadows, finding fault with every idea that occurred to her. The only thing she could do was give herself up, hope that was enough to uphold whatever agreement Ruby had made to keep Jake safe.

Melissa rose, and she walked back to Dr. Steve's house.

She felt numb inside, the distress of fate, weirdly reminded of the time she'd received that scholarship rejection, the way it seemed to reiterate that she would never obtain a bachelor's degree. The same certainty in Chris's voice when he assured Melissa that she was going to die. Living in a controlled world, meeting whatever end others wanted for her.

Ruby emerged from Dr. Steve's house. Jake's arm was over her shoulders, his feet dragging, stumbling sleepily.

Melissa's heart surged.

Somehow Jake was with Ruby. And alive.

She watched Ruby struggle to sit Jake in her car, the taillights flicker on as the engine started, as they drove away.

Jake was safe, but Melissa knew she wasn't.

She hurried from the house, kept walking next to a narrow, hilly street, nothing but shadows of trees on either side, scurrying deep into them whenever headlights appeared.

Movement gave Melissa strength, even if she wasn't sure where she was going.

Chapter Twenty-Nine

Lucky

Lucky watched the Vigilante finish tying up Marley in the kitchen.

"I didn't think you were real," Lucky said again. The Vigilante hadn't responded to him the first time.

"Yea, verily." The Vigilante flicked open an automatic baton, opened the door leading to the basement. "Want to see the rest of the house?"

Lucky did, and he stepped over Marley's unconscious body and Spence's corpse to follow her downstairs.

Lucky wondered if the Vigilante—a somehow mythic figure, discussed in hushed tones—was actually Melissa Cruz. The idea was a puzzle piece slipping neatly into place. The Vigilante had crippled the Winterses, and it made sense that the person who had done that had insider information about the crime family. And no one had ever suspected, or would have suspected, that it was a woman. Only her voice, and maybe her height, revealed her sex. A canvas mask with three vertical stripes down the front concealed her head, and she wore a black hooded sweatshirt, dark-gray jeans, and black boots. Gloves covered her hands.

If she suddenly disappeared, Lucky couldn't have proved she'd even existed.

In the basement, the Vigilante knelt next to two bodies, executed sitting next to each other against a far wall. One was Dr. Steve Debko. The other was a young Asian man Lucky didn't recognize. The left half of his head was gone.

"You know these two?" the Vigilante asked Lucky.

"One of them. Steve Debko."

"Who was he?"

"A doctor," Lucky explained. "My guess is he was treating Jake Smith. We were supposed to find him and his girlfriend."

The baton rose, almost imperceptibly.

"We?" the Vigilante asked.

"I worked with the Winterses," Lucky confessed. "I don't anymore."

"Why not?"

"I got tired of seeing things like this," he said. "Doing things like this. That's why Marley was trying to kill me."

The baton lowered. The Vigilante headed back up the stairs. Lucky followed her. He helped the Vigilante carry Marley out into the dark, cold, quiet night, noticing how the Vigilante stepped smoothly while Lucky strained. They reached an old Civic, and she unceremoniously dropped Marley's upper body on the street to open her trunk. Lucky lifted the other man on his own and, with a heave, dumped him inside. Marley was stirring awake, eyelids fluttering, but the Vigilante reached into one of her pockets, pulled out a small case, and removed a syringe. Injected something into Marley's neck. Moments later, he was back asleep.

"Well," the Vigilante told Lucky and slammed the trunk shut. "I'm going to bounce."

She climbed into the front seat of her car. Lucky stared after her, unsure what to do. In one day his secrets had been exposed to his family and the Winterses. The former probably wanted nothing to do with him. The latter, to kill him.

He needed help. And there was only one person who could help him.

Lucky followed the Vigilante.

A couple of times he called Renee and Marybeth, but neither of them answered or returned his messages. He wasn't worried that the Winterses had found them; the cabin was a secret, hidden and remote and barely connected to Lucky.

Renee and Marybeth, he realized, must have run from him. Were too scared to even speak with him.

And so Lucky drove in silence.

The truth about Ruby dejected him. She had either been working for the Winterses this entire time, even after he thought he'd helped her escape. Or perhaps she'd returned to them once Jake was in danger. In either case, she'd betrayed him.

And Ruby was the only person he'd ever known who had left the Winterses.

But, in truth, no one had ever left.

He was so lost in thought that he didn't realize nearly an hour had passed since he'd been following the Vigilante. Lucky had been too distracted to pay attention to where they were driving, but he assumed that, by now, they were somewhere in Virginia.

They drove onto a dirt road, and then turned onto another, narrower road. An old, decrepit barn came into view. Lucky slowed to a stop in front of it, glanced around the empty lot. He had no idea where her car had gone, wondered if she'd driven into the barn. Lucky cursed himself for his distraction, his age, his carelessness, whatever had caused him to lose focus.

His door was suddenly yanked open, and Lucky was pulled from the car. He caught himself on the dirt, palms burning from the impact.

The Vigilante stood above him, her striped mask lit by moonlight. "Why are you following me?"

Lucky lifted himself slowly to his knees. "I need you to tell me how you've fought them. How you've won."

The Vigilante walked to her car, half-hidden behind a pair of trees. She popped the trunk. "You want advice, then give me another hand with this guy."

"I can't work for them anymore," Lucky told her as he helped her pull Marley's bound body out of the trunk. Marley was still sleeping, and Lucky wondered what she'd drugged him with. "The Winterses aren't just going to let me go. They're going to come after me and my family."

"Yea, verily." The Vigilante grunted as they dragged Marley out, dropped his body on the ground. She indicated the barn. "Over there."

Lucky reached under Marley's arms.

"What are you, what . . . ," Marley slurred. "Lucky?"

Lucky ignored him as he and the Vigilante half carried, half dragged Marley to the barn. Marley kept talking, his words becoming clearer, sentences filling out.

"You double-crossed me," Marley said, struggling, but feebly.

The Vigilante pushed open a door leading inside the barn with the back of her foot.

"You're gonna die, Lucky," Marley said.

"He's probably right," the Vigilante agreed. "Also, your name's Lucky? Weird."

The barn was dark, but the Vigilante dumped her half of Marley on the floor and turned on a lantern next to the door. She walked around, lighting lanterns until a dim glow filled the space. This looked like the kind of structure that had been built as part of a larger property, and then that property had been torn down, the barn left for some other purpose that had never been realized, until it was forgotten. It might have been, Lucky considered, a neglected historical landmark, a remnant of the slavery days that left Virginia's land drenched in blood. The floor was dirt, and the wooden walls were full of holes, some chewed by animals, some ripped by weather. The only thing in the barn that wasn't aged or rotted was on the other side of the room, and when Lucky saw it, he knew what the Vigilante intended to do.

"How have you stayed alive this entire time?" he asked her.

The Vigilante grabbed Marley's bound feet, dragged him across the dirt. "The secret's in being the hunter, not the hunted."

"You're going to die too," Marley told her, and then he looked up. Saw what waited.

It was a gallows, three long brown boards. One had been plunged deep into the dirt. Another board protruded from its other end, close to nine or ten feet, the height of a basketball hoop. The third board was supportive, stretched at an angle between the other two. A small metal loop had been fixed to the end of the highest board, and a rope ran through it. A noose hung.

"Lucky, help me."

Lucky ignored Marley. "Are you ever going to stop?" he asked the Vigilante.

"Twelve men from the Winterses were in a room when someone I loved died," she said. "Marley was the last one there. He's the last one I needed to find."

"What do you mean?" Marley asked. He was gaining strength as death neared. "What do you mean?"

She pulled a rope hanging over a low rafter in the middle of the room. The noose rose.

Marley had recovered enough to scream, so she grabbed a wadded ball of paper towels on the floor and stuffed them into his mouth.

"Talk to me," the Vigilante told Lucky. "What's your deal?"

Lucky told her about his early days with the Winterses as he helped fasten the noose around Marley's neck, as she wrapped the other end of the rope around her hand and pulled it, slowly walking away, the rope over her shoulder.

Lucky told her about the anguish he'd suffered recently as Marley's body rose and thrashed.

And Lucky explained how he'd left the Winterses as the Vigilante grunted, and Marley was lifted until his feet couldn't touch the ground. The Vigilante wrapped her end of the rope around a hook on the wall.

"Well, Lucky," she said, rubbing her hands, staring up as Marley's body kicked, "you sound like a real a-hole."

"I just need to make sure my family's safe. Is there anything I can do to help them?"

The Vigilante didn't respond. Just kept staring at Marley. She and Lucky looked up at him like people gazing at stars.

"Do you know who Medusa was?" the Vigilante asked after Marley's feet had finished kicking and his body hung like a pencil mark in the middle of a blank page.

"Greek myth, turned people to stone with a look, Perseus cut off her head? That Medusa?"

"That's the one." The Vigilante walked back to the hook.

"You know," she went on, "all those myths are really just stories about how people are supposed to act or behave. And I always thought Medusa was so interesting. A woman so powerful that just looking at her turned men into stone. That's crazy. I read up on her."

There were no sounds except for the Vigilante's voice.

"Medusa had two siblings, and she was the only one of them who was human, and she was beautiful. After the god Poseidon raped her in the temple of Athena, Athena was so mad about it that she changed Medusa into a monster so hideous that just seeing her turned men to stone."

The Vigilante started to unwrap the rope from the hook.

"And I was thinking about that, why Medusa was turned into something so gross and violent? I think the truth is something different. Medusa froze men when they realized the evil of what they had done.

"Men looked at her, and they couldn't look away. That was their curse."

Marley's body fell to the ground like an invisible hand had thrown it.

"If you want to defeat them, Lucky, then you have to look at my face."

"You mean," Lucky asked, "under the mask?"

The Vigilante knelt, loosened the noose from Marley's neck.

"When I left who I was," she told Lucky, "I lost everything in my life. My family was either killed or abandoned me; my friends are gone. Even though no one knew who I was, I couldn't keep these two sides separate after a while. You have to look at my true face."

Lucky stared as the Vigilante undid the noose. He didn't understand what she meant, but now he knew this couldn't be Melissa Cruz. This was someone with no connection to anyone in the world, and he felt an immense, overwhelming loneliness at that thought.

"I still don't get it," Lucky said.

"You have to look at my true face," the Vigilante said a third time, and she turned toward him. "That's the only way you can be helped."

He just stared at her mask, into the three black stripes, the stains that darkened it like water.

"I think it's too late for you," the Vigilante said.

Chapter Thirty

Jake

Sunrise battered Jake's face.

Pain throbbed through his chest, so much that it hurt to breathe. He didn't feel like he could sit up and didn't try. Instead he gingerly touched the source of the ache, felt the soft cotton of a wrapping and the coarse texture of medicinal tape.

He recognized the arched ceiling above him. Ruby's bedroom. That was enough to tell him where he was.

Enough to tell him, finally, they were safe. Somehow he knew it.

Jake marveled at that. Billions of tiny experiences happen over a lifetime, sights and sounds and smells, yet it's the moments from childhood and adolescence that remain. He couldn't even figure out how he remembered the ceiling. Maybe summer days when Ruby was drunk or asleep, and he would come up here and watch television.

Jake tried to sit up, and his shoulder felt like a saw was chewing through it. He gently rolled to his side, taking deep breaths as the pain subsided to something manageable. Lowered himself to the floor.

Jake stayed still for a few minutes, then lifted himself from his hands and knees, teeth gritting.

I can stand.

He did.

I can walk.

Barely.

Jake crept to the bedroom door, paused at the full-length mirror hanging on its back.

He was shirtless, just that white bandage over his shoulder. He looked even more gaunt than normal—he'd always been naturally thin, but now his stomach was withdrawn, sunken.

He still had on the same jeans he'd been wearing over the last several days, and, Jake realized with embarrassment, at some point he'd peed on himself. He wondered if Ruby still had some of his clothes here, if he could even fit into them anymore.

Jake doddered down the hall, his hand pressed against the wall for balance.

Ruby was sitting at the kitchen table. A coffee cup next to her.

"Hey," Jake said. He was suddenly aware of his breath after days of unbrushed teeth, and grimaced.

Ruby didn't look up.

Jake walked around her and the table, to the chair on the other side, using the kitchen counter for support.

The kitchen had changed. There always used to be a half-empty bottle of something alcoholic on the counter. At first Ruby had hidden the bottles, and then they'd been left out as her drinking had increased. Jake used to sip from them when he was ten or eleven or twelve, shyly and secretly, just tasting the brown liquid. He didn't enjoy the taste or the uneven feeling afterward, but he did like the way his face contorted, like eating a sour candy. Not something you tasted because it felt good, but because it didn't.

Those bottles were gone now. Jake assumed Ruby had hidden them, hoping to present some sort of dignified appearance to him and Melissa. Not that Ruby had ever cared what people thought of her, but Jake could sense a change in her. It was in the house. The sign above one of the windows in the kitchen that read, "He hath blessed this home." The pictures he'd passed in the hall from the bedroom to the kitchen, colored illustrations, six on each side, depicting Jesus as he was being led to his own crucifixion. The Bible on her nightstand, a rosary draped over the cover.

Jake couldn't remember a time when Ruby had mentioned religion, but he wasn't surprised she'd found it. She'd always been given to excess, attracted to the idea of surrendering to something greater than herself. The Winterses. Alcohol. God.

Jake pulled out the chair and sat, carefully, his breathing louder as he lowered, a sudden moment of pain nearly causing him to cry.

Ruby's head was down, eyes closed. Her lips were moving, but she wasn't saying anything he could hear. A rosary was in her hands, beads passing through fingers.

She'd aged. A little heavier, her face rounder. Thinner hair.

After a few minutes her lips and hands stopped moving. A cross dangled off the rosary, and Ruby brought it to her lips, kissed it. Opened her eyes.

"You have a rosary in the kitchen and one in the bedroom?" Jake asked. "Why two? Prayer emergencies?"

"I was praying for you."

"Where's Melissa?"

"Not here."

"She went out?"

Something about Ruby's pause made Jake uneasy.

"She left you."

Jake felt a flash of alarm and pain. "What?"

"The Winterses came, and she ran off. You were asleep. Steve had put you under. You didn't wake up when they were there."

The comfort Jake had felt had vanished, his world overturned.

"Steve? The doctor?"

A rosary bead between her fingers, her fingertips pressed against it. "Steve didn't make it."

"Where's Melissa?"

The beads continued. "Not sure. They're looking for her."

"We have to find her!"

"We're far from wherever she is," Ruby told him. "In a different state."

Jake was standing, hands on the table for support, crumbs under his palms, tiny points pressing into his flesh before crumbling.

"You left her?"

"She left you."

"She's in trouble! They could have her!"

Jake couldn't stay still any longer. He had to do something. He gripped the edge of the table, and his legs buckled.

Ruby set the beads on the table, the rosary curled.

"Jake," she said slowly. "I need to tell you something, and it's not going to be easy to hear. You should sit down."

"What?"

"It's about Eric."

"Eric?" The word so faint it seemed like someone else had spoken it, someone far away.

"They killed him."

A demon writhed inside Jake's chest, tried to pull itself through his ribs, through the bullet wound, tear itself free.

"How did . . . how did we . . . ?"

"They showed mercy. I begged for your life, and so they showed mercy. But I have been told that, after we left, they were attacked by an old friend of mine. Lucky Wilson. He was with the Vigilante."

Jake felt like he was swimming under a sheet of ice and searching for air. "Was it Chris?" he asked. "Did Chris kill Eric?"

"It was his men."

There was something in Ruby's voice that Jake remembered, something plainspoken and honest, the same way he remembered the ceiling in her bedroom. The way, when he was a child, she'd calmly tell him at night, "Stay here, I'll be back," and she always was. The tone she took when something needed to be believed.

"I was asleep through . . . through Eric?"

"Like I said, Steve gave you medicine for the pain. I have it here."

"We have to find Melissa. I have to find her. I have to go back. I can't lose her too."

"I think it's too late, Jake," Ruby said.

Jake's breathing worsened, breath coming loud, wheezing. Ruby stood, and her arms were open and around him. He nearly sank to the floor. She held him up.

Chapter Thirty-One

Melissa

The door was open but the chapel was empty. A sign outside listed a 7:00 a.m. service. Melissa didn't wear a watch, and her phone and handbag were in Dr. Steve's basement, but the light from daybreak led her to assume services were close to starting.

Melissa slipped inside. Didn't see anyone watching her as she closed the door.

It had been years since Melissa had been inside a church.

Her mother made her go every Sunday, communions and confessions and Sunday school, standing next to her and singing loudly as Melissa mumbled along. There had always been that distance between the two of them, and Melissa wondered if it affected her relationship with religion, her reluctance a reaction to her mother's urges.

Truthfully Melissa had always felt a calling to church, some compulsion that may have come from all those hours of kneeling in pews, or the surety her mother and the priests and her Sunday school teachers had in their beliefs, or the beauty of the congregation slowly walking forward to receive communion, their heads humble and bowed. The embrace of Jesus, the grateful abandonment of an exhausted life.

She'd always imagined returning to church. But, as Melissa pushed open a door to a restroom, she'd never expected it to be like this.

Melissa locked the door to the bathroom and quickly unfastened and slipped off her shoes, pulled her jeans off her waist, ran water over the knees. No matter how much soap she used, regardless of how briskly she rubbed paper towels against her jeans, Melissa couldn't remove Dr. Steve's and Eric's blood. The stain deepened.

Melissa caught a glance of herself in the mirror and expected to see a haunted figure, lost and frightened, but what she saw surprised her.

Determination.

The surprise reminded her of how she'd felt when she saw Jake's photographs of her. Melissa always saw herself differently than others did. She knew she was attractive, but when Melissa looked at herself, she spent more time obsessing about what didn't work. And it tied into an overall feeling, somewhere deep inside her soul, that she simply wasn't good enough.

Her mom had died disappointed.

With Chris, she'd always been secondary to him and his family.

Even with Jake, she was less important than his photography.

But seeing herself now, the resolve . . . her own image gave her strength.

Melissa put on her jeans and left the restroom, her pants legs wet, but at least the dark splotches didn't look like blood anymore. She passed the entrance to the chapel, couldn't help peeking inside. The nave had been decorated for the holidays. Green wreaths hung from red ribbons over stained glass windows, poinsettias sprawled around the base of a Christmas tree. A priest thumbed through an oversize gilt-edged Bible.

He looked up, smiled.

"About a half hour," he told her.

Melissa kept walking, into an area marked "PRIVATE," past an unmanned desk. She entered a room with a large table and an orange cooler and pamphlets and plastic cups. There were three doors here, one open, the name "Father Bob Price" on the outside. Melissa searched Bob Price's desk until she found what she was looking for.

Wallet, keys, phone.

She left the wallet.

There was only one car in the parking lot. Melissa assumed it belonged to the priest.

She climbed inside, turned on the engine, plugged in his phone.

Melissa felt something she'd never felt before guiding her, almost like a gentle but insistent hand on her back, as she stole the priest's car and pulled out of the parking lot. She knew exactly what she needed to do.

Chapter Thirty-Two

Lucky

"Renee?"

"Hello, Lucky."

Lucky slowed. He'd been driving ten miles above the speed limit. "Is Marybeth with you?"

"She is." Renee's voice was low. "She showed up a few minutes after you left."

"Did you . . . did you tell her about me?"

"She didn't take it well."

"I understand." Lucky stared out the windshield, at the brown weeds on either side of the road and a dead deer on its side, white underfur shining. "Can I talk to her?"

"No." Firmly, and then, "She's not ready."

"Okay," Lucky said and added meekly, "Renee, I'm really sorry. We shouldn't keep secrets. I should have told you earlier that I kill people for money."

"You're insane."

"I'm not," he insisted. "I promise."

"I don't think you know that you are."

Lucky rubbed his right eye with one hand, glanced at the GPS. He was only a few minutes away from the cabin.

"I'm not crazy," he said.

"How much danger are we in?" Renee asked. "And don't lie. Not anymore."

"You're not in danger at all," Lucky lied. "It's me they're after. I thought I could reconcile things, but I can't."

"What does that mean?"

He pulled over to the side of the road. "It means they're going to try to kill me."

"Why don't you give them what they want?" Renee asked desperately. "You said you're protecting someone. Give her up!"

"That won't work anymore." Lucky's knife brushed against his leg as he walked up the dirt road toward the cabin, past brown and bare trees, some white, as if they'd been skinned.

"How many people has it been?"

"I can't tell you that."

"You said no more secrets."

"No, I know, it's because . . ."

Lucky let the sentence wither away.

He didn't know the number.

There were the men in that village. And the two people he'd killed although he hadn't been hired to do so—the pedophile who had been fired from Marybeth's school, the man who'd attacked him after a light traffic accident.

And then there were the people he'd been hired to kill, and that number was at twenty. Or it had been, a long time ago, when he'd still kept count.

And now the military man with Marley, but he fell into the self-defense category. And it would be important, Lucky felt, to make sure that Renee knew the difference between the two categories.

What about the couple the other night that he'd tied up and interrogated? Had he killed them?

Lucky couldn't remember.

He'd been so distracted by the possibility of Renee having an affair, and then Marybeth's involvement with William McKenna, and then . . .

"Lucky?"

Renee's voice. He'd almost forgotten she was on the phone.

"I'm here."

"You understand, right?" Renee asked, and Lucky had no idea what she was talking about. He hadn't even realized she was still speaking.

"I do," he agreed blindly.

"Really?" Renee seemed surprised at that. "You're going to let us go?"

"Wait, what?"

Lucky saw the cabin through trees, the late dawn lighting it.

Marybeth's car wasn't out front.

"Renee," Lucky said, crouching. "Did you and Marybeth leave?"

"Yes." A pause. She was finding defiance. "I called the police."

"You did?"

"What did you expect?"

"What did the cops say?" Lucky stared at the cabin through the trees, stood to get a better view. It looked quiet but not lifeless. Lucky couldn't figure out why.

Renee's voice faltered. "The police didn't believe me. They said a lot of people have called claiming they work for the Winterses. Like when there's a serial killer and people call to confess it's them."

Were there tire tracks in the cabin's dirt driveway?

"Lucky?" Renee asked.

Despite his name, Lucky had never had a specific moment where luck played a significant role in his life. Never a time when it seemed like fortune had slipped into his life and reshaped it. The winning lottery ticket, the chance meeting.

Until now.

Lucky accidentally dropped his phone and bent to pick it up.

As he did, a knife sliced the air where his head had been and plunged into a tree.

Lucky turned, phone in hand. Adriana Rusu stood behind him.

At least, he thought it was Adriana. Maybe she was Bianca.

"Lucky?" Renee was asking. "Lucky?"

He hung up.

"How did you know I was behind you?" Adriana asked.

"Turns out it was just—"

Lucky didn't bother finishing the sentence because Adriana reached for the gun on her hip. He grabbed her around the waist, and they fell together in a heap, the smaller, lighter woman underneath him. She cried out, still struggling to free the gun, but he pinned her arms at her side.

"We don't have to do this," he said.

Adriana didn't respond, just kept struggling.

Lucky pulled back a little, still trapping her arms, looked her in the face. "Adriana," he said. "I want out."

They paused in their struggle, gazed at each other, their faces inches apart.

This was the closest, Lucky realized, that he'd been to a different woman's face in years. He felt as if his eyes had been absorbed in hers, wounded and angry and scared. The emotions he saw revealed his own, the shared intimacy from their fight.

And then Adriana headbutted him in the mouth.

Lucky's hold relaxed. Adriana pushed him off and yanked her gun free from its holster.

Lucky recovered in time to grab it. For as many people as Lucky had killed, he couldn't recall actually ever being in a fight. And this was one he could well lose. Adriana was strong, fast, skilled.

And her sister was probably somewhere out here.

Lucky felt the kind of dread a child feels when he's alone and dark is coming. It took all his strength, accompanied by a cry he hadn't expected, but he managed to pull the gun loose. It sailed somewhere into the bushes.

"We don't . . . need . . . to do this," Lucky told her, dismayed that he was wheezing.

He had a sudden sense of how he looked to this twentysomething woman as she lightly bounced in front of him, her ponytail flapping to each shoulder, fists ready in front of her face. Older, out of shape, struggling to breathe.

"You can walk away," he offered, hoping she'd accept.

She kicked him in the stomach.

The next thing he knew, Lucky was on his knees, trying to breathe in air. He looked up just in time for Adriana to knee him on one side of the head. He listed to the left, and she hit him with her other knee.

Lucky shakily held up his hands in front of his chest to protect himself.

It was like trying to put out a fire with a cup of water.

Her boot hit him flush in the nose, and he fell, hard enough to hear the wet sound of the back of his head smacking the ground.

Something exploded in his ribs, twice. Two quick kicks into his side that turned him over.

Adriana's arm wrapped around his neck.

She'd climbed on his back, Lucky blearily realized, as if he was a web and she, the spider. Adriana's legs wrapped around his waist, her heels pressed into his thighs. That arm around his throat squeezed tighter.

Air trickled in and then slowly stopped, like a memory he was forgetting.

Lucky's elbows collapsed, and he lay on the dirt, distantly aware he was dying. One hand reached up, searching for her face, a cheek to punch or an eye to poke, but her face was turned away, protected. Lucky tried to pull himself forward with the other hand, tried to find the phone, anything that could help.

He found her gun.

Lucky didn't even attempt to aim. He just grabbed the gun and twisted his hand and pointed it above himself and squeezed the trigger, and it didn't matter, Lucky thought, if he hit his own skull. Death was coming regardless.

The arm around his throat fell away. Lucky gasped in air, like a dying plant soaks up rain.

He couldn't move for a few moments, even though he heard Adriana behind him, scrabbling. He slowly rolled over and saw her feet kicking.

Lucky rose and coughed, clutching her gun.

Adriana lay before him, as if floating on her back in a dark lake of blood.

"Where's Bianca?" he asked, his words a creaking door.

It sounded like Adriana was trying to respond, but she couldn't. Or maybe she was just trying to breathe. Lucky couldn't tell.

But he knew, suddenly, Bianca wasn't here. If she had been, then she wouldn't have let Adriana fight alone.

And he wouldn't be alive.

Daylight was beginning to peer farther through the trees. An unseen bird chatted. Adriana gasped wet breaths.

Lucky stepped into the blood and reached into her pocket. Pulled out her phone. A message on her locked screen.

B: With them, come after.

Lucky knew who Bianca meant by *them*.

Somehow the twins had found this cabin. Maybe they'd followed him when he'd driven Renee. Maybe there was a tracker on his car. Maybe this cabin wasn't as much of a secret as he'd hoped. But when his wife and daughter had left, Bianca had followed them. Adriana had stayed behind, waiting in case he returned.

He looked down at Adriana, at her stark white face. She was dying, but Lucky didn't have time to wait for death.

This was the feeling Lucky had forgotten, the assuredness of a path, the sense that he was doing what must be done. There was no question of good or evil, only necessity.

He aimed the gun at Adriana's head. Behind him a dead sun rose in the winter morning.

CHAPTER THIRTY-THREE

JAKE

And this was where Eric's body was going to lie, in the shadow of Ruby's house. Ruby had told Jake that the Winterses were going to bring Eric here tomorrow, bury him in her backyard. A shovel was plunged into the dirt, waiting.

To Jake there was something unbearably cruel that he'd been asleep when Eric had been murdered. His closest friend dying just a few feet away. Jake knew he couldn't have stopped it, but he'd been robbed of the chance. Helpless to do anything.

Another unspoken betrayal of his best friend.

"Are you cold?"

Jake didn't turn toward her voice.

"We don't have to put him here," Ruby went on. "We can take him to a cemetery."

Put him here.

Jake stared at the dirt, felt Ruby behind him. She draped something over his shoulders.

"It's your old jacket," Ruby told him. "I can't believe all these old clothes fit. Are you eating enough?"

"Tell me what happened," he said. "Tell me what happened when Eric . . ."

"No," Ruby replied firmly. "You don't want to know that. You don't want to see that whole picture. There's nothing there that will help you."

The pain in his shoulder, which had been softened by painkillers, ached. "That doesn't feel honest."

"I barely knew Eric or that girl, but I don't think either of them would want you to carry their wounds. Trust in healing; it comes from something greater than us. For He is the Lord, who heals us."

Jake jammed his hands into his jeans' pockets. "When'd you get religious?"

"When I stopped drinking. He guided me out. I followed a path, lit by—"

"So how come you never tried to find me?"

A beat passed.

"You're blaming me," Ruby said, "because you're sad right now, and you feel abandoned. Remember, the Lord guides us—"

"What did you give up for me?"

Ruby didn't answer.

"I gave up my childhood for you," Jake said heatedly. "Those nights you left? I should have been sleeping in my bed, knowing you were there for me. All those times when I was in middle school or high school and had to take care of myself because you were too drunk. And then when I found out what you did to Eric's mom—"

"I couldn't let her go to the police," Ruby interrupted him, but calmly. "She would have put all of us in danger. And whatever she confessed wouldn't have mattered, for the Winterses would have killed us all."

Jake kept talking as if Ruby hadn't spoken. "And I kept it a secret from him. Knowing you arranged that hit-and-run with the Winterses. I kept that to myself!"

"And what would he have done? What choice did you have?"

Jake didn't answer.

"All of us would be dead," Ruby said decisively. "A foolish man's heart engages in folly. I did it to keep you alive, and I'd do so again."

"Hi, Ruby," Melissa said.

Jake watched Ruby tense, shock cross her face. Her small eyes widening.

Jake suddenly remembered how sharp the blue in Ruby's eyes was. How he'd once longed to capture it.

He'd forgotten that. The impulse that initially led him to photography.

Ruby turned toward Melissa.

"You escaped."

Melissa didn't respond, and Jake saw that change in her, the difference he'd noticed in her voice when she'd called him earlier that day, the way Melissa had walked toward him when he'd met her an hour ago down the road from the house, the strength in her shoulders and arms when he'd held her.

"How . . . how did you get here?" Ruby asked. "Who did you tell, who drove you? Do the Winterses know?"

"I drove myself," Melissa said. "Stole a car and a phone from a priest."

"Wait, what?" Jake asked.

"And I told Jake what you did."

Ruby took a step back, bumped into the upright shovel. "She's deceiving you!"

"Don't lie, Ruby," Jake said tiredly. "Not anymore."

"I didn't want Eric to die! I didn't know he was going to be there! Just her!"

"Jesus," Melissa said.

Ruby was acting like a frightened animal between Melissa and Jake, frantic for escape.

"You told me you left the Winterses," Jake said. "You said after you told them about Eric's mom, you left them."

"I did!" Ruby exclaimed. "But I had to return. I had to bring the Word. The world will be overcome with weeds and poison, unless the scythe is told where to slice. I had to help them find the righteous path."

"What are you even saying?" Melissa asked.

Ruby looked wildly at her. "Before the Lord, the whore is confused."

Melissa sighed.

"I rid the world of its evil!"

"You're a monster," Jake told Ruby. He felt like he'd been asleep for almost his entire life, but now he'd been shaken awake.

"I'm not! Everything I did was justified! Every time someone suffered, it was to save you." Ruby's voice lowered; she spoke faster. "I did what I had to. I committed sin, imperiled my soul, all for you. I'd do so again."

"None of this was for me," Jake replied flatly. "I barely had a mother or a home, and I've had this sense for so long, this feeling like, like, I wasn't worth anything. If I wasn't worth a mother who could stop drinking for me . . . who could find the same strength she found in alcohol and criminals and now, I guess, God or something else, in me. But you never did, or you never could, and I took that out on myself. Sometimes I think that's why I like photography so much, so I can see the world the way I want to see it. The way it should be."

"I have always loved you!" Ruby declared.

"If you loved me, Eric would be alive. If you loved anyone, his mother would still be alive. You can't love. You can only serve."

Ruby inhaled sharply.

Jake was surprised that his body was trembling.

"But I know what to do now," Jake said, and he felt poison filling his words. "I'm going to make all of you pay. You and the Winterses. You're still part of them."

"They'll kill you," Ruby replied darkly. "You think your anger is going to guide you? It's going to lead you to death. Anger greets us in the desert, anger and desperation and fear. And you're too soft to walk through the desert, Jake. I had to be strong for both of us. Because I love you."

"Jake," Melissa said.

He hadn't realized that he was advancing on Ruby.

Jake turned away from her. Walked away, Melissa next to him.

"You won't survive in the desert!" Ruby called, her voice an admonishment. "You won't survive without me! You will succumb!"

Chapter Thirty-Four

Lucky

Lucky drove faster than normal, even though he couldn't risk getting pulled over, not with the small armory of weapons sliding around in his trunk. The AR-7. The shotgun from Spence. Adriana's Beretta.

He'd left her body in the woods. There was no time to hide her from anyone who might walk by, no time to erase her existence. Or his involvement.

He called Renee again, let the phone ring until her voice mail came on.

Lucky didn't even know where he was driving, had no idea where Renee and Marybeth would run. But his mission was clear.

He had to keep them safe.

His life had been so complicated, but now it was simple, even exhilarating, in the way sudden truths often are. This was how he was best, Lucky knew. Uncomplicated and assured. Duty bound with a clear objective. He'd been lost in a fog, but the fog had lifted.

A sign for the interstate was ahead. Lucky had a decision to make. He figured Renee had taken Marybeth either to her family in Philadelphia or hidden somewhere else in Virginia. Maybe with friends.

He chose Virginia, decided to drive to his house. There was no chance Renee and Marybeth would return there, but someone from the Winterses might. Someone he could question.

His phone buzzed.

Lucky almost swerved off the road in his haste to answer. "Renee?"

"This is Jake."

"Jake?" Lucky had no idea who was calling, wondered if it was some sort of telemarketer. He glanced at his phone, didn't recognize the number.

"With Ruby," Jake added.

"Ruby's . . . son?"

"I got your number from her phone. She told me you know who the Vigilante is. Can you help me find him?"

It took Lucky a moment to respond. "The Vigilante is a her."

"I need to find her," Jake went on. "I heard that you saw what happened in the basement. They killed my . . . they killed Eric. They tried to kill Melissa."

"The Vigilante won't help you," Lucky said. "That's what you want, right? Help?"

"Yes."

"What did your mother say?"

"We had, we had a falling out."

So Jake knew, Lucky realized. Ruby's son knew she'd turned on Melissa. And now he was striking out alone, in that impetuous rebelliousness of youth. The kind that parents know their children will eventually experience, and they can only hope their children avoid the ramifications of their most reckless actions.

"Can you help me?" Jake asked. "I just need to know where the Vigilante is."

Lucky pondered it. On one hand, despite Ruby's betrayal and her continued employment with the Winterses, he didn't want to encourage her son further down this path. Jake was essentially telling Lucky that he wanted to play Russian roulette and asking where he could buy bullets.

Then again Lucky could hear the determination in Jake's voice. And not just determination, but anguish. Grief that needed to be sated, otherwise it would never be resolved. Lucky had heard this before, and he knew there was only one recourse, one conclusion to reach.

Death.

Better that the boy, Lucky thought, talk with the only person who could help. Maybe the only person who could convince him to abandon this plan.

"Lucky?"

"Here's what you need to know," Lucky began.

After he hung up with Jake, Lucky bit his thumb knuckle, wondered how to keep his own family safe. At this point, there was nothing he could offer the Winterses in exchange for their lives. Marley and Adriana were dead. There was no trade the Winterses would find fair.

But even if Lucky's family would never be safe here, there was a chance they could be safe somewhere else. Lucky didn't know where that would be, and he wasn't entirely sure about the mechanics of vanishing, but it was possible. It might mean a life of constantly being on guard, of assuming new identities, perhaps moving to some small remote town in Canada or Alaska, maybe an idyllic community where violence was a forgotten concept and the entire town agreed on everything and well-being for all.

A living Christmas Village.

He was nearing his neighborhood when Lucky called Renee again.

This time she answered.

"Renee! Where are you? Are you okay?"

"We're okay." Still with that monotone, as if the emotion had been wrung from her soul.

"Where are you and Marybeth?"

"We came back to the house."

Lucky almost dropped the phone. *"The house! Our house!"*

"Why are you shouting?"

"You went back to our house!"

"Please stop shouting."

Lucky was mashing the phone against his ear. He spoke low as he approached his neighborhood, grateful that he'd guessed correctly. "Renee, listen to me."

She was silent, and Lucky realized how he sounded, his voice low and dangerous, the kind of voice that trickles into nightmares.

He took a breath.

"These are dangerous people looking for us. We can't go to the cops, but I can keep us safe. I promise you. I can keep us safe. But you have to listen to me."

"I didn't know where to go," Renee said. "I thought about taking Marybeth to stay with my family, but I didn't want to put them in danger. I couldn't go to any friends. I don't know where to go."

Lucky should have anticipated this. He had tracked people running from the Winterses, and often they hid in their homes.

In a sea of sharks, often people would rather hang on to wreckage rather than risk swimming to an unknown shore.

"Someone's outside," Renee said quietly, and Lucky suddenly felt like he was listening to someone other than his wife, a lifeless narrator, the resignation people find after fear.

"I keep seeing her through the window. I don't know if she's going to come in or if she's waiting for us to come out. But I keep seeing her in different places, like I'm imagining her."

He'd never heard Renee like this before. "Where's Marybeth?"

"Upstairs. If I give them me, they'll let her go."

"No, they won't. They will kill you both. I'm almost there!"

Lucky swerved onto the street parallel to his own, passing basketball hoops on driveways and trash containers on curbs. A neighbor walking a dog glanced curiously. Lucky screeched to a halt, hopped out of the car. Grabbed Spence's shotgun from the trunk.

"Okay, Renee," he said, speaking into his phone as he jogged, trying to keep his voice calm. "I'm here. I need you to open the door. Just a little. Don't show yourself. Just open the door halfway."

"But she'll come in."

"You have to trust me. Wait one minute and open the door. Just halfway and *do not show yourself.*"

Between two houses, and across the street from his own, Lucky set the shotgun down. Held Adriana's phone close to his mouth and, to avoid figuring out how to unlock her phone, whispered to Siri to text Bianca a short message:

come in

Lucky felt someone watching him, wasn't sure who it was. There were windows everywhere, windows above and behind him and across the street. Thousands of eyes were on him, examining Lucky, waiting for his next move.

The front door opened.

A figure emerged from a gap between houses. Walked quickly, purposefully, toward Lucky's home.

He picked up the shotgun.

Lucky felt his neighbors watching him as he strode behind Bianca, the shotgun pressed into his shoulder. As he aimed it at her narrow back.

Chapter Thirty-Five

Melissa

"You're not DoorDash."

Melissa and Jake had walked into the center of the empty barn, but Melissa had known it wasn't empty. It *looked* empty—a tall time-beaten structure, dirt floor, wooden walls with holes torn through. But Melissa could sense something else, like a song you're listening to with nothing but instruments, and you somehow know a vocalist is about to sing.

The Vigilante stood behind them, in the doorway they'd just walked through, wearing a canvas mask with three stripes down the front, gray jeans, black hoodie, boots, and gloves. She loosely held an extended baton in her right hand.

"I wasn't sure you'd be here," Jake said.

"I'm always here. Why are you here, Jake?"

The way the Vigilante said his name was disconcerting to Melissa, but Jake didn't seem to notice. "Because it was Ruby," he told her. "She's the one who got Eric killed. And almost Melissa."

The Vigilante cocked her head. "Who's Ruby?"

"My, my mom."

"And Melissa?"

Melissa raised her hand.

"And Eric?" The Vigilante looked back and forth at Jake and Melissa. "Oh, wait, was he the guy with half a . . . the guy next to the doc? Okay, I'm all caught up. Wait! Your mom set up your girlfriend? Amigo, I thought my family had issues."

"She's not my family."

"Sure she is. Family is always family."

Melissa noticed Jake shaking, even if it was almost imperceptible. He had told her he was physically recovering, but she'd driven here while he sat in the passenger seat, his hand occasionally pressed to the bandage, hunched over and grimacing as the priest's car lurched over dirt roads.

"I can't let them walk away," Jake said. "Even her."

"So what do you want?" the Vigilante asked. "To kill your own mom? That's weird, Jake. And, I promise you, it isn't going to fix a thing."

Melissa noticed discolored dark patches on the mask, like the bloodstains on her jeans.

She had never suspected that the Vigilante was a real person, much less a woman. Chris had told her the rumors after his uncle's murder, Victor Winters a larger-than-life figure, nearly a revered myth, maybe a demigod the way Chris and the other men described him. Happy to kill when necessary, so powerful and relentless that death itself feared coming to his door. In some ways, the notion of a secret masked vigilante taking down Victor had made sense, a rumor the only thing capable of ending a rumor, the idea inciting dread and worry. But those were just stories. Everyone knew it was just a rival gang, a secretive police task force, maybe the government.

But now the Vigilante was real, and something about that terrified Melissa. It allowed for the sudden belief in other myths, disproved falsehoods. A child seeing a claw emerge from under her bed.

"What I want is—" Jake started.

The Vigilante abruptly turned and left. It happened so suddenly that Jake and Melissa were taken aback, glanced at each other in surprise.

"I don't think we should be here," Melissa told him. "There's something wrong."

Jake didn't reply. He just walked after the Vigilante, toward the front door. The response was rude, but Melissa accepted it. She could almost feel Jake's pain and anguish reverberating, a rushing wave that needed somewhere to crash.

Or was she just making allowances for another man in her life to pursue evil?

She followed Jake outside and around to the back of the barn, to a field of dirt and weeds.

The Vigilante was peering into a large white plastic bucket placed against the building. Others were lined up next to it. A shovel lay in front of them.

"What do you use this place for?" Jake asked.

The Vigilante ignored him. "If you're going to stay, grab a bucket."

"Why?" Melissa asked.

The Vigilante was fastening down a lid. "It's a long story, but I've buried a bunch of the Winterses' men out here in shallow graves. And now I need to dig them up and burn their bodies."

"What?" Melissa asked.

"Got to burn up some bad guys," the Vigilante said. "Too many people know about this place. Give me a hand?"

"I'm not . . . ," Melissa said, and she and Jake glanced at each other. She was relieved that he seemed as startled as she was. "I'm not going to dig up and set fire to dead people?"

But Jake followed the Vigilante, and Melissa followed him, out to the field as the Vigilante carried the sealed bucket in one hand, a shovel in the other. She stopped at a small pile of three stones.

Jake saw other piles scattered around the field.

"The guy buried here is missing a nose," the Vigilante said. "Don't ask."

Her shovel plunged into the dirt.

"You're not well," Jake said faintly.

The Vigilante ignored him. "Good thing the dirt isn't packed. It's a lot easier to move than I thought."

"This, this isn't what people do," he went on, still speaking softly.

"It's what people did, are doing, and will always do."

"How can you . . ."

The Vigilante stopped digging, rested for a moment. "Do you know who these men were? Do you know what trafficking is?"

"I'm sorry, I just . . ." Jake touched his chest.

The Vigilante turned toward Melissa. "You're Latina, right?"

"Yeah, from Panama."

"No joke? Me too! I thought I was the only one!"

"You're Panamanian?"

"Yea, verily," the Vigilante confirmed. "I can't imagine we have anything else in common whatsoever . . . but that's nice. You hablo?"

"I do," Melissa said although she knew her Spanish was rusty. "Do you?"

"Not anymore," the Vigilante replied regretfully. "Anyway, I really do need to burn up these bodies."

"Why did you do all this?" Jake asked.

"Because of what those men did to me." The Vigilante spoke easily, unbothered. "But I've reached the end."

"So you're done now?" Jake asked. "You got your revenge, and it's over?"

"Sí. That's for you, Melissa. Español."

"But you're the only one who was able to do anything," Jake said. "The cops never got to them until you came along. No one even knew about the Winterses. And you exposed them and took them down, and now they're finally reeling. And you're just going to walk away?"

"You trying to get me to keep killing?"

"I'm trying to get you to help me!"

"Help you with what?" The Vigilante didn't wait for him to answer, straightened and stretched her back. "Don't look down."

Melissa glanced into the hole and quickly turned away. Closed her eyes.

She heard the Vigilante unfasten the plastic lid of the bucket.

Smelled the sharp scent of gasoline.

Liquid splashing down.

Three scrapes of a match before it lit.

Heat, the way it both pulls and repels.

And then Melissa smelled something awful and heard the wet sound of fire consuming, and she opened her eyes.

Jake was following the Vigilante to the next marker.

"Why are you following me?" the Vigilante asked, and there was a tiredness to her tone. "I told you I'm done with all this. If you need help, then you've come to the wrong person."

"You can't let evil men walk away," Jake argued.

For a moment, Melissa realized that he sounded exactly like his mother.

"I was running at those men," the Vigilante said, tight and direct, the lightness left. "And they caught me, and because of me, my sister died. They shot her in front of me. That was my fault, and killing the men who killed her still made it my fault. There's no peace, there's no place to return to. There's nothing to return to.

"My sister's name was Melinda. She was a former social worker who dedicated her life to helping people, to doing things the right way, as frustrating and terrible and slow as the right way always is. She was living with a person who loved her—super-boring guy, but he loved her, so whatever—and she was entering a new phase in her life, and she was kind of funny and lovely, and she died because she followed me. She died because she came back for me."

Melissa had assumed those faint dark stains in the mask were from blood.

Maybe they were tears.

"You might not die," the Vigilante went on. "You might actually kill the person who killed your friend. You don't look like much of a fighter, but maybe you'll get lucky and accidentally give him mumps or something. Fun fact: the Wintereseeses—sorry, I never figured out the plural form of their name—are terrible at keeping up with their vaccines. I know, I do my research."

Her dialogue, Melissa noted, had taken a strange trip, from the acidity of emotion to someplace unpredictable.

"But if you do go after revenge," the Vigilante concluded. "You'll lose more than you realize. There's no change without loss."

Melissa watched Jake. He'd been quiet this entire time, not even exhibiting the anxiousness of waiting to speak.

When he did reply, it was slow, measured.

"I can't let them just get away," Jake said.

"And what do you want for them?" the Vigilante asked. "Death?"

"I don't know," Jake said.

Throughout the conversation between the Vigilante and Jake, Melissa had almost forgotten where she was. But now she felt the heat behind her from the burning body in that hole, the flames surging, as if they were trying to escape but were being pulled back.

"Oh Jake," the Vigilante told him. "They're going to kill you."

◆ ◆ ◆

"She's right," Melissa said.

Jake sat in the passenger seat, sullenly staring out the window. Strange how, ever since she'd seen him with Ruby, something about him seemed younger. There had always been a youthful motivation in Jake, something childlike about his infatuation with her and the pursuit of photography, but there was an excitement and charm to that. This was something different. Adolescent and angry.

He didn't respond.

"She was right," Melissa said again, "and so was Ruby. You're not a killer, and because you're not, they'll murder you."

"That's because that's all Ruby and that vigilante know. They don't know any other way but death."

"Do you?"

"I'm trying to find it."

"I remember what Chris became," Melissa told him. "It's like he went into war or something, and there was a moment where he could have come back, but he didn't. He went deeper, and then he became something else. He grew into something else."

"They shot me," Jake said with a quiet intensity. "They killed Eric. They hunted you and me like dogs."

"I know."

"They won't let you go, and all you want to do is run."

"I want to live. With you."

Jake's hand had found his shoulder. "Running's not living."

They didn't speak for the rest of the drive.

CHAPTER THIRTY-SIX

LUCKY

"Marybeth?" Lucky shouted once the ringing in his ears from the shotgun had subsided. "Renee?"

His wife and daughter peered down from the top of the stairs as he hurried into the foyer, Bianca's body lying behind him.

Marybeth took a tentative step down. Renee pulled her back, wrapped her arms around her. Marybeth didn't resist.

"Was that an explosion?" Renee asked.

Something about that was astonishing to Lucky. Renee had never heard a gunshot.

"We have to go," Lucky said. "More will be here soon."

They didn't move.

"They'll find you if you stay here."

The women looked at each other uncertainly but descended the staircase.

"Dad," Marybeth said admiringly, when she saw the dead assassin in the doorway. "You're like Rambo!"

Lucky blinked.

Marybeth was screaming and trying to run back up the stairs, and Renee was holding her. Lucky slung the rifle over his shoulder, helped Renee lead their daughter toward the back door.

"Oh my God," Marybeth was saying over and over.

Outside, in their backyard, the neighborhood was deathly quiet. A dog had been barking insistently after the report from the rifle but now stopped. Lucky could imagine the fear from the dog's owners, the worry about attracting violence to their own doors.

His wife and daughter held hands as Lucky crept forward, the shotgun heavy. Bianca had probably been here by herself, but he wasn't taking any chances.

He opened the Jeep's door for his wife and daughter, glanced around as they climbed in. A window shade across the street shifted. Lucky knew he was being watched, probably recorded.

He walked back to the driver's seat.

"I think we should talk about what just happened," Lucky said and started the engine. "As a family."

Marybeth had been crying silently, and now it was as if she had decided to stop holding back the sound. She cried loudly and helplessly.

He glanced into the rearview mirror and met Renee's eyes. She stared back at him.

There was a calmness in Renee that Lucky found surprising. He marveled at his wife's strength, Renee's resilience, despite everything she knew being upended, the murdered woman in the entryway of a home, her chest blown out of her body. It would have been fine for her to have a complete collapse—Lucky had seen it happen to others.

Instead, Renee was detached, rubbing their daughter's shoulder, softly saying words he couldn't quite hear.

"Where are we going?" Marybeth asked. "What are we going to do?"

"Well," Lucky said. He didn't see any cars trailing them. Didn't even hear police sirens although, after the shotgun's blast, he assumed most of his neighbors had called 911. "I have a few ideas. I think it's best that the two of you hide somewhere. And then—"

"Did you really shoot that woman?" Marybeth asked.

It was a curious question to Lucky. It meant that she was resistant to the truth. Marybeth still hoped there was an answer she hadn't yet realized.

"I had to," Lucky said. He spoke slowly, the way he'd explained to his tear-streaked daughter, when she was just four or five, that her pet fish, Cheetoh, had died. "Listen, honey, that woman was going to murder you and your mother. And me. She was not a very nice person."

"Jesus, why are you talking to me like I'm a toddler?" Marybeth asked.

"Language," Renee warned her.

"Dad just shot someone in the back, and you're telling me to watch my fucking language?"

"Wow," Lucky said. "That's unnecessary."

"I agree," Renee said, and Lucky's spirits were buoyed by her support.

"I don't understand," Marybeth moaned. "I don't understand anything."

"Do you guys want to listen to music?" Lucky offered. "Maybe that would help."

"What do you have in mind?" Renee asked back.

"Stop the car!" Marybeth suddenly screamed, and she wouldn't stop screaming. "Stop the car! Stop the car! Stop the car!"

Lucky ignored her, like he had when she was a baby and would cry at night in her crib; he'd hated doing that, but Renee had insisted. Now he turned on the radio, spun the volume wheel to the maximum. He always listened to a station that played old pop love songs, and Air Supply's "Almost Paradise" filled the car.

Tears came to his eyes as his daughter wrestled to open the door, despite the speed at which they were driving. Renee did her best to hold her back as Marybeth cried and struggled.

"It's going to be okay," Renee was saying as Air Supply's monotonous drums reverberated, as the duet soared. "Mommy and Daddy will take care of you."

Lucky glanced approvingly at his wife in the rearview mirror, but he couldn't shake the feeling that something seemed off. This was so close to what he'd wanted—complete exposure, followed by vulnerability, and then acceptance. Renee understood everything, and he was certain Marybeth would come around, but Lucky felt like seeing them through the rearview mirror was giving him a distorted view. He watched Renee wrap her arms around their daughter's body to stop her from lunging to the door, Marybeth's expression contorted and her hair wild.

"Honey," Lucky advised his wife, "you should wrap your legs around her waist."

Neither of the women heard him as they struggled.

A shrieking warning from his car's sensory system. Lucky looked forward and saw the back of a semi looming in front of them.

He slammed on the brakes, and his Jeep swerved into the next lane, almost colliding with the rear of the semi. Another car's horn beeped, and its tires screeched as it narrowly missed them. Lucky fought to regain control, steadied the vehicle.

"Everyone okay?" he asked.

Renee had been thrown on top of Marybeth. She sat up, and Marybeth did the same, shakily. Renee seemed fine, but Marybeth had a bloody nose. She touched the blood and looked at her finger.

"Honey, your father asked if you're okay," Renee said.

Their daughter nodded. Didn't say anything else.

The near accident seemed to have mollified everyone. Marybeth looked out the window, quietly crying. Renee opened her handbag and gave her a Kleenex. Marybeth took it without a word, held it to her nose.

Renee sat with her hands in her lap, her breathing slowing after the exertion.

Another horn. Lucky realized again that he was focused on his family rather than the road.

"Drive carefully, honey," Renee told him. He felt her hand on his shoulder, her warm, steady hand.

Chapter Thirty-Seven

Jake

Jake rang the doorbell of the house where Melissa had lived with Chris, listened to the metallic chime.

A man opened the door. Squints for eyes, pockmarked cheeks.

"I'm here to see Chris," Jake said.

The man regarded Jake.

"I'm Jake Smith, and he—"

"We know who you are."

The door opened farther, revealing another man. They let Jake in, checked him for weapons, ran their hands down his arms and legs and back and stomach, pulled his wallet and keys out of his pockets, tapped his crotch.

Straight ahead was a sun-filled kitchen and a doorway leading to a shadowed dining room. Jake remembered the two staircases past the door, awkwardly close to it, one leading up to a hallway with two bedrooms where he and Melissa had spent an entire weekend.

Jake wondered if she had truly left him.

"I'm going to clear us," Jake had told her as they sat in the stolen car, parked behind a gas station hours earlier. "There won't be more killing. I know what to do."

"It's not going to work," Melissa said softly but resolutely. "When it involves the Winterses, the story only ends one way."

"What are we supposed to do?" Jake asked, anger flowing into his words. "They're going to keep looking for you. And who knows what Ruby's planning! We can't hide forever."

"I'd rather hide than kill."

There was an insanity to this, something unreal, as if Jake was living in a slightly altered existence. Eric gone. Ruby zealous. The Vigilante real. Melissa leaving him after he'd just found her. These were events and decisions that belonged within the realm of dreams, a world you pondered after waking, relieved you'd escaped.

Perhaps he was still anesthetized on that table in Dr. Steve's basement.

He touched Melissa's wrist. She held his hand. Ran her thumb over his, examining it sadly.

No. This was real.

"I'll find you after," Jake said.

Melissa turned her face away when he embraced her.

"I don't think I'll be here when you get back."

The men led Jake downstairs.

A pair of circular poker tables were in the basement with a rectangular table between them, like a pair of glasses. Six men sat at each round table. A doorway opened to a hall on the far side of the room. A television hung in a corner showed some boxing match, the volume low and indiscernible.

Two disinterested naked women sat on stools placed on top of the rectangular table, their legs uncrossed.

Jake saw bruises on the women, purple circles on their stomachs and thighs and backs.

"Well," he heard Chris say, "look at that."

The three men at Chris's table held playing cards, and they set the cards face down on green felt. Colorful poker chips were piled before each of them. The men at the other table kept playing. The women leaned toward each other, whispered.

"I didn't expect you to show up here," Chris said. "Then again, no matter what deal we made with your mom, I knew I was still going to kill you someday."

One of the men raised his arm at Jake, made the gun motion with his fingers.

There was a faint odor in the air, the musky smell men got when they've been outdoors for too long.

Jake wondered if he'd made a mistake, stepped too far over the line.

He wanted to rush back up the stairs but forced himself to stay.

"I have something to tell you," Jake said. "But I don't want to talk here."

"One time when I was a kid," Chris said, "I found this wasp in my backyard. The wasp had a broken wing, and it'd fly a few feet in the air and then fall back down to the ground. So I caught it and trapped it in this shoebox. No idea why, just stupid stuff kids do. I put it in there with a spider I'd found earlier. Back then I always collected bugs."

No one but Chris spoke.

"I forgot about the shoebox until a couple of days later. Went back on the porch and saw it. I opened it up, and I remember I'd forgotten what I'd put inside there. But I still haven't forgotten what I saw."

Jake's shoulder throbbed.

"The wasp and the spider were both dead," Chris went on, "and they'd eaten parts of each other. There were loose dead legs in there, and their bodies were torn apart. I think part of the wasp's head was in the spider's mouth."

One of the men swore loudly and slammed down his cards, and all the other men at his table laughed. He swore again, reached out for one of the women. She climbed down off her stool and bent. The angry man smacked her. She fell to her knees, stunned for a moment. The man sat back in his chair.

The woman touched her cheek, gazed at her fingers.

After a few moments she climbed back on her stool.

Jake's throat burned, a complaint or cry aching to emerge. But this was a world in which he had no footing, a different language than the one he spoke.

"You come here," Chris said, gesturing at Jake, "and you see yourself as a wasp and me as a spider. You with the broken little wing."

Everyone laughed, except for the sullen one who'd had the outburst.

And the women.

"You think you and I are going to be trapped together, maybe kill each other," Chris said. "But that's not what's happening. Melissa's the spider."

Jake started to speak. Chris raised a hand.

Jake stayed silent.

"Melissa and I almost killed each other. I took your mom's offer because I figured that out. I left that box. But you and Melissa, you two are going to stay inside it. And when someone looks inside, they're going to see that you're both dead."

"That's not what's happening," Jake said.

"That's because you don't know you're already trapped."

Jake felt unsteady suddenly, almost dizzy, as if he was about to lose his balance. "Like I said," he told Chris, "I have something to tell you. But I don't want to talk here."

More of the men turned toward him. The two women watched him.

Chris glanced down at his cards, grimaced. He tossed them to the middle of the table and rose.

A man rose with him.

Chris pointed at Jake. "Look at him. Chris is good."

The man sat back down.

Jake followed Chris across the room, toward the small hallway at the other end.

The basement tasted of fighting, of anger, and this was something Jake inherently recognized, even if he'd never been drawn to it.

Jake often wondered if that was why he'd fallen into photography. The reactive nature of the art, not taking part in what was happening, but standing aside and observing it, a journalist's detachment.

But then he'd met Melissa and realized detachment was impossible. He couldn't photograph Melissa in any way other than one that showed his love. Humanity was inescapable.

And he thought about what Melissa had said, as he walked through the group of criminals, what the Vigilante and even Ruby had said. Murder was inescapable.

Chris led Jake into an empty, unfinished storage room with cement floors and silver tape on overhead ducts and a dusty plastic wrapping taped over the one window. Green eggshell soundproofing panels lined the walls. A washing machine and dryer were in the corner. A dark shadow was on the floor.

It was the room in the recording Melissa had told him about.

The room where Chris had killed that man. But now there was something else in the air, another smell.

Sweat and semen.

"You'd better have something good for me," Chris said. "Because—"

"I can give you the Vigilante," Jake said.

Chris didn't say anything for a moment.

"Why would you do that?"

"Because the Vigilante is Ruby."

It took almost a minute for Chris to respond. He kept opening his mouth to say something, then stopping.

"How?" he eventually asked. "She's so fat. And old."

"That didn't stop her from taking out Seth."

"Yeah," Chris admitted, and he thought again, and as he did, the tip of his tongue poked out of his mouth. To Jake there was almost something childlike about the gesture.

In that moment he deeply missed his camera.

The moment passed.

"I saw the mask at her house," Jake went on. "I asked her about it, and she told me the truth. She worked for the Winterses for years, knows everything about what you all do. And when she left, it wasn't on good terms. She never completely came back, and blamed all of you for what she did. You had to suspect the Vigilante was someone you trusted."

"A woman, though?"

"You thought it was Lucky, right?" Jake asked.

"I did."

"Lucky knew the truth, maybe helped her, I don't know, but he wasn't the one wearing the mask. It was always Ruby."

Chris turned his back to Jake, walked over to the wall, studied the soundproof panels.

"Messed up for you to turn on your own mother," Chris observed. "Then again, no one hurts you more than your own family."

"Ruby hasn't been my mother for years. She's the one who killed Eric, and she tried to kill Melissa. I know your men pulled the trigger, but she's the one who used them as a bargaining chip."

"Why are you telling me this?"

"So you'll let me and Melissa go. You can take down the Vigilante and Lucky. I can give them both to you. I have the proof."

"And now that I know all this, I can just find them and kill them. And then I'll find Melissa."

"You could, but I'm offering a man's agreement. That's all I have. Nothing but my word. And I think that's good enough for you. Especially with what you can do with this."

"What's that?"

Jake took a moment before he went on. This had to be phrased just right, otherwise he wouldn't make it out of this house.

"Melissa told me about the power struggle with you and your uncle. If you take down the Vigilante and Lucky, then there's no question anymore about who's in charge."

A shout outside. Chris's eyes didn't leave Jake's.

"Maybe Chris is starting to think," Chris said softly, "that you know too much."

"All I want," Jake said, "all *we* want is to be free. Me and Melissa to be free from the Winterses. We'll leave the area, and you'll never hear from us again."

Chris kept staring at him.

"Tell me where to find Ruby," he said.

Chapter Thirty-Eight

Lucky

"Are me and mom ever going to be safe?"

"Soon," Lucky said. He told himself this wasn't a lie because he believed it.

It had been two days of driving without stops, the three of them alternately taking turns sleeping in the car, Renee and Lucky driving through Maryland and Virginia, eating at small tucked-away restaurants or in parking lots, stopping at rest areas to walk and use the bathroom, once paying for a motel room with cash so they could each shower. Lucky knew better than to stop and stay in any one place or drive in one particular direction. He left no pattern.

But there was another reason Lucky didn't want to stop: Renee still seemed to be in a state of shock and easy compliance. Marybeth had given up on escaping and was instead reconciling herself to acceptance.

Lucky worried that introducing some new sense of stability, of permanence, would wake something in them. Potentially turn them against him.

He needed more time.

And so he kept driving and offering the promise of eventual safety, the false confidence that he knew exactly what he was doing. They'd given themselves to him, he understood, in a way Renee never had and Marybeth hadn't since she was a small child. Lucky savored it. For years his hidden identity had grown in strength privately, like a small tree he was tending in a secret grove, and when his family had finally seen it, they'd discovered it to be an oak.

"But *how* are we going to be safe?" Marybeth asked. Renee slept in the passenger seat as they drove down I-95, halfway between northern Virginia and Richmond. "Do you even have a plan?"

It was a fair question.

"The plan is to keep you and your mother alive," he said.

Marybeth flounced back into the back seat of their new car, a used Toyota RAV4 that was, admittedly, far less comfortable than his Grand Cherokee had been. Lucky had seen the Toyota for sale on the side of a dirt road near the town of Dumfries, stopped at the house, and paid for it in cash. Parked his Jeep off a side road, stripped off its plates, removed everything from inside.

He hadn't been surprised that his picture was missing from the media, the story of what had happened in his neighborhood unreported. Because that was how it was to work for the Winterses. The story had died before it could emerge.

"I need to pee," Marybeth announced. "Can we stop there?"

Lucky glanced into the rearview mirror, didn't see anything suspicious, although it would have been hard to tell in the constant stream of cars on I-95. He took the exit to the rest area Marybeth had indicated.

Pulled to a stop as Renee stirred awake.

"Are we home?" Renee asked sleepily.

"I'll be back," Marybeth said. She left the car, hurried toward the building.

Renee rubbed her eyes, sat up. "I shouldn't have said *home.* I just keep thinking we'll be back there soon."

Lucky noticed redness in her eyes and worried it was from sadness rather than sleep. "We will," he assured her.

"The first thing I'm going to do is take a long shower," Renee went on. "And then fall asleep in my own bed. And then call the cops on William. It's nice to have goals."

Lucky chuckled appreciatively, although the idea of returning home left him feeling uneasy.

"Is there someplace where we can stop for a few days?" Renee asked. "Maybe a resort in North Carolina? By the beach."

"A beach?"

"It'd be nice to go to the beach," Renee said. "We haven't been to one for years. Remember how we used to go to Cape May when Marybeth was little? We'd stay at that hotel and walk around and see all those bed-and-breakfasts painted in so many different colors? And we'd talk about owning one someday. You making breakfasts for the guests and me running the finances. And we'd tell Marybeth she'd have to clean all the rooms. She used to get so mad."

Lucky was only half listening. He'd been scanning the cars in the parking lot, and his attention was focused on one parked on the far side. It was some sort of squarish sedan, entirely nondescript, completely forgettable.

And that worried Lucky. He couldn't figure out how he'd missed it. Hadn't even seen the car pull in.

It'd been days since he'd slept more than an hour, and there had been moments when he'd almost fallen asleep at the wheel. Renee had driven, too, but, when she had, Lucky had found sleep difficult, like chasing someone ahead of you in a race, someone you had no hope of catching.

"Lucky?"

"I'm sorry," he said. "I'm just so tired."

It was a weakness that felt surprisingly good to admit. Strange how, despite the intimacy he felt with Renee and Marybeth, this simple statement was the most honest he'd been in days.

"If we do go to North Carolina, we should visit colleges," Renee said. "We could do it now instead of in the spring."

Something else stirred within Lucky, a rustling he hadn't felt since before he'd been worried about William McKenna. Tears.

"Lucky?" Renee asked, alarmed. "What's wrong?"

"I think I'm just happy," he told her.

Lucky wept into Renee's arms, felt her fingers in his hair, a hand patting his back the way she always touched him, as if her mind and body weren't connected.

Lucky wondered if he was the reason for her disconnect. Maybe his lies had always struck something in her, some subconscious part of Renee realizing she couldn't truly trust him, a Darwinian instinct of self-preservation. Maybe he'd created this divide, and Renee deserved more, the chance to give herself completely to someone.

"Lucky, where's Marybeth?"

He sat up, wiped his eyes.

"I'll check." He opened the glove compartment, gave Renee the Beretta. Pulled his knife from the sheath around his ankle and slid it into his jacket pocket.

He tried to remember when Marybeth had left the car and had no idea.

He needed rest.

Renee's suggestion of the ocean was appealing, the retreat to water and the soothing sound of surf. Floating on caressing waves.

Lucky walked to the women's restroom and opened the door, one hand holding the knife in his pocket.

Marybeth was sitting on the counter, her back to the mirror. Her face was bruised, lips bleeding.

And there was something else in her face Lucky recognized, and it was a terrible thing to see.

It was the expression of someone who is about to die, all pretenses violently stripped away. Nothing but childlike fear.

"Hey, Lucky," Seth said.

Seth's gun pressed Marybeth's neck.

"Dad," Marybeth said, her voice filled with tears, "I'm sorry."

Lucky didn't move.

He hadn't seen Seth in years, not since their mentoring had ended. Lucky remembered the burn marks that covered the young man's body and the hate that always simmered under the surface. But there was something new to Seth now, in addition to a wrapping that covered half his face. He had an awkwardness to his stance, a grimace underneath his glare.

He was in pain.

"I thought you were dead," Lucky told him.

"Maybe I am," Seth said. "I've been burned and stabbed and run over. Or maybe you and I both are."

Lucky didn't know how to respond. He looked at the blood trailing down his daughter's chin, and his heart felt lost.

"You were just the worst teacher," Seth said.

"I was?"

"Didn't you hear me?" Seth pressed the gun harder into Marybeth. She flinched. "Burned and stabbed and run over?"

"Two of those things happened before I met you."

"Don't make excuses."

Marybeth was crying freely now.

"If you let her go," Lucky said, "you can take me in. Take me to them, and they can do what they want."

"They told me in the hospital what you did," Seth went on as if Lucky hadn't spoken. "What happened to Marley and his man. How you helped the doc. Double-crossing everyone in your life. Me, the Winterses, your daughter, your wife. Anyone else?"

"No, I think that's everybody."

Lucky saw the handle of the door on the other side of the restroom, the one behind Seth, turn.

"Seth," he said, so that his former mentee wouldn't be surprised and accidentally pull the trigger. "Someone's coming in behind you."

A woman hurried into the restroom, impatiently ushering in her younger daughter, a girl of about six. Both of them stopped.

"You two, don't go anywhere," Seth said without turning around, catching everything in the full-length mirror.

"Walk in front of me and sit down," he ordered them.

Long ago, Lucky had learned that there was a process to killing someone.

During his days in the army, he'd had a friend who kept a pet snake, a four-foot-long boa constrictor named Henry. Lucky had found the idea of owning a snake entirely bewildering and had constant questions for his friend. One of the things he'd learned was that the snake had a diet of frozen mice and rats.

"I can't use live rodents," his friend had explained. "They might kill Henry."

In his first assignments for the Winterses, that wasn't something Lucky had understood, and the killings had been sloppy, the cleanup extensive, the risk almost equal for both Lucky and his victim. It had taken time to remember and understand the lesson he'd learned from Henry: the victim should, in all practical matters, already be dead.

That meant subduing any sense of hope by the time they realized death had come.

But this woman had something to fight for.

Lucky could see it in her eyes, the anger, determination. The way her hand tightened over her daughter's shoulder.

She threw herself at Seth, and Lucky shouted something, not words, just a sound, at the fear that Marybeth was going to be shot. But Seth's gun stayed quiet as he swore and fell, the woman on top of him, she screaming for her daughter to run. The little girl stayed still, staring, her mouth open but no sound coming out.

Lucky ran forward and grabbed his own daughter's hand, yanked Marybeth off the counter, her body dead weight at first, frozen, then coming alive. The woman on the floor kept screaming and then stopped abruptly, as if she was surprised when Seth shot her twice in the chest.

The full-length mirror Lucky had been standing in front of shattered as he and Marybeth ran out of the door, as he heard the little girl screaming behind him.

Lucky's knife was in one hand, Marybeth's hand in his other. The RAV4 was close, and he glanced back at the restroom, expecting to see Seth emerge. But the restroom door stayed closed.

Lucky started the RAV4 and pulled into reverse and saw Seth leaning against the building, barely able to stand. The impact from Ruby's car had injured him more than Lucky had realized. Lucky watched Seth raise a gun, his arm shaking.

But Lucky sped out of the lot before Seth could fire.

Renee and Marybeth were shouting as he pulled onto I-95.

And into gridlock.

"What happened?" Renee was asking. Marybeth was making a hoarse shrieking sound. Lucky smelled the sour acidity of vomit. He took the Beretta from Renee's shaking hand and stuffed it in his pocket next to the knife.

"We're going to the beach," Lucky said.

He looked around but didn't see Seth or the nondescript sedan. Instead, Lucky studied the drivers and passengers and families around him, bored and resigned, and Lucky felt a sudden ache to belong. These people with their quiet lives and successes and tragedies and families and neighbors.

This lovely moment, this pause of life when he was sitting in the car with his wife and daughter, all part of the same inexorable march forward, souls driven to the horizon.

If only, he thought, Renee and Marybeth would stop screaming.

"We're going to be okay," Lucky told them, and he turned and tried to wipe the blood off his daughter's chin. She reared back, eyes wide. "Everything's fine."

But something had broken in both Renee and Marybeth. Whatever control he'd held, whatever trust they'd given, was gone.

Someone was tugging his arm. Lucky hadn't realized his door had been yanked open or that Seth's face was next to his.

"We're going to the beach!" Lucky shouted, and he pushed Seth in the chest.

Seth cried out and stumbled back, his gun falling to the ground.

The people in the cars around him were opening their windows and staring, phones recording.

Lucky stepped out of the car and tried to pull the Beretta from his pocket. Even with the younger man's injuries, Lucky knew he might not be able to take Seth without a weapon.

Lucky couldn't free his Beretta before Seth tackled him. They fell against some other car, and Lucky's lower back felt like it had caved in as a rearview mirror dug into him, Seth grunting like an animal.

Lucky finally pulled his gun loose, and he and Seth fought for it, both their hands over it, and one of them shot twice and the window behind Lucky broke and someone screamed.

Lucky hoped it wasn't Renee or Marybeth.

Anyone else but them.

A wave of worry filled him, and he drove Seth backward, both men falling to the ground. Lucky placed his knee on Seth's chest, and Seth's face turned in agony. Broken ribs, Lucky guessed, and there was pleasure at Seth's pain, a sadistic glee Lucky had never felt before. He watched his protégé's face contort, the helplessness in his eyes, the way his hand stopped fighting and let go of the Beretta.

Lucky tossed his gun away; he wanted to use his hands.

He pummeled Seth's face, kept smashing until, finally, Lucky's fists were pounding into the hard pavement.

Lucky rose and staggered back in the direction of the RAV4, but it was gone. He looked around, his legs rubbery, and realized that cars on the interstate had pulled off the road in an effort to get away. Traffic was flying past now, people staring at him and Seth's body.

Lucky held up one hand to stop the cars rushing toward him and stumbled to the side of the road, toward the trees lining it. He didn't know where Renee and Marybeth had gone, but he was happy they had escaped. They were free of him, free of the blood dripping down his fingers, leaving a trail on the pavement. He kept his other hand up as he walked dumbly toward the side, into the cars screaming past.

Renee and Marybeth had gone to the beach. Lucky imagined them there, and the picture filled his mind.

The sun a child's yellow ball in the sky.

Birds soaring.

The two women before the water.

A ship's sail like a petal.

Lucky imagined this image as he stepped into the final lane before the trees, now seeing cartoon crabs cavorting and jellyfish rising above the water and a mermaid's shadowy head emerging and a sea turtle crawling across the sand and digging a hole to lay its eggs and dolphins lunging and a whale submerging and rain gently falling and he heard the sound of rain as it tapped tapped tapped against a wide, tilted beach umbrella and he smelled the heady scent of barbeque potato chips that Renee always had a craving for during these vacations and Lucky pictured everything there, everything except himself.

CHAPTER THIRTY-NINE

JAKE

In the darkness among the mass grave behind the Vigilante's barn, Jake watched Ruby arrive.

She parked next to the building and lumbered out of her car. Jake sent a quick text, shoved his phone into his pocket, and headed down the incline, the slope forcing him to jog. His shoulder ached but less than it had.

Ruby stood inside the barn, her hands jammed into a hoodie.

"I wasn't sure you wanted to see me again," she said.

"Just this one last time."

They walked toward each other, stopped a few feet apart.

"We'll never be finished, Jake," Ruby told him.

"What's that mean?"

"Children spend their whole lives trying to understand their parents," she said. "Loving, blaming, forgiving. Hating. And that's different than everyone else. Almost every other person you know is going to be like a single note you hear in a song, but parents are a whole song that children hear in parts their entire lives. I turn my ear to the scripture; with an instrument I solve its riddles."

"You rehearse all this?"

"Maybe."

"You killed Eric."

Ruby slumped, and now she averted her eyes from Jake's hostile glare. She said something he didn't hear.

Jake asked her to repeat herself.

"The Lord only allows so much control," she said, "over the choices we make."

The front door to the barn opened, and Chris Winters walked inside. He walked purposefully, striding toward Jake and Ruby. He had a gun in one hand, brushed his hair out of his eyes with the other. And there was that sudden longing again in Jake for his camera, the feeling so sharp he nearly reached to where the camera always hung on his chest.

But his camera wasn't with him. Jake didn't know where it was.

"Lucky here?" Chris asked.

Ruby stepped in front of Jake, placing her body between him and Chris. "What are you doing?" she asked.

Chris ignored her. "I scouted the barn. Didn't see him."

"Jake." Ruby turned toward her son. "Why's he here?"

"For you."

Ruby looked back and forth between the two men, and now Jake was the one to glance away. "We made a deal," she told Chris.

"That was before I knew who you really were," Chris said.

"I don't understand," Ruby said. "What did I do?"

"The real question," Chris replied, "is when did it start?"

"I don't understand," Ruby said again, and her voice was higher.

Jake refused to meet her eyes.

"Jake," Ruby said simply, quietly. "What did you do?"

His wound felt like it had reopened, blood running down his arm and side.

"I told him who you are," Jake said. "Who you really are. The Vigilante."

A zip tie landed at Jake's feet.

"Tie her up," Chris said. "She's walking out of here. I don't want to carry your mom's fat ass to the car."

Jake picked up the tie. He'd never seen one before, heavy plastic, stiff loops like mouse ears. He grabbed Ruby's hands, pulled them toward him, placed the loops around her hands. Pulled the loops until the plastic pressed into her wrists.

She watched him. He looked down, eyes averted.

Jake desperately wanted to say something, to offer whatever assurance he could . . . but he forced himself to remember Eric.

Her hands trembled as he tightened the loops.

"Why?" Ruby asked quietly.

Chris's hand on her shoulder before Jake could respond. He still held the gun in his other hand.

And that gun rose as a new voice came from the front door, the person Jake had texted when Ruby first arrived at the barn.

"Interesting," Frank said.

Chris froze.

Unlike Chris and Ruby, Frank hadn't come alone. Three men walked in behind him.

"What's happening?" Chris asked Jake.

"Oh Jake," the Vigilante had said the last time Jake had been in this barn, "they're going to kill you."

"Maybe," Jake replied. "I know I'm not strong enough to beat any of them. But they can kill each other. And all you have to do is walk away."

"Walk away?"

"Retire, like you want. Leave this world behind. Let yourself forget all this and become that other person you keep talking about. Just give me the mask."

"You're going to become a vigilante?"

"No," Jake said. "Someone else is."

"Like I said on the phone," Jake told Frank. "It's him."

He pointed at Chris.

A moment of silence.

Chris swore and raised his weapon. But one of Frank's men grabbed Chris from behind, forced his arms down. The gun clattered to the floor.

"Melissa told me the truth," Jake said. "She'd known early on it was Chris. Why do you think he needed her killed after she left him?"

Frank rubbed his chin.

"After Victor died," Jake continued, hoping Frank believed him, "Chris told Melissa he wanted to undercut you, show you weren't effective. And no one knows the Winterses better. He hurt them to hurt you, to get your job."

Chris shouting now, denials and threats, but it was like Jake barely heard him, dull noise in the background.

"We found the stuff where you said it was," Frank said.

"All we want," Jake had told Chris in the basement of the town house, "is to be free. Me and Melissa to be free from the Winterses. We'll leave the area, and you'll never hear from us again."

Chris kept staring at him.

"Tell me where to find Ruby," he said.

"There's a barn in Manassas. That's where Ruby's buried the bodies and where she hides out. She'll be there in two days. You go there, and you'll find her, the mask, and the bodies. I'll send you the address."

Chris led Jake out of the soundproof room. Walked him back to the poker tables and the men and the naked women, and someone sighed and stood and escorted Jake upstairs and outside.

Jake waited for the door to lock, then reached behind the hedges lining the house. Grabbed the mask and baton he'd hidden earlier, stuffed them into his pants.

Knocked on the door.

"Any chance," Jake asked with a sheepish smile, "I could use the bathroom?"

Upstairs, in Chris's bedroom, Jake hurriedly hid the Vigilante's mask deep in the dresser.

Lifted the mattress and slipped the baton inside.

Then he left.

Chris was on the ground, struggling as one of Frank's men held him down, trying to shout muffled threats through a large palm covering his mouth.

"You could have hidden those yourself," Frank said. "You went to the house. This doesn't mean anything."

Jake had known that the evidence wasn't much, that his plan was largely based on accusation. But he'd hoped Frank took that on faith, enough faith to act against the person who coveted his position.

The man holding Chris down yelped and drew his hand back from Chris's face.

"He bit me," the man exclaimed.

"Of course he planted it on me!" Chris yelled.

"Melissa told me where to look," Jake insisted.

"Because she probably put them there herself!"

Frank looked at Jake, and Jake couldn't read what was in his eyes.

"You can't trust a woman," Frank said eventually, and he turned toward the man guarding Chris. "Let him up."

Chris shook himself free, glared at Jake.

"I'm going to kill you," Chris told Jake. "Tonight."

"What about Lucky?" Jake asked desperately. "What if he was working with—"

"Lucky's gone," Frank said. "And his family didn't know a thing about what he did. Even if they do now, they're too scared to ever speak up."

"I can prove Chris is lying," Jake told Frank. "I can prove it. He killed your men and buried the bodies out back."

"No," Ruby said.

Everyone turned toward her.

"You're calling your own kid a liar?" Frank asked.

"I don't owe Jake a thing anymore," Ruby said.

The world seemed like it was slipping away from Jake. He looked at the gallows against the far wall.

"But he's not the one lying," she finished. "Jake's right. Chris is the Vigilante."

"What?" Chris exclaimed.

"How do you know that?" Frank asked.

"Because I helped him," Ruby said.

Chris cursed and lunged at Ruby.

She raised her bound hands, pushed Chris to the side. He sprawled past her, landed hard on the floor.

"What do you mean you helped him?" Frank asked.

"No one knows the Winterses better than the two of us," Ruby said. "And no one had more reasons to take you down. I told him to attack, and he attacked. Jake found it all out. He's telling you the truth, just not the whole truth."

"Mom?" Jake asked unsteadily.

"She's lying!" Chris shouted.

Frank studied Ruby. The two of them regarded each other for a long moment.

Finally Frank nodded, looked down at Chris. "You're too dumb to have done this on your own."

"I'm not!"

"Just take Jake outside first," Ruby said. "Please. For him. If he sees this, he'll never forgive himself."

She knelt, using her bound hands for balance.

One of the men took Jake by the arm, started walking him to the door. Frank pulled out his gun.

“Mom?” Jake asked, and he could suddenly see everything that was about to happen, and he fought wildly to return.

But he was dragged to the door.

“We’re family,” Chris was saying as Frank’s gun pressed into the back of his head. “You’re Chris’s—” And then there was a gunshot.

Ruby watched Jake serenely, her eyes wet.

Jake had a thought, a flash of hope as they opened the door to the barn. A chance the Vigilante would be waiting, under a new mask and holding a new baton, rushing in to help.

There was nothing but the night.

No one was coming to save them.

Jake fought and looked back just before they closed the door. He saw Ruby’s lips moving, but he couldn’t understand what she was saying. It sounded like she was telling him to cut his hair.

Chapter Forty

Melissa

It was near night when Melissa found Jake, sitting on a bench a mile away from the same gas station where she'd left him. He was hunched over and small.

She sat next to him and gave him a plastic shopping bag. Jake looked inside, took out his camera. Held it uncertainly in his lap.

It took him a while to speak. But when he did, he told her everything.

Melissa listened and watched his face, although he didn't look at her. It was as if he couldn't bring himself to, a sinner unable to raise his eyes.

Jake talked about his mother, about how she'd always returned those nights when he was a child. About how, a couple of times, she stayed in with him, and they played games together, and she laughed with him and, once, how she couldn't help herself and leaned over and kissed his nose. And, in that moment, it had felt like enough, like everything.

He asked Melissa if she remembered his mother's blue eyes, the blue that was like no other blue in the world, and she told him she did.

Epilogue: Four Years Later

Melissa watched the woman step out of the Arizona heat and into the air-conditioned gallery. The woman wore a blue beautiful sundress, a pair of large sunglasses she took off, and a floppy hat she left on. She stopped by the door, letting herself adjust to the air-conditioning and the change in light.

Melissa always liked watching people enter the gallery, the way they slowed as if wading into deep water. And she was always interested in what pieces struck their attention first. On the occasions that Arizona Sun Gallery had a sculpture, that's always where people immediately went. Something about sculpture had a certain quality of allure. Sam, the elder owner of the gallery, once told Melissa it was because sculpture was so daunting. Everyone has experience to some degree of taking photographs or drawing a picture, but molding a figure from clay is beyond their capabilities.

That made sense to Melissa, but she thought there was another reason as well: the permanence, the way the creation was destined to last. The reason we stop and look at any monument. They will remain long after we are gone, stories left in clues for the future to decipher.

It had taken Jake a long time to resume photography; truthfully, despite her encouragement, Melissa hadn't been sure he would. They'd decided to leave the DC area and move as far away as possible—almost as if, blindfolded, they'd tossed a dart at a map—and picked southern Arizona, a small, quiet town named Bisbee, dominated by hills and dirt.

Melissa had wondered if the move disrupted Jake too much, if the change had come too soon after the deaths of Ruby and Eric. There was a heaviness to Jake she'd never noticed before, and she worried it was the kind of change Chris had undergone, this darkness wrapping around him, pulling him into its depths.

They'd found jobs in Bisbee, she at the gallery and Jake at a bar, lived in a house that the owner was renting out while his military son was stationed overseas for three years, but their new lives hadn't begun in the way she'd hoped. They were both wounded, forever tense, near panicked when they heard a sound outside the house at night; Bisbee nights, compared to DC, were pitch black. And Jake seemed lost, destitute, even after his great sadness had finally started to ebb away.

Melissa worried that the person he'd been was gone.

The woman who had entered the gallery walked over to her, and Melissa caught a slight whiff of an intoxicating eucalyptus-scented lotion the other woman had applied. They gazed at a photo detailing the mountain ranges of nearby Tucson, the way the mountains encroached upon the city—no, the way the city encroached upon the mountains. It had been taken just before evening, and there were stars looming in the purple sky.

This photograph was called *Sunset Eyes*.

"Do you know his work?" Melissa asked the woman.

"A little," the woman replied. "I saw one of his photos in a collection of the year's best nature photography."

"He's done well for himself," Melissa said. "My name's Melissa Cruz. I'm the assistant manager of this gallery and Jake's girlfriend. And I also manage his career."

"Do you really?"

"And a few other artists. No one you would have heard of. They're new, just starting out."

The woman looked around. "Is Jake Smith here?"

"He can't handle hearing people discuss his work." Melissa smiled. "We're working on that."

"I get it."

"So what brings you by? I haven't seen you around town."

"I'm just driving through," the woman replied without looking away from the picture. She didn't give more of an answer than that, and Melissa didn't press.

The two women moved to another photograph. This image showed rising gray rock outcroppings among mountains of sparse green trees. The evening sun was visible, fat and sinking into a Y-shaped gap in the mountains, like an egg about to be broken along the edge of a glass.

Melissa remembered the day she'd come home and found Jake peering into the back of his camera, looking at this photo.

"I'm not ready to take pictures of people," he'd said.

"I know."

"But it turns out that I'm not ready to stop taking pictures."

"Those are rock hoodoos," Melissa explained to the woman. "At the Chiricahua Monument. Some people call them earth pyramids. They have roots in Native American mythology. Some say they're lucky, others that they're spirits of evil men."

The woman looked closely at this photograph.

"What do you think they are?" Melissa asked.

"Yea, verily," the woman said. "I just think they're some pretty rocks."

Sometimes Melissa and Jake fought, and they'd never fought before. It helped that she knew why he suddenly grew so angry, understood that he'd gone through so much pain that his anguish needed an outlet.

Jake understood so much, but deeper emotions still escaped him.

It had taken him a while to realize he'd always be sad about Ruby and Eric.

And Melissa could tell he didn't yet understand that she would always love him.

But it was a wonderful thing to see him slowly realize it.

The last photo the two women looked at was called *Ruby*, and it showed blue-black water wrapped around a large red stone.

"This is just so beautiful," the woman breathed. "This is the one I saw in that collection. There's something so lonely about it."

"Lonely?"

"I'm thinking outside of the picture. I mean, this is just some guy standing with a camera by himself, alone taking a picture at night. It's a photo about missing something."

Melissa didn't reply.

"Is that wrong?" the woman asked.

"It's whatever you need it to be."

"What do you think it is?"

As a rule, Melissa never discussed what she personally found so captivating about Jake's work, but she made an exception this time.

"I think it's the moment before violence."

The woman looked sharply at her. "What do you mean?"

"All of his photos," Melissa said, "are right before the sun or moon comes out, before the whole complexion of the world changes. I think that's what makes it sad. Jake's capturing the moment before that happens."

"I hadn't thought of that."

"People ask me all the time why his photos are popular," Melissa said. "Some people say they're beautiful; some say they're sad; some say they're scary. But they're just human, too human, trying to return to the moment before something is forever gone."

The End

ACKNOWLEDGMENTS

There are so many people I need to thank for *When She Left*.

There's really no one I owe more to, professionally, than superstar agent Michelle Richter. There's no partner in publishing more devoted to her writers, or more caring, or honest. I can't imagine working with someone else and never want to.

I've called Jessica Tribble Wells a dream editor before, and, happily, I have yet to wake. I owe her everything for helping me find the voice for these books, as well as for her resolute optimism and remarkable insight.

Of course, Jessica doesn't work alone, and the entire Thomas & Mercer team has been an absolute force. All the love and thanks to Sarah Shaw, Miranda Gardner, Rachel McClure, Alicia Lea, Michael Jantze, and Amanda Hudson.

And to Peggy Keegan for her generous and selfless time and insight. Everyone needs a Peggy.

Every crime-fiction author makes a point of thanking the crime-fiction community, and for good reason. They're wonderful people. From Bookstagrammers like @Bonechillingbooks; to groups and organizations like the Thrill Begins, Crime Writers of Color (CWoC), Sisters in Crime (SinC), Mystery Writers of America (MWA), and the International Thriller Writers (ITW); and book festivals and conferences that pointedly feature crime fiction, like the Gaithersburg Book Festival, Fall for the

Book, Virginia Festival of the Book, the Washington Writers Conference, and more. I've long been fortunate to be part of this writing community.

Special thanks to Alison Gaylin, Hank Phillippi Ryan, Tracy Clark, Cate Holahan, Alma Katsu, Jess Lourey, and Wendy Corsi Staub for their early reads and enthusiasm. It's a lovely feeling to have the support of my favorite writers and heroes.

Thank you to Lydia Kang, a wonderful writer and doctor, for her medical advice about the best way to injure my characters. And to Mark Bergin and Micki Browning, similarly wonderful writers and former cops, for their explanations of crime scenes and the workings of a small-town police force.

I owe so much to my close friends in writing, and there's no way I can mention all of them, but all the love to Jennifer Hillier, Eliza Nellums, Tara Laskowski, Art Taylor, Kathleen Barber, Angie Kim, Christina Kovac, Louis Bayard, Yasmin Angoe, Susanna Calkins, Carrie Callahan, May Cobb, Hilary Davidson, Sian Gilbert, S. A. Cosby, Sarah M. Chen, Dan and Kate Malmon, Hannah Mary McKinnon, Kellye Garrett, and Alex Segura.

Thank you to everyone who hangs out with me on *Crime Fiction Works*. That newsletter is a mix of the personal and professional, and it's become a joy, something I look forward to writing every month. I hope, similarly, you look forward to reading it.

Thank you to two of my closest friends, Michele Greene and Carl Hagenbrock, for always being there.

Of course, thanks to Nancy and Noah. Life would be nothing without the two of you.

And all the love to my parents, and to my family, both in the States and Panama.

And thank you, of course, to everyone who has taken a chance on one of my books and returned for more. Sharing your work with someone is like inviting them into your house, and nervously hoping they enjoy it. I hope you feel at home.

—E.A.

About the Author

Photo © 2019 Marian Lozano Photography

Anthony Award–nominated E.A. Aymar's thriller *No Home for Killers* was published to praise from the *New York Times*, *Kirkus Reviews*, *South Florida Sun Sentinel*, and was an instant bestseller. His thriller *They're Gone* received rave reviews in *Publishers Weekly* and *Kirkus* (starred) and was named one of the best books of 2020 by the *South Florida Sun Sentinel*. He is a former member of the national board of International Thriller Writers and is an active member of Crime Writers of Color and Sisters in Crime. He runs the DC Noir at the Bar series, was born in Panama, and now lives and writes in—and generally about—the DC/MD/VA triangle.

E.A. Aymar runs *Crime Fiction Works*, widely considered the most important newsletter in crime-fiction history by E.A. Aymar. It's free, runs once a month, and includes author interviews, book recommendations, events, prizes, cool stuff happening in crime fiction, and puppies.

He does his best to make sure it's not annoying or too frequent because that's just the worst.

To subscribe, visit eaymar.substack.com.